Bookworm

She'll Bury Herself in a Book

KL Griffiths

Published by Cottonwood Fire LLC

www.klgriffiths.com

FIRST EDITION

Cover design by Creative Paramita

Library of Congress Control Number: 2024919544

ISBN 979-8-9887038-2-2 (pbk)

ISBN 979-8-9887038-3-9 (eBook)

Chapter 1

Three Years Ago

Later, Lyn would recall a dark premonition, though she didn't believe in such things, had never had one before.

Her arms were browned with topsoil up to her elbows. She picked at the dirt moons entrenched in her nails where her glove fingers were worn away. Several hours of weeding the front flower beds had painted a sunburn on her back and arms, but one last flat of petunias remained to be planted. She surveyed her work and was catching her breath when the sound of a car barreling up the county road caught her attention, raising the hair on her neck. "Don't Fear the Reaper" blared from stereo speakers, the tune warped by speed.

On that beautiful spring day, Lyn held the flowers in quaking hands, the frail violet heads shivering for a few never-ending seconds while she listened. It was about the time Jude should be home from his thirty-mile bike ride. She heard a crunch and a whoosh, the chime of metal on metal, the hiss of lost air, and the car's engine still gunning. Later it would bother her that she didn't hear the squeal of brakes or the screech of rubber drawing on asphalt. No tire tracks of any kind.

She prayed she'd heard a fox or a deer get clipped, but in her heart she knew the grotesque metallic whisper meant nothing would ever be the same again.

"Please," she whispered. Lyn's guts turned into a bowl of gnashing snakes. What if Jude was hurt, what if he needed her? What if—she dropped the flowers and ran toward the road, straight through the narrow strip of trees, her face slapped and scratched by jagged branches. Lyn didn't register her ankle twisting on a root as she plunged through the ditch and into the tree-lined road.

There. Lyn's breath hitched. She nearly dropped into a boneless heap. The bike was in the drainage ditch on the other side, one wheel still spinning, the other, gone. Jude's shoe was attached to the pedal, the racing bike shoes that clicked in. His leg was attached to the shoe up to where a gray-white splintered bone jutted out. Lyn lost the feeling in her arms and legs. A blackness seeped into the edges of her vision.

"Jude?" she called, begging against what her eyes told her. She spun in a circle, scanning the road ahead and behind and the forest hemming the parkway. Again and again she called his name.

She spotted him. "Oh, Jude..." Her hands flew to her mouth and she stomped her feet in protest. To where her husband lay, she forged, still stomping, clumsily picking her way through the thicket. A car slowed as Lyn burst from the woods, and the driver leaned his head out the window, began to ask if she needed assistance. The man was interrupted by the hair-raising screams of his female passenger, who spotted Jude at that moment. She shook his shoulder and violently pointed. The driver made the 911 call.

Lyn dropped to her knees in front of what was left of her husband. She removed his helmet and weaved her fingers through his hair. The impact had sheared him of clothes and skin, heaped in a blood soaked pile at the base of a tree. Eyes open, he stared indifferently at the sky.

Lyn had no idea how much time elapsed while she sat rocking Jude's lifeless body in her arms. Someone approached from behind, put a hand on each of her shoulders, and asked if he could take her away. *No.* She didn't want to go anywhere, ever. The person dressed in blue—an officer then—was patient, although Lyn didn't know it or care. The sun sank low, darkening the shadows around the patrolman. She was dimly aware he had waved back the first responders so she could stay with Jude a little longer. When the darkness made it impossible to see Jude's features anymore, she continued to resist the arms that towed her away, away from her world to a loss unthinkable.

Chapter 2

Lyn's eyes widened. Her jaw dropped. She hurled the library book from her lap as if it had stung her. It skidded over the coffee table and landed on the hardwood floor in a page-crimping straddle.

"What the...Jude?" She called her dead husband's name out loud, but why? She didn't believe in ghosts. Warily, Lyn stared at the book on the floor. She sipped her coffee. The hot liquid down her throat was bitter and smooth and real.

Yes, I'm awake.

She slopped some coffee on her wrist as she set the mug down.

Ow. Awake.

But what she read was impossible. She touched her forehead. No fever. She gave her cheeks a light smack and noted the sting. Yes, everything seemed to be working properly.

Yet there it was, a regular book on the floor. Before she could change her mind, Lyn lunged for it, squeezed it hard enough to turn her knuckles white. She closed her eyes and took several deep breaths as if she were about to jump from a great height. In her hands the book trembled as she reread the impossible words again, out loud.

The souped-up Plymouth Duster barreled up Sandy Ridge Road with a phlegmy roar. Although a band of forest separated the woman from the road, she straightened at the sound. The flat of petunias in her hands trembled as she listened. The sound felt dangerous at this specific time; she cocked her head and focused.

There.

Oh no.

A drum crash, jarring and wet. She dropped the flowers and ran straight through the narrow strip of trees, not feeling the prickers slice her face or the slap of branches. She almost wiped out on a root as she raced toward the road.

There. The bike was in a ditch on the other side, one wheel still spinning, the other, gone. A racing shoe was attached to the pedal. A leg was attached to the shoe up to where a gray-white splintered bone jutted out.

"Jude?" She spun in a circle, scanning the road ahead and behind and the forest that lined the parkway. Again and again she called his name. She saw—

Lyn snapped the book shut. How could these words be here? They were about her, *exactly her*. Three years ago. She touched her lips and set the book down, carefully this time with fearful reverence. There had to be an explanation. She went to the kitchen and with shaking hands poured herself a second cup of coffee and added a generous splash of Bailey's. On second thought, she added more, made her way to the kitchen, and splashed cold water on her face.

It had to be coincidence.

But it couldn't be. Besides the character having Jude's name, everything, down to it being a Plymouth Duster—well, she didn't know what sort of car it was because she never saw it and they never caught the driver, but the words were...*souped-up*. And earlier in the book, she was sure it mentioned a Pinarello road bike—her Jude's—and a blaring song, "Don't Fear the Reaper" —the same one that played in her nightmares, the one she heard seconds before Jude was killed. She clamped a hand over her mouth.

Caesar padded over and nuzzled her lap with his moist nose. He wagged his tail and regarded her with mismatched Husky eyes—one blue, one brown.

"I've lost my mind, Caesar."

Lyn got up, and he followed her to the sliding door. Cleaning the door tracks was on Jude's honey-do list when he died. It had faded, but his writing still greeted her each time she went to the fridge: SLIDER TRACK. She grunted with the effort of opening the door. Caesar wedged himself through, never waiting for her to open it fully. Through the glass door, she watched her beloved Husky frolic in the snowy, wooded lot. Suddenly, he sniffed the air and darted off. Something behind the woodpile must have gotten his attention. The hair on the nape of his neck stood and his tail stiffened. One paw hovered in indecision.

"Caesar!" Lyn opened the slider. "Come." The last thing she needed was for him to get sprayed by a skunk or get into it with a coyote.

Caesar glanced her way before taking off for the rotting pile of partially-cut firewood. It was one of many shrines to Jude. The wood lay where he left it three years ago, the ax head still stuck in the block, the half-stacked pile, and the just-hewn pieces in a jumble. When Lyn needed firewood for herself, she cut it fresh with her own ax on the new chopping block. To disturb Jude's wood, to stack it, or—God forbid—burn it, would take away what she had left of him.

Caesar stopped short of Jude's memorial woodpile, although he clearly wanted to break through the invisible fence. He barked and ran back and forth, reined in by the electric current. He took a few steps forward, got the warning beep from his collar, and hustled back, all the while snarling and snapping.

Lyn jammed on her rubber boots and dashed back to the door, boots squealing on the wood.

A thought brought her up short. *What if the animal is rabid?* She ran back to her bedroom and yanked open the sock drawer and swiped the larger of the two pistols, banging her fingers hard enough to make them bleed. She squeezed and flexed her hands and willed them steady while Caesar barked and barked, intent on whatever was behind the woodpile.

If anything happens to Caesar...

She couldn't pull the sliding door open, jammed as it was with years of leaf bits and sticks, so she dropped the gun into her robe pocket. It weighed the pocket down and untied the knot, allowing the icy wind to bite her legs. She dug it out and readied to shoot.

Caesar didn't even look her way as she waded through the mud and snow, fingering the trigger and attempting to cinch her robe.

"What is it, boy?" Lyn halted just shy of the woodpile. The animal behind it made no sound. Between lusty barks, Caesar's nose worked overtime, so Lyn sniffed too, noting the freshly scraped earth where Caesar had scratched and the pungent leaves and wood pieces in various stages of decay. The snow had been marred by scrapings and shoe prints.

Not hers. Too big. She couldn't think straight with Caesar's barking.

"Caesar, quiet."

He never listened.

Lyn picked her way around the pile, not looking down, feeling with her boots so as not to trip on the cut logs. She didn't know what she expected to see, but what she saw rooted her to the spot, gun leveled. Caesar barked and snapped, but his calls were drowned out by the ringing in Lyn's ears, the rush of her blood.

At first, she thought it was a scarecrow lying in the snow, dressed in a red and black flannel shirt. But it had hands, honest-to-God hands. The wrists peeked out between the flannel and the black gloves. And the legs in faded jeans had the sculpt of muscle. And ended at a pair of hiking boots.

But that *head*.

The head was round and gray and...was a hornets' nest. Little medallions flaked off the nest or fluttered silently, weakened and broken by time. The head-sized pod was the work of hundreds of hornets. The largest nests could hold seven hundred hornets, Lyn knew, and this nest was enormous. The open shirt collar revealed a knobby Adam's apple and the...man? lay unmoving with arms and legs spread wide. A chunk of nest was ripped from the whole, and splintered medallions were strewn about the snow like coins. It gave the appearance of a head, blown away by a kill shot.

"Hello?" Lyn whispered. Her trigger finger itched to squeeze.

No response.

With her boot, she nudged the shoulder. It gave at her push, but showed no signs of life. She should take a pulse, should put her fingers on the wrist. But the hornets' nest stayed her. She kicked this time, into the soft place beneath the ribs. Again, nothing. No sign of life. She considered shooting the body, just to be sure, but how would that look, her unloading into a corpse? She backed away.

A hornet's nest. That was no coincidence. She fled back to the house and dragged Caesar alongside her by his collar.

Chapter 3

THE POLICE ARRIVED IN the time it took Lyn to down an espresso martini in a lowball glass, wash her face, brush her teeth, and pace the kitchen a few dozen times.

Upon hearing the doorbell, it was Caesar's habit to become silent, pad over to the door, and wait for Lyn to open it. No barking. Like he knew what dogs were supposed to do and refused. Caesar could only be counted on to stop a burglary if the thief had a squirrel perched on his shoulder.

Lyn peeked out the bay window. A pair of officers stood on her porch, and behind them her magnolia tree was garlanded with ribbons of toilet paper, likely a "gift" from her students.

Oh, how'd I miss that? Lovely.

The white loops danced and swayed in the winter wind. The pieces that tore loose blended in with the snow. Lyn's yard was hit by students at least one time during the school year. She figured it was because her house was remote, and Caesar never ratted them out, never even barked.

Loud, less patient knocking. "Police."

Lyn opened the door.

"Lyn Darrow?" One officer had Irish all over him, freckles and wavy ginger hair that rebelled against everything. He looked cold.

She nodded.

"You reported a body on your property?" Irish thumbed behind him. "That's no small patch of woodland. Could you point us in the right direction?"

"It's close, behind the woodpile."

The second officer was taller. His gaze swept the room behind her, taking in details and somehow also giving Lyn his attention. "Do you know the deceased? A neighbor? Recognize him—or her—from any-where?"

"It looks like a *him*."

Both officers' brows furrowed. "It?" Irish asked and continued, "Could be a dead animal."

"He's wearing clothes." Lyn pulled her robe tighter against the cold, but she remained behind the threshold. Behind her, Caesar panted and wagged his tail. She could hear the swish of it against the floor.

A third squad car showed up. The tall officer, *L. Andrews*, according to his badge, spoke into his radio that he copied their arrival. The two men exchanged a mysterious look Lyn guessed was meaningful because Irish blurted, "Fine," and stomped off toward the arriving officers.

"What was that?" Lyn asked.

"We were discussing who would question the caller." L. Andrews wiped his shoes on the mat. "I won."

"Neither of you said anything."

L. Andrews smiled but didn't elaborate. "We're letting out the heat. Mind if we continue our conversation inside? "

There was no legitimate reason not to invite him in. Lyn almost responded with the reflexive *yes-come-in-would-you-like-some-coffee,* but when she opened her mouth, she found her tongue was lead. Visions from the book, the toilet paper tree, and the thing in the backyard were muddling her mind. She thought she'd feel better when the cops arrived, but for some reason, now that they were here, she wanted them to go away. What? Had she thought they'd take the thing from her yard and done deal? That she wouldn't be questioned? She resisted the urge to tell this L. Andrews *never mind* and shut the door. Lock it. Go back to her books. Just not *that book*.

"Uh...my house is a mess." Lyn could only eye him for a second.

"Suit yourself." He pulled out a tiny spiral notebook. Caesar pushed by her and wound around his legs, turning his polyester pants into fur pants.

"Caesar, come back inside."

"He's no trouble." The patrolman scratched Caesar behind his ears. "He probably smells the stray we dropped at the pound this morning."

"He'll never leave you alone now."

"That's alright." His name was Leif, he said, pointing to the *L. Andrews* above his badge. Lyn tried to wrangle Caesar away from him, and her gun banged into the door handle. The officer's gaze fixed on her gaping pocket, and his eyes flashed with strain.

Lyn made sure her hands were splayed and visible. "I meant to put it away. Sorry. Is it okay if I take it out of my pocket?"

"If it's all the same, I'll do the honors." Without so much as brushing her body he slipped the gun from Lyn's robe pocket. She folded her robe tighter and re-tied the knot.

"Dumb of me," she mumbled.

L. Andrews's cheek showed some heat. "Is it your habit to carry a firearm in your pajamas?"

"No." She didn't like how defensive she sounded.

"So you were expecting trouble?"

"No. I mean. Yes. I thought it might be a rabid animal behind the woodpile. I was going to put it out of its misery."

He almost smiled at that. "You don't want to have a concealed weapon when you call us. You could get shot by a jumpy officer—"

"—who fancied himself in danger?"

Irritation flashed across his face. "We don't *fancy* anything. A hand goes to your pocket and we have half a second to decide whether you're going for a tissue or a handgun."

"I understand," Lyn said.

The officer's stony eyes said he didn't believe she did.

"Sorry." Lyn opened the door. "I'm not myself. Please, come in."

L. Andrews' gaze roved her living room and kitchen. She could see him cataloging and analyzing. Did he see dust and decide she'd let her house go? Let everything go? Did he see the post-it notes and deem her scatterbrained? The books. He saw a bookworm for sure. Did he think she had an overactive imagination? One thing he surely thought: her gun etiquette was lacking.

He ejected the magazine and set Lyn's gun on the end table, but stood just inside the door, since she hadn't invited him to sit. Caesar kept putting his furry body against L. Andrew's legs, adorably demanding to be petted. L. Andrews obliged.

"Did you hear anything unusual, either last night or this morning?"

"No. Nothing." (He didn't ask whether she'd *read* anything unusual.)

"How'd you find the body?"

Lyn explained how Caesar's barking had alerted her. She left out the book. Why she didn't bring it up, she couldn't say, except she didn't imagine herself explaining the situation without coming off as a nut case. And why did she care if this cop thought she was crazy? She didn't. But she *did* want to be believed. Anyway, she couldn't prove there was anything wrong with the words in the book. Only *she* knew why they were impossible. She, and her husband, Jude, who was dead. With that thought came the familiar stab, the one she'd never learned to parry though Jude was three years' gone. The cut was unexpected and a gush of *why* always spilled out, usually audibly, but this time Lyn managed to hold her tongue.

"Are you okay?"

"Er, yes," Lyn said.

The door burst open and would've slammed into both dog and man if Leif hadn't thrown up a hand to block it. In blew an icy gust and the Irish officer. A frown creased his face and forehead.

"Ma'am. There's no body behind the woodpile."

"Yes, there is."

He scowled. "I assure you there isn't. We checked the whole yard."

Lyn shook her head, at a loss.

"We checked the backyard. Nothing. Just tracks."

"But. I—I kicked it. Surely…"

Irish put up his finger, indicating she wait. He spoke into his radio. "Dispatch, we're a code 4 here." To Lyn, he resumed, "Somebody, or probably somebodies, was screwing around behind your woodpile. There's tracks everywhere." Irish nodded at the magnolia tree festooned in toilet paper. "And I noticed you got fans."

"I teach at the high school."

"They come all the way out here to get you? You must give some pretty harsh grades."

Lyn started to protest that her students liked her. The toilet paper was done in fun, but Irish had his mind made up.

He continued, "The footprints lead off the property and come out at Sandy Ridge Road—it's kids being stupid." He ran his sleeve along his red nose. "They left you a present, a hornet's nest."

"Yes—I forgot to tell the 911 operator, but the body…it was headless. The hornet's nest was the head."

Irish frowned, as if her credibility had gone the way of the body.

Lyn sat straighter and forced calm into her voice. "There *was* a body. I saw it. Are you telling me it got up and walked away?"

"I'm telling you it walked to Sandy Ridge Road. I can show you the tracks. Somebody's having fun twisting your noodle. Juveniles, like as not."

Irish's assessment was wrong. Her students would not pull a prank like that. They wouldn't. She knew them. He didn't. Which meant someone else had posed as dead in her yard. Someone who knew exactly where Caesar's electric fence ended. What if she had knelt down and felt for a pulse? But no, this someone knew another fact: Lyn Darrow was so petrified of hornets' nests, that she'd never get close to one again. Her eyes welled and she blinked away her thoughts.

Irish continued, "You sure like your privacy, living way out here."

"I like the quiet," Lyn said.

He eyed her again. "We can take a statement, but it's a waste of time."

She gritted her teeth. Not being believed was ticking her off.

Leif studied her throughout the exchange. His eyes on her made her uncomfortably warm. With another one of those loaded glances at Irish, he pulled up a chair and poised his pen. "Mrs. Darrow, I'm going to make a report. Would you tell me the events of the morning, all of them one more time from the moment you woke up until you called us?"

Lyn sat.

Irish sighed.

His partner ignored him.

Irish made his consternation known by shifting his weight from foot to foot, not stepping off the welcome mat, sighing, and tweezing his reddish mustache with his thick, freckled fingers. Eventually he pulled out his phone and got lost in the glow.

L. Andrews asked more pointed questions about the body. Was it prone or face up? What color were the fingers? Had she noticed any footprints? Anything strange?

Somebody lay in her backyard playing dead, someone who knew about the hornets' nest, after all this time. That part, Lyn left out.

Irish received a phone call and took it out on the front porch. They were alone. Lyn was in mid-sentence when she was quietly interrupted.

"This isn't the first time I've been here." His careful tone said it all.

"You mean the day...Jude...?"

"First on the scene." he nodded. "I'm sorry for your loss."

The memory cut through the fog of three years. It would cut through thirty years, three hundred years. This patrolman, Leif Andrews, was here the day Jude died. That might explain why she didn't want to invite him inside.

"I don't remember you," Lyn said.

"That's okay."

"I don't remember much."

Irish blustered back in, breathing hard, hiking up his belt and stomping snow all over the rug. Another look passed between the officers. This time, Patrolman Andrews shook his head and stood. "We'll put a watch on your home for the next few days. You'll see more of our cruisers driving by. We'll talk to the park rangers, too, so they know to watch out for any unusual activity."

Lyn thanked him.

"And maybe you should get this licensed, as a precaution." He indicated the gun on the table and gave his notebook a last scan. "Oh...and the hornets' nest. Kind of an unusual prank. Any idea what's up with that?"

Lyn caught herself before nodding. "No."

"No? You sure?" Leif leaned in.

Suddenly the wood grain on the tabletop was extraordinarily interesting. Lyn traced it with her finger.

"Mrs. Darrow?"

"I just hate hornets."

Irish cleared his throat. It was time to go.

Chapter 4

After the officers left, Lyn made herself another espresso martini in a rocks glass. This time she filled it to the top. On the couch with Caesar, she had a good, long cry into the cottony fur behind his ears.

Lyn Darrow, widow and hater-of-hornets, high school English teacher and lover of books had but one *ask* of life: leave her alone.

Now that Jude was gone, what more was there? In fact, she often asked to be mercifully taken out of this world. A bolt of lightning. A brain aneurysm. A tree falling on her head. Even an accident like her Jude's would be welcome, for it was clear he didn't suffer.

Swift and consummate and brutal was Jude's death. It was Lyn who suffered when she beheld his broken body, flayed and ground and shattered. His helmet had preserved his beautiful head. She had combed her fingers through his long curls and cried into his unseeing eyes and open lips.

Was it any surprise she wished to escape into books? There were worse ways to cope. She considered the drink in her hand, enough to slay Goliath. Well, books—one in particular—had let her down, had mown her down, in fact. So liquor was the next right thing under the circumstances. She picked up the dreadful book, half expecting it to burst into flames but not caring all that much if it did. Yesssssss, the Tito's was doing its job. Her mind had a little fuzz going. It gave her the courage to pick up the book again.

The cover art was on the creepy side: a silhouette standing in an evergreen forest. Not much could be discerned about the man except that he looked capable and threatening with hands at his sides open and ready, like they itched to grab a throat.

Bookworm's author, EM Snow, was not pictured, not on the back cover and not in Wikipedia, so Lyn had no idea whether EM was a he or a she. A Google image search returned many pictures of both women and men, snowy scenes, and a picture of a children's book. There was nothing to suggest the author was someone Lyn knew—except for the terrible scene, the description of what happened to her, exactly.

The librarian, Nolan. He had given her the book. He always gave her great books, until this, of course. Surely he'd have more information.

But that would involve an awkward conversation with him (all conversations outside of school were awkward). She and Nolan had an unspoken agreement. She would approach the reference desk and ask, "How are you?" He'd say, "Fine. Ready for another book?" She'd say, "Yes, please." He'd ask how she liked the last book, and she'd say, "I enjoyed it very much. Thank you." He'd pull out a book from his drawer, hand it to her, and say, "Our next book discussion is Thursday if you'd like to join." She'd say, "Maybe," which translated to *not-on-your-life*, and off she'd go with her book.

But to have an honest-to-God conversation with the librarian? She hadn't done that since they set up their arrangement three years ago. Besides...Sunday. The library was closed. Thank God the library was closed.

And Sunday meant she could have another espresso martini in a low-ball glass.

Chapter 5

Monday morning, like every school day, Lyn's Land Rover was the second car to pull into the staff parking lot. She and Silas had an understanding. He started the coffee and Lyn brought him a cup. Some days, the only thing stopping Lyn from hitting the snooze button was the idea of her cheerful, sarcastic boss sitting at his desk wondering where his cup of coffee was.

The teacher's lounge was cold as usual (something to do with the ductwork), and the enormous dry-erase board boasted the remains of last week's staff meeting notes. An angry hand with splayed fingers crossed through and mostly-erased Silas' bullet points on the Teacher Dress Code. The tattooed décolletage of one particular teacher came to Lyn's mind. Perhaps someone was expressing her disagreement with the *draconian*—was that the word used at the meeting? –dress code.

The drip coffee machine filled the room with the roasted smell of morning. Lyn gave herself a splash of cream and a heavy-handed pour for Silas. With a mug in each hand, she pushed Silas' door open with her backside and entered the principal's office.

"Ahhh, my favorite." Silas said as she handed him his coffee. "And you're not bad, either, Darrow." The principal of Park High wore a bow tie with school colors, a mostly-ironed Oxford, and skinny jeans.

Lyn tried to smile at his good-natured ribbing. "My cheeky boss... how are you?" Her face felt frozen in a grimace. Silas was tuned into her moods and couldn't be fooled, so she gave the fakest laugh ever and quickly turned to leave.

"Uh-uh." He shook his head and held up a finger as he took a sip. "Fess up, or I start a rumor about you."

Lyn didn't want to kick off Monday by talking about the "body" in her yard. She needed the coffee to unknot her hangover-brain. And quiet. She needed more of that before her students arrived. Silas would ask gobs of well-meaning questions and add finding the culprits to his already ceiling-high pile of work because he was a friend and her boss.

"I uh...met someone." She did. Two someones. Police officers.

"Oh my gosh you didn't!"

Such exuberance. She never would have guessed Silas would be this happy to think of her dating. He never said she should date. He wouldn't dare. He knew how much she loved Jude. But here, he was obviously happy about it. Even though *it* wasn't true.

She tried to backpedal. "It's nothing. Honest." *Honest.*

"Ok, you get a pass this morning, but we have a standing appointment for you to give me all the details, or else I'll go crazy in my imagination, thinking of something scandalous which nobody will believe because you're so bookish and strait-laced. But I love that about you. I have enough problem-children teaching my children. But you, you never give me any problems."

"How's Tom?" Lyn deflected.

"Tom's painting the kitchen. Canary yellow. And he's a bear about the whole thing, which is lunacy because it was his idea. I thought the cream was subtle and classy, but he's not happy unless he's changing something. And of course Peaches rubbed all over the fresh paint and furred it up. No way are the cat hairs ever coming out of there. I told Tom he'd better get sanding, and he said the fur adds texture, and I could sand it if I wanted. The *sass* of that man."

"You know you like his sass," Lyn teased.

"Ah, true, true, and it didn't hurt that he made it up to me with take-out from La Kabob, which was the one ray of sunshine about the whole thing."

"Your kitchen will be a ray of sunshine when Tom's done with it."

"Just like you. Now what gives?"

"You said I got a pass."

"Changed my mind. Your face is turning into a chili pepper."

Lyn touched her cheeks self-consciously. "I told you, I met someone."

"Thank you, Captain Obvious. Now, the good stuff."

"He's a cop."

Silas grimaced. "You? I don't believe it. Cops aren't your type."

Lyn stared, blinking, but Silas didn't back down. He bugged his eyes out.

"Okay. I met two cops. They came to my house because I got rolled and there was a body in my backyard but it wasn't a body because it got up and walked away when I wasn't looking. The cops came and obviously they couldn't find it. But they asked me lots of questions. Well, the one did."

"Lyn that's awful."

"I know—"

"Being in the vicinity of a straight I-take-it available man. However did you manage?"

Lyn rolled her eyes and stood to go.

"Oh, Darrow, let me guess. You graded a stack of essays to purge him from your mind."

Lyn arched an eyebrow.

"Here's a funny thing." He held a white envelope, "I found this under the front door this morning. It's full of dead wasps." He shook his head. "Senior pranks. We were *so* much cleverer than this. I mean, c'mon...they're not even *live* wasps."

Hornets, not wasps, Lyn thought. And Lyn *had* been much cleverer than that. But that was many years ago, long before Jude, even.

Silas was wrong about her grading, for twenty-eight essays on the significance of Vincent van Gogh's ear awaited her. She offered what she hoped was a straightforward smile and took off down the hall, the click of her shoes echoing in the empty halls.

At the threshold of her classroom, she lurched.

The coffee cup slipped from her hand and shattered on the linoleum. Hot liquid splattered all the way up her legs, on her pencil skirt, on her sweater, even up her neck. Lyn didn't feel the burning liquid. In her frantic flight to get away from her classroom, her high heel skidded in the coffee puddle, and she fell forward, spilling her purse and tote. Her hands smacked the floor. She was unable to save her face from a thick, sharp piece of mug. Shards of ceramic bit into her shins, and some of the smaller bits stuck when she tried to get traction in the coffee mess and slipped. With the uneven gait of the terrorized, Lyn pounded back to Silas' office, purse and tote forgotten.

Silas stood so fast his chair toppled. "My God, your face."

"My room..." Lyn couldn't get out the rest.

He left her sitting in the plastic chair usually reserved for miscreants. She picked bits of ceramic out of her skin and took deep breaths until Silas returned, sporting a sheen of sweat. "I called the police."

The police. *Augh.*

"What kind of sicko does that?" Without waiting for an answer, Silas dug in his pocket for his phone. "I need a substitute teacher for Lyn Darrow. Yeah, all day. And an alternate room. Add the room change to the morning announcements..."

While Silas was deep in the details of cushioning the school day against her classroom, Lyn made her way to the nurse's office. The click of her heels against the linoleum made a racket that made her feel uneasy in the empty building. Her entirely illegal gun was in her purse, dropped in the hall and doing her absolutely no good there. Worse, if Silas found it, Lyn would cease to be his favorite teacher.

A noise down the hall made her stop. It sounded like the janitor's closet. Whoever vandalized her classroom could still be here, now, waiting for her. She wished for her gun. How could she be so thoughtless to leave it behind?

She turned back for it and caught her reflection in the mirrored window of the nurse's room. Her cheek was slashed with a hideous frown of crimson that dribbled down her neck. With a careful hand she touched it. She knew she'd been cut by a piece of mug but didn't realize it was still embedded in her face. When she bent to unlock the door, a drop of blood landed on the knob. With her palm she wiped it away and let herself in. She'd be safe enough locked in the nurse's office.

The nurse's office had two beds with curtains for privacy, one open and one closed around the bed. Could someone be behind the curtain? It wasn't sheer enough to see through. She held her breath and listened.

Nothing.

Before she lost her nerve, she swiped open the curtain, nearly pulling it out of the ceiling track.

An empty bed. She folded herself into it and pulled the thick curtain closed, screeching the rings along the iron tube. She wanted to lay back on the cot, but her legs would bloody the white sheet. Instead she leaned forward and studied the flecks in the tiled floor, the bits of dust and dirt collecting in the corners, and a thin, yellowish spider with threadlike legs.

Her gore-painted classroom pushed back into her imagination.

Sirens neared the school, a sound that usually filled Lyn with memories of Jude, but today made her blood flow faster. That sound would bring help. She had just mentioned the enigmatic police officer to Silas and maybe a small part of her wished to see him again, but this was like a wicked genie's answer. *You want him? You got him, Lyn. Be careful what you wish for.* Before she could let her thoughts linger too long on officer L. Andrews, Lyn helped herself to a large bottle of peroxide and dumped it over her cheek, being careful to lean over the sink. The wash revealed the piece, and Lyn tweezed it and gently tugged until the shard, the size of a dime, came free with a little burst of pain. Without the shard to cork the flow of blood, it ran faster. She grabbed a paper towel and stamped it against her cheek.

Apologizing to future hand-washers, Lyn slipped off her shoe and put her foot in the sink. The hydrogen peroxide set first one shin on fire, then the other. She dried her feet and legs with paper towels and wiped a clean paper towel across her face, keeping away from the gash. Good enough.

The hallway was long and empty between the nurse's office and her classroom, and she could both hear and see the cluster of police officers huddled in conversation with Silas. Where had they all come from? She'd only been gone a few moments and was surprised at the swift response.

One, a mustached man in plain clothes and wearing a badge on his belt looked at Lyn but addressed Silas. "This the teacher?"

Silas turned and nodded. "Lyn Darrow, Officer Barnfeld."

"*Detective* Barnfeld." He made no move to shake. His eyes roved over Lyn's cheek, her legs. A fat tongue roved over his lip. He scanned her the way one would assess a racehorse he might bet against.

Paramedics arrived carrying duffle bags and wearing white gloves. Behind them, at a respectable distance, lurked teachers, arriving for the day and pulled toward the drama. Among them was the gym teacher, who mouthed, *What the hell?* Lyn could only shake her head. The whispers of her fellow teachers sounded like hornets.

To the arriving teachers, Silas held up the calming it's-under-control hand.

Lyn sized up *Detective* Barnfeld, who carried a lot around his midsection, and it spilled over his gun. The flat-top military buzz cut was all that remained of a more disciplined youth. He gnawed at a piece of gum, but it didn't mask the rotten tang of cigarettes wafting about. The chewing made his thick, squarish mustache spasm.

As he studied her face, his expression clouded. "Excuse me a sec." He entered the classroom, then returned and took another look at Lyn. To Silas, he said, "That's her, alright."

"What?" Lyn asked.

"You mean you didn't see it?" the detective asked.

Silas took Lyn's elbow and whispered. "It's okay. You don't need to go in there." He shuddered. "Once is enough."

She hadn't analyzed the reddish-brown slashes and splatters all over her classroom. Why would she? It was surely paint, but it looked like blood. Was there a rhyme or reason to it? She inched into her room and took in the scene. The "blood" on each of the desks was slopped with Jackson Pollock abandon, the hornets' nest centrally placed on her desk like it was an apple for the teacher. Red hand prints on the book posters and—she spotted something else she had missed the first time and was drawn by macabre curiosity—to the photo of Caesar ripped into tiny pieces and scattered in a puddle of blackish paint. She only knew it was Caesar's picture because the picture wasn't on the poster anymore.

But what Detective Barnfeld referred to was the enormous dry-erase board Lyn used for quotes and writing prompts. Lyn hadn't entered the room before, so she missed it entirely. The board was on the hallway wall, not visible from outside the room. What should have been on the board was a quote from W.B. Yeats. She had written it after one student was particularly harsh toward another's writing. The word *suck* had been bandied about. The writer had cried. Lyn stopped the class and wrote the Yeats quote. She asked everyone to pen some stream-of-consciousness thoughts on a dream they held. Each time they weren't sure of what to write next, they were to re-read the quote until something came.

But I, being poor, have only my dreams;
I have spread my dreams under your feet;
Tread softly because you tread on my dreams.

That was the quote she'd left on the dry-erase board when she went home for the weekend. Now the quote was gone. In its place was a larger-than-life rendition of a woman's face: unquestionably Lyn's.

"You don't look well." Barnfeld had come in behind her, had touched her lower back. The unexpected contact zapped her already-coiled nerves.

"Now you see it, don't you? Your boss said it was a painting of you, and I didn't believe him. I figured he was traumatized—you know how those effeminate types are—but he was spot on. It's you, alright. You got yourself one pissed-off student, Miss Darrow."

Mrs. Darrow. I'd be married if he wasn't dead. The detective's use of *Miss* angered her. Or maybe it was the way he emphasized it.

He got right to business. "Does any particular student come to mind? Any of them made threats against you lately?"

Lyn clamped her lips together. Like she was going to rat out a student on a hunch.

"How about we take this conversation outside? Let the guys take a look at you." Barnfeld ushered her out the door.

The paramedics—they were for her? She didn't need them. The paper towel showed thinner and thinner blood C's when she dabbed her face. She shook herself loose from Barnfeld. "Is that necessary—can't we just clean it up?"

Barnfeld thumbed his belt loops and rocked back on his heels. "Probably animal blood, but we have to be sure. Crime lab's slower than geriatric slugs on a salted street, but I put in a rush."

An officer was busy cordoning off the area around her classroom with yellow tape.

"Blood?" Lyn asked. "Surely it's paint?"

"Don't you smell that? Like pennies. I've smelled enough crime scenes to know the difference between blood and paint. Once the labs are back, we'll give the okay for your people to clean. Otherwise, we could be scrubbing away evidence. Miss Darrow, you got any haters?"

"Doesn't every teacher have students with grudges?"

"Sure, sure. But not every teacher gets her portrait done in blood. You've got yourself an artist here."

Silas, breathless from putting out the administrative fires, joined them in the hallway. His bow tie was askew. "We have cameras that should have picked up whoever broke in. Guess what? They're smashed."

A no-nonsense paramedic got right in Lyn's face. "Now, I brought this all the way up here. Don't you make me take it back down without at least setting on it." The marinesque woman patted the gurney with a gloved hand. "Give me a minute of your time. I won't bite," she said.

Lyn laughed sardonically. She didn't even correct her grammar. *...setting on it...*"You look like a wrestler."

"Close. MMA. Mixed martial arts. But we only punch people. We don't bite."

"I do."

"You do what?"

"I bite." *Where did that come from?*

"Hmph. Thanks for the warning. I'll be careful." She pointed to her chest. "Tawny, at your service."

Something about Tawny made Lyn like her instantly. Lyn submitted to the examination. Tawny the MMA fighter said leg shaving would be out of the question for a few days, and the face gash was on the edge of needing stitches. "If it was me, I wouldn't do it. Scars are good for my image. But with your face, I'd do it."

"You switch into paramedic mode and treat yourself after a hard fight?" Lyn asked.

Tawny laughed. "I treat the *other* girl after a hard fight. Nobody treats Tawny."

Barnfeld was back. "Tell me about this Delaney Lucas. I hear she's a live one. She been acting strange lately?"

"Strange is Delaney's usual."

"So I hear. She angry? More quiet than usual? She write any threatening stories or talk tough to her buddies?"

"Delaney has no friends. And no. She's—"

Tawny tipped Lyn's face so she could spread ointment on the cheek gash. Tawny's makeup was thick and perfect, as was her braided hair. She was one-part goddess, one-part thug, the sort who looked like she wanted to save the world *and* start a bar brawl. So she got a sleeve of tattoos and—it would seem—did both.

Barnfeld inserted himself between Tawny and Lyn. "Your boss says Delaney has mental problems."

"Silas would not say that."

"Fine. He said she's an introvert with abandonment issues."

"Delaney's dad got cancer and her mom self-medicated with alcohol and prescription drugs before she moved on to harder stuff."

"So?"

Lyn rolled her eyes. "So, Delaney became the caregiver to her mom when her dad died. Delaney's mother has mental problems. Delaney has problems."

"How do you know all this?"

"Essays."

"Officer Andrews tells me you're pretty jumpy."

Lyn scoffed. How could he? Right or not, she felt betrayed by the officer.

"Is it true?" Barnfeld asked.

Lyn clamped her lips shut and suddenly hated Leif Andrews.

A hive of blue-coated glove-wearers took over her classroom. Not a single poster would be salvageable. Every desk had blood marks. Another detective prodded the hornets' nest on her desk, rocking the proverbial apple for the teacher.

Lyn closed her eyes. The would-be artist, he made the image...complimentary. Lyn in blood against a white board was striking. Larger than life. Her lines fell pleasant to the eye. Dark against light. Her gaze was cast down as if the world were below her. Her hair a lion's mane of red and black fire. Her lips, unhinged with a ready word. Surely the way she was depicted was not how she appeared: Beautiful. Sensual. Enigmatic. Next to the blood image were finger-painted words: *I have dreams, too.*

Chapter 6

THE SHOCK OF SEEING her classroom painted in blood pushed the impossible book about Jude's death to the back of Lyn's mind. Silas sent her home for the day. Told her to take tomorrow off too, if she wanted. On her way home, she passed a Park Hill police vehicle headed in the opposite direction, lights flashing. As she drove the winding country roads, she asked herself over and over who would want to kill some poor animal to send her a sick message? Who pretended to be dead in her yard while she looked on? Someone wanted to terrorize her.

They succeeded.

Lyn did what she determined to be the next right thing. Normally, that would be curling up with a good book and pretending the real world didn't exist. Reading was always *the next right thing*—until her latest book had sent her straight back to the terrible moment Jude died. Today, there was a more practical way to cope. She sat at the kitchen table and cleaned her gun with a toothbrush and hydrogen peroxide, the 9mm Smith & Wesson in parts on the kitchen table, old dishrags protecting the wood. Caesar lay at her feet, panting, tail tucked beneath him, apprehensive. He knew what was coming.

Lyn pushed cleaning cloths through the barrel and spoke to him. "Sorry, I know you hate this."

He looked at her with big, wet, fearful eyes.

Years ago, after a bad thunderstorm, Lyn had come home from work to find the front door trim ripped off up to the knob, and Caesar guiltily gnawing on a piece of it. She had been tempted to yell, but the puddle of pee told her Caesar wasn't himself. He never lost control in the house. The same thing had happened when she did target practice and left Caesar in the house, but it was the wooden sofa leg he'd chewed up. Loud noises were Caesar's enemy, and chewing was his comfort. Lyn had curtailed her target practice after that. It felt cruel to subject Caesar (and her house) to it.

"You're coming outside. If you want to grind your chops on a thick tree branch or a piece of firewood, go for it."

Caesar padded toward Jude's woodpile. A perfect chewing log tempted him from a foot beyond the shock line. Caesar knew if he stuck his neck out for that bone-sized log, he'd get zapped. Caesar whined longingly at the stick until Lyn found him another one from the woodpile she had cut herself, not as thick, but it would do.

Lyn's phone buzzed with a number she didn't recognize. She ignored it and resumed arranging her targets, pushing paper plates onto nails in the tree trunk. A few minutes later, another call from a different unrecognized number. Then the first number again. Solicitors? The blood mural came to mind. Maybe it was the artist, calling to see how she liked her portrait.

The next time her phone went off, she answered.

"Lyn Darrow?" asked an unfamiliar male voice.

She didn't respond, didn't want to admit who she was.

"Lyn Darrow? I'm Chuck Higley from Channel 5 News. Do you mind—"

Lyn ended the call and sighed, in mixed exasperation and relief. The news. Of course. Word got out it was her classroom.

Another buzz. The same number.

Oh, she'd be popular now. Had reporters already called Silas? Lyn might not be her principal's favorite teacher anymore.

The third time a call came from that number, she blocked it. She removed the hollow points and loaded the practice ammo. Pushing the bullets into the magazine always made her fingers ache, and the cold made it even harder. At least the snow had melted. She backed away to range distance, eyed her target, and exhaled.

Gun-thunder filled her mind, crowding out her fear and memories.

She emptied the magazine as Caesar slunk around like a hyena, weaving behind Lyn in the erratic manner of the unhinged. She reloaded. Shot. Reloaded. As the reports grew steady, so did Caesar. Lyn reminded him of the thick piece of firewood he could wrap his furry white paws around and take out his terror upon. Teeth flashing, he debarked the hunk in no time and crunched on it till it broke in half and he'd reduced it to pulp.

By the time she paused shooting, Lyn's fingers were blue with cold, and the smiley face she'd drawn on the plate with marker was shot away. Nothing remained but a jagged scrap around the nail. Lyn picked up her shell casings so Caesar wouldn't put his nose into them. As she dropped them into the bucket they made satisfying, metallic chimes.

Lyn shot until her fingers were numb. Then she shot some more.

Every few rounds, she replaced the shot-through plate with a fresh one. She was setting up to begin again, when the wet, sucking sound of footsteps froze her. She had the gun loaded with her practice ammo, which wasn't ideal. Practice ammo would rip cleanly through a body, would not do the damage regular ammo would.

Her shooting hand shook. Caesar's ears perked up, but he didn't rise, a log held casually in his paws.

From the side of her house, the footsteps closed in.

Lyn raised the gun in the direction of the steps. She considered saying hello, but that would give the intruder knowledge of her location. Better to outshoot. To be the surprise. Her *hello* would come from the Smith & Wesson if whoever approached her meant any harm.

Caesar scrambled up and bounded past Lyn, wagging his tail as Patrolman Leif Andrews emerged into view. His hand rested on his gun holster, and he waved with the other. "Whoa. I come in peace."

Lyn narrowed her eyes and flashed him a look of annoyance.

He halted, confused. "Is something the matter?"

"I'm going to set my gun down because I'm feeling angry right now," Lyn said.

"What for?"

Lyn rolled her eyes. She was not going to play his games.

"I came to update you on your classroom."

"And then report back to that detective on my mental state?"

Leif shook his head, appearing to not understand.

"So update," Lyn snapped, sharper than she intended.

"The blood was human. Your school will be closed for a few days while CSI combs over it."

All the strength went out of Lyn. She wobbled to the picnic table and dropped onto the bench. "Human...whose?"

"We won't know until forensics analyzes it. We may never know. But it means your classroom—and your school—is a crime scene."

Lyn wiped her nose with her sleeve and blinked to keep from crying.

"Under the circumstances, you're using your time wisely." Leif gave an appreciative nod to the ring that was once a paper plate, now more of an asymmetric snowflake. Caesar circled him and rubbed white fur all over his pants. He patted Caesar's head and scratched behind his ears. "You've got yourself quite a range here."

"I'm not much good."

The pitted tree trunk agreed.

Leif surveyed all her misses, divots in the dead tree. "Hey, you're practicing, aren't you?" He flipped through a stack of plates. "A hell of a lot of practicing."

Lyn blushed and shoved her hands into her pockets.

They stood a hundred yards from where Jude's body had landed, where Lyn and Leif had met three years ago. Her eyes flicked to his arm. She could dimly recollect this man's feel, his smell, and his breath on her neck as he asked her to come away and let the first responders take him, take away her Jude. Forever. There was something troubling about this Leif, specifically his...arm? ...something out of reach. She shuddered but didn't know why.

Her body still sort of wanted to punch him. Her now-empty fists clenched, but not just because of what he had said to Detective Barnfeld. Something about him sent her straight back to the moment of Jude's death.

"Why'd you tell that detective I was jumpy?"

"Is that what he told you?"

Lyn didn't answer.

Leif laughed, but Lyn didn't see what was funny.

"He was testing you. He read your statement. Cops do that. Like waving something red. If the animal charges, it's a bull. He wanted to see how you'd react, that's all. He's kind of a—let's just say, him and I aren't close."

"He. It's *he* and I."

"What?"

"Forget it, you didn't tell him I was jumpy?"

"No, ma'am. You were calm, especially under the circumstances."

Hmph. And this cop had no idea, *no clue* about the totality of the circumstances—the book describing Jude's exact death and the hornets and what they meant to her.

Chapter 7

Park Hill High School was closed for the second day in a row, thanks to Lyn's classroom. After yesterday's excessive target practice, her entire supply of practice rounds was used up, and Lyn's hands were swollen, blistered, and generally useless. She needed to make a trip into town for more ammunition, and croissants from Bear's Bakery were the day's bright spot. Lyn ordered a half dozen bright spots to go.

The counter was manned by a grinning girl with a tattoo sleeve and a dusting of flour on her cheek, a prior student. What was her name? As Lyn chewed on her croissant, struggling to remember the student's name, the girl rescued her from the awkward moment.

"You'd be so proud of me, Mrs. D. I'm reading *Anna Karenina* in Russian Lit this semester. Have you, ever?"

Lyn nodded. A slow death by spoons wasn't as torturous as *Anna Karenina*, but with the croissant in her mouth, it was too much to say. All she could manage was a thumbs-up and "Russians are wordy." It came out *ushens aw urdy*. Lyn shrugged and saluted her ex-student with her half-eaten croissant.

Pam Bear (who went by Miss Pam because, well...Miss Bear) flitted around the kitchen, kicking up flour and humming. When the bakery owner saw Lyn, she wiped her hands on her apron and approached the counter.

"Russians are…" Miss Pam made a chef's kiss to communicate what she thought of Russians and held out what looked like peanut butter fudge. "Here, try this." She often asked Lyn's opinion of this or that confection she'd dreamt up, but Lyn knew Miss Pam was generous and wanted to give her the gift of something sweet.

Lyn closed her eyes and allowed the fudge to melt in her mouth. "I'll take this over a Russian any day."

After making small talk about the books she'd been reading, Miss Pam went back to her dough, and another clerk appeared from the storeroom, obviously a new hire—and a surprise.

"Delaney." Lyn said, "When did you start working at Bear's?"

"A couple weeks ago."

Lyn wondered if Delaney had been contacted by one *Detective* (don't you forget it) Barnfeld. She seemed her usual self, so Lyn guessed that no, she had not. Lyn avoided the elephant in the room—her bloody classroom—and asked about the toilet paper.

"Hey, you and your friends didn't pay me a visit Saturday night by any chance, did you?"

"I don't have any friends," was her Delaneyesque comeback. It was sadly true. Like Lyn, the girl didn't seem to have any close friends, and also like Lyn, didn't seem to want any. "They roll your place again?" she asked, cracking a smile.

"Uh-huh."

"That sucks." Said like it did not suck one bit. Lyn's galactic assignments stole swaths of Delaney's evenings that could've been spent watching Netflix or reading something she liked, so Delaney had written in one of her essays.

Lyn eyed her. "Hey, does Miss Pam give her employees free samples?"

Delaney's answer was to snatch a donut hole and pop it into her mouth.

"You're lucky," Lyn said. "I'd quit teaching for a job that got me free croissants from Bear's."

"So, if I convince Miss Pam to hire you, you'll quit teaching? All Miss Pam and Heather talk about is books, constantly." Delaney thumbed to Heather, the girl who had said she was reading *Anna Karenina*, and the name clicked. *Right. Heather Bentley.* How could Lyn have forgotten?

"Besides," Delaney lowered her voice, "after what happened to your room, it only makes sense, Mrs. D. Teaching's too dangerous."

Lyn sucked in a deep breath. Of course. How could she think they wouldn't talk about it?

Heather-the-Russian-lover leaned in. "I heard, but I didn't know it was *your* room, Mrs. D. I'm soooo sorry."

Lyn pretended to shrug it off, and Delaney said, "Hey, I got to pick up a shift today because we're off school. Works for me. Mrs. D, you should quit teaching and work here. You three could talk books all day and eat scones or whatever you like. I could teach your class. I have some people I'll be failing."

"And miss out on your sardonic essays? Not a chance."

"I don't even know what that means."

"Good thing we have dictionaries. Bonus points for using it correctly in a future essay. Or ask Heather." Lyn saluted both girls and winked at the chipper Heather, who'd run the gauntlet of Lyn's class and come out, not only unscathed but better for it, loving, *loving???* Tolstoy.

Delaney gave the peace sign, one of the small gestures that proved she didn't hate Lyn—just her assignments.

Lyn waved back and continued on her way. Everywhere she went, she ran into someone she taught, either now or in the past. In the years since

Jude died, holding casual conversations had become harder and harder for her. Other than books, Lyn didn't have anything to talk about. She didn't mind talking with her students about books because she loved them. The books *and* the students. Not to mention, teaching paid the bills.

Resting on the passenger seat of her Land Rover was Leif's business card. Lyn stuffed another bite in her mouth and read the letters of his name, tracing the insignia.

Leif Andrews, Patrolman. First on the scene when Jude died. It was all a blur. Lyn's eyes had stopped working after seeing Jude. She remembered only the feel of ironlike, indifferent arms wrapped around her as she thrashed. She hated the arms that dragged her away from her love. But wait. Something new came as she fingered the business card: the taste of blood. Where'd that come from? Oh...right. She cringed. How could she forget? But then, how could she *not* forget? Lyn had been so crazed by the sight of her beloved's broken body, she bit the arm of the person who tried to pull her away.

One Leif Andrews.

Did he have a scar on his arm? And how did he feel about her taking a bite? Peril of the job, she guessed. No wonder he was so antsy over her gun. At least he didn't bring it up, her biting him. Now it made sense why she wanted to run when she saw the officers. It brought it all back, Jude's death, the smells, the tastes, the horror of losing her best friend in the whole world.

Oh, but she needed a book. A good one this time. Something to get her mind off the present. And the past. Lyn needed to escape her world. And she *would* escape, right after she confronted a certain librarian.

She wiped her mouth with a napkin and realized she'd bitten the side of her cheek. The taste of blood wasn't only in her imagination.

Chapter 8

The library was situated atop a bluff overlooking Woden's Creek. The few non-handicap parking spots on the street were always taken, so Lyn drove around back into the lower lot and took the many, many thigh-paring stairs up to the rear entrance—not that she minded. The steep steps were good exercise, and she caught her breath on the landings, enjoying the creek's burble and sometimes catching sight of a cardinal in the bone-colored birches along the creek bed. Once inside the sliding doors, she tipped her face to the blast of heated air that welcomed her.

Salt crystals carried on the treads of shoes sprinkled the black industrial carpet, crunching underfoot. On both sides of the entrance were corkboards studded with flyers and notices for babysitting services, Girl Scout meetings, book clubs, and a missing black and white cat named Bleep (who was overfed and looked more like a panda bear). Enormous skylights poured natural light into the spacious area. Plush chairs and couches lined the walls, and in the farthest reaches of the library was a nook with a gas fireplace, Lyn's favorite spot. Everything about the library was a comfort, except the book in her hand.

As Lyn crossed the main foyer, she remembered the croissant in her other hand. No food allowed in the library. She halted, unsure if she should cram the rest in her mouth or turn around and finish it outside. Buttery flakes sprinkled her coat sleeves like dandruff. The floor too.

Oops. She decided to give it to the birds and squirrels, and when the doors whisked open, she chucked it out. Her gaze followed the half-eaten hunk into the chest of one Leif Andrews, in uniform.

"Double oops..."

He arched an eyebrow.

"I wasn't expecting...I thought the squirrels...are you following me?"

"No, ma'am. I'm checking out a book. I've been accused of being a donut-lover, but this is the first time I've had one thrown at me."

"It was a croissant."

"You shouldn't litter."

"I'll go grab it." She darted for it as he bent down. Their heads clunked and he laughed.

"I got it." He handed her the chunk of dirt-dusted croissant, and she put it in the trash. With this Leif in her vicinity she did feel a little safer, but also, unsafe, as if she were standing by a fire on a winter night. One side was toasty warm, almost too hot, and the other side trembled with cold.

She nodded her thanks and hurried inside.

The library was Lyn's sanctuary, a cathedral where the smell of books was incense, and the whispers of books sliding into place were vespers. Library shelves were full of the souls of people long gone and far away, like Jude.

How Jude had loved books.

Shortly after his death, Lyn decided to read every book in Jude's personal library and every book he checked out of the Park Hill Library. The only problem was the privacy laws that prevented the librarians from giving her access to his check-out history, even as his widow. Nolan was the only librarian willing to break the rules by "suggesting" books to her. It was a kindness that moved her in the darkest weeks following Jude's death. She had explained to him that she was in the mood for a very niche, very particular type of book. And Nolan had asked, "What genre?" She whispered, "The Jude Darrow genre," and with only the smallest hesitation, he pulled up Jude's checkouts. He gave her a book her Jude had read. She had asked for other books from then on, sometimes from the Jude genre, sometimes not. His suggestions had never let her down, until *Bookworm*.

Before *Bookworm*, it was as if Nolan could read her mind and knew exactly the sort of books she'd prefer. Sometimes she'd do her own choosing, for variety. Being an English teacher, Lyn had always enjoyed reading, but after Jude died, reading became her world. Her obsession started with the stack of books on his bedside table. Lyn had read each one and replaced it, had taken a picture of the stack so she didn't forget the order, even the way a few of the books were askew. She finished *East of Eden*, which Jude had been reading when he died. Next up was *Leave the World Behind,* which he was also reading. And on and on.

And then Nolan helped keep her tethered to Jude in the one way she could be: books. Her present TBR stack topped out at two feet. She could never have enough books on the nightstand. But what felt holiest were the books she knew had been read by Jude. Those made her feel like he wasn't gone, not truly. This way, she and Jude could still share stories.

She fished her returns out of her bag. As the books tumbled in the mostly-empty bin, they made loud, hollow knocks. She winced and searched for Nolan. Not seeing him, she scanned the shelves, grabbed a book. It seemed like Nolan was always at the library. Maybe he was on a break.

While scanning, Lyn spotted Leif Andrews searching the non-fiction section, his finger dragging along the spines as he walked the row. She quickly looked away to avoid eye contact and was happy for the distraction of Nolan appearing from behind a bookshelf. A woman with a tote full of books smiled and gushed her thanks at him for the book. Nolan was a favorite with the ladies, his athletic build apparent even in his button-down oxfords and khaki pants. He was a favorite with Lyn too, but not for the same reasons. She wasn't looking for a pretty face. She was looking for access to Jude's books.

Lyn met him as he returned to his desk. Nolan had a boyish habit of running a hand through his wavy hair, grabbing fists of it and tugging when he was deep in thought or figuring out a problem. Lyn spent much time with Nolan in her field of vision while she pored over the books he suggested, seeing him but not seeing him. She didn't start with her usual mechanical *How are you?* but instead pulled the book from her bag, her sweaty palm leaving a fog on the protective cover. Lyn bit her lip and held out the book.

Nolan frowned. "What's wrong?"

"This was from the Jude genre, right?"

"I don't remember. Why? You didn't like it?"

Lyn struggled to form a phrase that didn't sound crazy. Nothing came. *Spit it out, Lyn.*

"You didn't like the book?" He repeated.

Lyn flushed. "No. I mean no. I...look." She flipped open the book to the chapter about Jude, to where her photograph of Caesar held the page. She splayed the book out to Nolan. "Would you mind reading a few pages?"

Nolan, perplexed, fixed his eyes on her. "I recommended it."

"I know."

"I read everything I recommend."

"Even the Jude genre?"

"Even that."

Lyn flushed a deeper shade of red. "There's something *off* about it."

She handed over the book and he fumbled it.

"Sorry," Lyn said.

He picked it up. "I'm afraid I lost your page."

Lyn re-found the chapter and held it under his nose. He scanned the pages, his lips moving slightly as he read.

Nolan glanced up and blinked. "I'm not sure I understand."

"Did you get to the part about the..." Lyn trailed off, immersed in scanning the words and flipping pages. "Augh. Can't find it. There was a part..." She trailed off, earnestly searching for the page. Her brow furrowed. "I don't get it."

"Are you alright?"

Lyn took a few steps back and silently waved him off. He called after her but she ignored him. The back corner of the library was usually empty. She made her way to the fireplace and crumpled into an arm chair. She fanned the pages, searching for the words about the cyclist who got hit by a car and the woman, *herself*, holding a flat of petunias. That was what she'd been holding. Petunias. Perhaps she remembered the wrong chapter and put the bookmark back in the wrong spot. But no. She remembered. The very page. She had tossed it onto the passenger seat, the plastic crinkling when it landed. She'd glanced at it again and again during the trip into town. A venomous snake slithering through her car would not get as many furtive glances as that wretched book.

Except for the stop at Bear's Bakery, the only time it was out of her sight was when the officers were at the house. She'd left it on the couch, upside down. Even if her page was lost, the story was in there somewhere. Lyn scanned and scanned. It was as if someone took a thread ripper to the story and wove in a new one.

Huddled with it by the library fire, Lyn skimmed from the beginning to the halfway point. Nothing. No sign of the scene. Lyn pressed the open book to her face and inhaled deeply. A few hours ago she could barely touch this book because of what was inside, and now she wanted more than anything to locate the horrible passage, if only to prove she wasn't mad. She flipped and skimmed, reading backwards and forwards. Finally, she decided to start at the beginning. It *had* to be there.

Hours passed. Lyn pushed frustrated palms into her eyes and massaged her cheeks, not wanting to give up on finding the passage. The small of her back ached from sitting so long, and her belly cramped with hunger. The fire had been shut off. She became aware of the rustle of fabric and a quiet tread.

Nolan.

"Mind if I sit?" He had the low-volume librarian voice down.

Lyn held the book open in her lap and motioned to a second plush chair, which he took. On his button down shirt, the faint mark of the iron showed Nolan had used too hot a setting. She stared at the burn mark.

When Jude was alive, Lyn had ironed his shirts.

After Jude died, Lyn pulled all his clothes from the hamper and piled them beside her on the bed. The few shirts that had been in the washing machine, she dried and ironed. Why? He wasn't going to wear them. Ever. Again. As the weeks passed, the freshly-ironed shirts hanging untouched in the closet mocked her. She told herself it was out of boredom that she ironed them a second time, a third. And on and on until the fabric gave way and split, and the collars were ruined. Even the finest shirts could hold up only so long under heat and starch. Lyn forgot herself one day while mindlessly running the iron over a shirt. Back and forth, back and forth went the iron, the piney smell of burnt cotton becoming more and more intense. Jude's favorite movement of Carmina Burana, "O Fortuna," blasted from the radio.

Lyn's hand had been on the iron, but her head was in her Land Rover, speeding down the highway. In her imagination, shafts of light from the setting sun crashed into the trees flanking the highway. *This way*, Jude said. *This way to where I am.* A blink away.

Anything solid beside the highway would do the trick, a broken-down car or a telephone pole. All Lyn had to do was keep the pedal depressed, yank the steering wheel.

Boom. Problems solved.

Lyn imagined the cement column in her front window growing larger and larger and blotting out all else as it tore through the engine block, through—

Nolan cleared his throat, pulling Lyn out of her reverie.

"I used to iron Jude's shirts. For some reason seeing your shirt there..."

He frowned as he inspected his shirt. "Oh...darn." Nolan nodded toward the wall clock, "I'm sorry, but we're closing,"

The library, closed? Where had the hours gone? *Into the book* was the answer, but Lyn hardly believed it. She snapped the book closed, harder than she intended. "I didn't see the time."

"You seem to be wrestling with that, not reading it."

"I'm trying to find the spot I read earlier."

"No luck?"

"None."

Nolan lightly touched the spine.

Lyn whispered, "I've always appreciated you breaking the rules for me, getting me Jude's books."

He waved it off.

"I don't know, maybe I'm losing my mind, but I'm telling you there was a scene in this book that described what happened to Jude."

"Your Jude?"

She nodded. "The accident."

Nolan's face became instantly unreadable. He tapped the cover with his finger. "Nobody dies in this book."

Chapter 9

It was dark Wednesday morning as Lyn pulled out of her driveway. A patrol car passed. The officer turned on his dome light and waved a greeting. Seeing the uniform brought Jude's death to the front of her consciousness, though the whole point of the patrols was to keep her safe. Books had kept her safe, until recently. She wasn't letting this inexplicable book out of her sight. How could there be a scene from her life in it? How could the scene disappear? It couldn't. The only answer was that Lyn was losing her mind. But she didn't feel crazy. Isolated sometimes, enough to own a gun and learn to use it, but no matter how isolated her life had become, and Jude's death was the worst of it, she never felt her wits slip. The Irish officer thought her strange for living remote and alone, but she had her books, her Caesar, and lots of buffer space between her and...everything. What did he know?

She kept the book beside her because she wondered if it would turn again, back into the story it was before. After Nolan had ushered her out of the already-closed library, she took *Bookworm* home and re-read it twice, each time thinking the words would magically go back to the scene with Jude, as they had that morning. But no. She couldn't see it in the dark car, but she touched the smooth cover and flicked the pages. When she arrived at school, she hustled through the empty, dark parking lot.

Lyn braced herself as she flicked on her classroom lights. The hush of an empty, bare-walled, scrubbed out classroom held its breath. Two hours before the opening bell, even Silas wasn't in the building. Was she scared to be alone in the school? Absolutely. But she reached into her purse and touched her Ruger, the littlest pistol she owned. The school wasn't open yesterday, otherwise she would've gone to assess the room then and put it to rights as much as possible. Barnfeld said her effects would not be returned. They were evidence. Silas had given her an allowance to purchase new wall decor and cushions to replace the bloodied ones. Yesterday, she'd purchased prints of Picasso and Pollock paintings and several other unusual prints with vibrant colors that begged for a story to accompany them. To inspire essays, she had purchased snapshots of the March to Montgomery, Kennedy's motorcade, Einstein and his wild hair, and even a replacement of the defaced Julius Caesar poster. She taped the photo of her beloved Caesar to the corner.

To find a replacement for her movie-size poster of *Watership Down*, she had turned to Etsy and found a whimsical print that boasted one of her favorite quotes. *Watership Down* taught lessons about survival and resilience. Lyn felt a kinship with the rabbit protagonist, Hazel, who lost everything familiar and was thrust, unbidden, into a harrowing journey. She was beginning to see herself as a rabbit, targeted and terrorized and (presently) unprepared for a fight. The rabbit Hazel was not naturally-inclined to leadership or even confidence, but he rose to the challenge before him. He did what was needed, the next right thing. What was Lyn's next right thing? Target practice? It was a step in the right direction, but was it enough? She arranged her newly-purchased wall art and left plenty of space for the print of Hazel.

Her cell phone vibrated against the desk, startling her. Silas. He asked if she wanted another personal day.

"I'm here. I came in early to fix my room."

"What?!" The alarm in his voice set her on edge. Should she be at school, alone, this early?

She sighed. Now being alone anywhere was bad? She was a thirty-two year old widow. *Alone* went with the territory. She didn't give him any pushback or acknowledge *to him* the angry piece of her mind, the part that groped for books and quiet and no human contact whatsoever because she knew Silas was on her side.

"Who'll get your coffee if I'm not here?" Lyn tried for levity. But it was more than that. She'd not be played like a pawn. Whoever defaced her room wanted to break her. Or more likely, to re-injure an old break. Hornets occupied Lyn's thoughts, flying into the open space whenever she wasn't focused on something else. No. Lyn did not need an extra day off. She needed the distraction of wrangling lots and lots of students. She thanked Silas and hung up.

The voicemail icon told her she'd missed a call yesterday, likely while shooting. It was a sergeant from the Park Hill Police calling to ask if Lyn wanted a recommendation for bodyguard services. "Just as a precaution" said his message. She was isolated out there on her property, he said in so many words. He knew a guy who'd do it for practically nothing.

No. And the next person to insinuate there was something wrong with Lyn living alone in the country would get a piece of her mind.

At the morning bell, students poured through the door and scrambled to their seats. Could any of them be responsible for painting her classroom in human blood? No. Just, no. Lyn couldn't help but eye them just the same, leaning on the front of her desk, legs and arms crossed. She knew she looked her most formidable with her hair swept into a chignon. And today, she had to look the part of blithe inquisitor, to radiate composure till she made it her reality, especially after what happened to the room. The students would want to be reassured all was well, though Silas had sent out an all-district communication that it was safe to return. He'd held an in-person meeting assuring parents and staff. Lyn had to be careful in her line of questioning, that it didn't set the students on edge or scare them. *Who toilet-rolled me last weekend? Who pretended to be dead in my backyard? Who left me a hornets' nest?*

She led with a wink and a half-smile: "Okay, who did it?"

The students stared ahead, sheeplike and unwilling to meet her eyes.

"I don't mean the classroom, and you're not in trouble. I'm talking about Sunday, my house. Who did it?" Lyn asked again.

Stephen Tobba, a whimsical genius with a flair for impersonating superheroes and donning their personalities during class discussions, raised a tentative hand. Today he was sporting combed hair and a Captain America T-shirt, which meant he was feeling charming and cooperative. He raised his hand and asked, "Is that a rhetorical question?"

"No. A rhetorical question doesn't require an answer. I do."

"But...Mrs. D...did what?"

"Someone left a 'present' in my yard." Lyn meant the body, but the toilet paper was a "present" too. She could not care less about the toilet paper. "And this." She held up the envelope with the hornets, the one Silas had given her the morning her class had been vandalized.

Stephen shrugged. Collectively, the students did the same or nearly so. Except for a faceless screen of dyed-black hair who raised a milk-white arm. The Sharpie she'd been using on it was still clutched in her palm.

"Delaney?"

"I thought you were going to put in your notice."

The class giggled.

"I couldn't bring myself to leave you uneducated."

"I did it," Delaney said.

"Really?" Lyn's voice dropped an octave, to the bullshit chord.

Delaney remained in the anonymity provided by her hair, but a sneer formed on her blackened lips. "It was me...can I go to the principal's office now?"

"Nice try. But no, I don't think you'd make it to Mr. Matthews' office. How about you write out your confession and give it to me after class? And a croissant wouldn't hurt your cause, either."

Delaney shrugged and breezily began writing. With Delaney, consequences weren't ever the punishment they were supposed to be.

Lyn strode over to the whiteboard and wrote a quote:

I get up and pace the room, as if I can leave my guilt behind me.
But it tracks me as I walk, an ugly shadow made by myself.
– Rosamund Lupton

She turned to the room, hands on hips. Her eyes, slits. "This isn't about my classroom." *Or was it?* "I'd like to know who rolled my trees last Saturday night."

Her students read the quote with furrowed brows and puckered faces, as if it was not written in English. She hoped Rosamund's words weren't skipping right over the surface of her students' brains like well-flung stones. Lyn had a roomful of zombies, and it was her role to bring them to life with Shakespeare, Steinbeck, and Dickenson. Not exactly *The Hunger Games*. As Lyn examined each face, she hoped she'd be able to read a few guilty expressions and investigate later, but only Delaney looked particularly smug because she was Delaney. Lyn would get no confessions this way.

She sighed. "Pull out your answers to the analysis questions for chapters..." And the class moved on. Lyn did her best to focus on teaching, which was difficult. Someone wanted her off-balance and hypervigilant.

She was.

During the lunch period, Lyn was at her desk with *Bookworm* open under her nose. If she couldn't find the car accident scene, she could at least find the place the book went in that direction.

Nikki leaned into her door. "After what happened to your classroom—you're reading?" Nikki made a yuck face. She was a first-year Spanish teacher whose students adored her, and the feeling was clearly mutual. Also, she leaned heavily on conversational Spanish as opposed to written form because it was most practical. And, score, no Español essays.

Lyn was in mid-chew on a huge bite of her veggie sandwich. She struggled to swallow a hunk of pretzel bun. "This is pleasure reading." Another lie, but it was supposed to be pleasure reading.

"How've you been holding up?" Nikki asked.

Lyn's bite caught in her throat, and she had to work to get it down. "Um...I escape into my work?"

"Maybe if you'd get out from under that mountain of student essays, you could join us at Whistlestop for drinks? Cures all ailments."

Lyn shook her head. "My students' internal monologuing about double entendre in *Romeo and Juliet* gives me pleasure." A piece of green pepper fell out of her sandwich and into the book, and she picked it out and popped it into her mouth.

"Hmph." Nikki wagged her phone showing the screen to Lyn. "*This is pleasure.*"

Lyn made out the shirtless bodybuilder sprawled in the sand.

"Um-hmm," Nikki raised her eyebrows. "Am I right? Art."

Lyn raised her eyebrows dismissively.

"What? You don't think that's sexy?"

"That lights me up about as much as the frozen meat section...*Lady Chatterley's Lover*, that's sexy."

"Lemme see."

"This isn't *Lady Chatterley*. It's *Bookworm*. Ever hear of it?"

Nikki waved it away.

Buck, the Phys Ed teacher and Park Hill's own hunk of muscled meat, walked by, saw them, and backstepped. In his hand was a bag of cheese balls. He wore a mischievous grin. "Hey, Lyn. You're famous. In a horrible way. Your classroom was like something out of a horror movie. I saw it myself. And you got rolled, too."

"How do you know?"

"Instagram," Buck said, "The shot of Caesar watching through the window. Even I liked that one."

Lyn massaged her face. Social media didn't hold interest for her. Too bad, because it had the answer to who rolled her house.

Nikki looked up from her phone. "I saw it, too. Caesar's adorable."

"You don't find it mildly bothersome that both of you have seen a picture of my dog that I didn't know about? Let me see."

"First the dirt, Lyn, you know we want it." Buck pulled out a chair and leaned in.

As a high school English teacher, Lyn was accustomed to being ignored by her audience when she opened her mouth. The attention was overwhelming.

"Like we're flies," Buck said, "Start at the beginning."

Lyn told them about finding the bloody room, the whiteboard, and her portrait. At first she felt unclothed and vulnerable, but as her story unraveled, she lost herself. Even as Nikki's or Buck's faces broke or puckered in empathy, Lyn pulled herself through the events as if each scene was a knot on a thick rope, and she could, by saying what happened out loud, relieve herself of the burden of it. Reach the top, ring the bell.

Buck let out the breath he'd been holding. "Damn, girl. How do you sleep at night?"

"I'm practicing my shooting and playing detective with Google. It's not working out." Lyn overturned the envelope and let the dead hornets fall onto the desk. Nikki picked one up by its wing and studied it.

"A mystery," Lyn said, "Somebody left that on my desk the day my room got a makeover."

"Be more exciting if they were alive," Buck said.

"How do you know they weren't—when the envelope was put in there?" Nikki asked.

"You should get another dog." Buck took a seat in the first row of student desks and crossed his feet on the seat beside him. "Your mutt watches them roll your house. I think he's why they come. The kids post pictures of him watching them through the window, not making a peep, like he's watching a movie instead of watching trespassers run all over the yard." He showed her the proof on his phone.

"Hey. Nobody talks trash about Caesar but me."

"If you say so," Buck said. "But he never barks, all the kids say so."

Lyn recalled how Caesar had barked his doggie head off at the thing behind Jude's woodpile. The "body" that walked away before the police came.

"I tried to get a confession this morning," she said, "Bunch of poker players. Delaney Lucas said it was her so I'd send her to Silas. I had her write instead. Know what she wrote? The title was: "Being Force-fed Mrs. Darrow's Books is Jim Jones Kool-Aid and Being forced to write Mrs. Darrow's Essays is Mind Rape."

"I don't even know what you just said," Buck threw a cheese ball and caught it in his mouth.

"Then she described toilet-rolling my home in great detail, which of course proved she has never been to my home or seen it."

"I don't know, Lyn. It might've been Delaney. She's the serial killer type. Solitary. Weird. Hates people."

Sounded like Lyn.

"Do you know what that little turd did in my class last week?" Nikki pointed with her phone. "We're conjugating like we always do on Wednesdays. I say the English pronoun and verb and the class says the Spanish. We're going along, fine, fine, when all of the sudden, Delaney gets up, stomps over to Maura—little Maura—and starts screaming in her face. In Spanish, 'Uno, dos, tres, quatro.' She does this to fifty before I can get Silas to help me pull her out of the room, still scream-counting. Maura looked like she was going to be sick right there. No tears though. That was impressive."

"A sudden." Lyn couldn't help herself.

"What?" Nikki asked.

"It's all of *a* sudden. Sorry. I didn't want to interrupt, but back there you said, 'all of *the* sudden.'"

Nikki's face scrunched up and she shook her head. "Whatever. Once we got Delaney in the hall she shuts up and is smiling. Not a sweet smile. More like a creepy clown smile. I'm telling you, that kid's a whack job. She did it. They say it's usually someone you know."

Buck nodded. "How do you spell psycho? D-E-L-A-N-E-Y."

Lyn instinctively snapped at them, "*Little* Maura snapped pictures of Delaney on the toilet and airdropped them to the gym class."

"How do you know?"

"Essays."

"Essays, huh? Well I know a thing or two as well. I got my intel about your house. Wanna know how? Wall sits." Buck playfully threw a cheese ball.

It bounced off Lyn's cheek and fell on her desk. She ate it. "I'm listening."

Buck checked around conspiratorially. "I had the kids doing a loooong wall-sit in gym today."

Nikki wasn't impressed. "So?"

"Hurts like a bitch. Good for the quads. I do it when they're out of line. Or when I'm in the mood to hurt them because they're young and cocky and I'm bitter over my lost youth."

Lyn gave an appreciative nod, and Nikki gave half her attention. She was getting aroused by her phone.

"They toss bunk to each other, trying to combat the pain, see? I couldn't get this much dirt waterboarding them. They get all red-faced and start moaning and bitching...then they go all peacock on each other with how fast-n-furious they were over the weekend, who slept with who, who had a party, who got pulled over. You know how it goes. It's waaaaay better than essays."

"I doubt that," Lyn said.

Buck tossed his wadded-up cheese bag into a garbage can across the room. It went cleanly in. "Yeah, it was Fiksel. And the McGee twins. Also a few cheerleaders, but I don't know who exactly. They would've done you worse, but your boyfriend scared them off. Put the fear of God into them with his—"

"What'd you say?"

"Your boyfriend. Your ears should've been burning."

Boyfriend?

"The boys went on and on about how finally Mrs. D got herself hooked up. And I'm not going to lie. I thought, *it's about time.* It's good to hear you're living life, instead of crawled up the ass of a book—no offense. Especially now, with what's going on. You need a man around. For protection."

Lyn would have rolled her eyes, but she was busy being stunned by Buck's revelation.

"They said he looked like a farmer and had a badass hulkish build—I'm paraphrasing here."

Lyn's breath hitched. *Farmer? Or scarecrow?* "What'd he look like?"

Buck arched an eyebrow at her, like, you don't know what your own boyfriend looks like?

"I mean, I have several...boyfriends, haha." She hoped the ridiculous statement would fly right over the bar of possibility.

"I don't know. They didn't paint me a picture."

Lyn's stomach made a U-turn at the idea of the "dead" scarecrow prowling her property. It was so much easier to think the scarecrow *was* a student, even if it made little sense in light of the significance of hornets to her and her specifically.

Buck continued, "What freaked them out the most was he didn't say anything. Not a word, just this guy with a ski mask. Your boyfriend sent Fiksel and his pals packing."

"I don't actually have a boyfriend," Lyn said.

"Now *that* I believe," Buck said.

Nikki glared at Buck, "Shut up." Her face softened for Lyn. "Some guy, hanging out around your place at night? And after what happened...creepy. Maybe Buck's right, you should get another dog."

And Lyn hadn't even told them how Caesar *did* bark, and how the man—for it *must* be the same man—had feigned death, right under her nose.

Chapter 10

The "Boyfriend"

ON A BLUFF IN the Park Hill Conservation overlooking the Darrow residence, the man stationed himself, giving him an unobstructed view of Sandy Ridge Road and Lyn's front yard. Any moment now, her Land Rover would crest the hill. He would hold the binoculars until his muscles cramped if that's what it took. He passed the time in a nebulous but electrifying dream of him standing over a tied-down Lyn Darrow.

Three days ago, he'd made contact. Unplanned, but oh, so exciting. Watching the book zap her like voltage—no, *like a hornet*—had aroused him. He'd gotten close, too close to the window, but when she flung the book across the room, he tossed up victory hands. He cried. He would get to play with her. Finally, Lyn in her white robe, her sweet, pink flesh visible as the wind pulled it back like a curtain.

What a fast-thinker he'd been when she unexpectedly came outside. He figured she'd be pretty much paralyzed after reading her life in a book, but her stupid dog wouldn't shut up. The hornets' nest was a stroke of genius.

He almost lost his resolve as he lay in the snow with her standing over him and the hornets' nest over his face like a bowl. They were all dead, but the paper scratched, and he couldn't see. He thought he could smell fear in Lyn, yes, but also anger. What if it happened again, what happened before? He didn't think he could stand it. All he had to do was nothing. Be dead. He had felt dead for so long it wasn't that difficult, even when she nudged him with her boot.

Even when she had kicked him.

As he had lain in the snow waiting for the sound of her retreating, he consoled himself with his imagination. A toothy, million-jawed hate plowed through scenes of him and Lyn. Though he'd learned to control his outsides, an ache festered on the inside. His heart twisted like storm clouds fashioned by howling winds, and always at the center was Lyn Darrow. *The* Lyn. Darrow. He waited and watched and imagined.

Today, as he surveilled her house, the binoculars didn't shake, though his arms ached from holding them for so long. From the bluff across the road, he'd worn the ground smooth while watching, always careful to leave cigarette butts and a beer bottle now and again for the park rangers so they'd think it was teenagers and not him staked out at the Darrow property. He knew every curve of the ground, every sandstone flake and quartz rock, every foot of the local terrain. He had several favorite places to sit and watch her house. He knew how to erase himself from the forest.

There. The Land Rover. So predictable.

The man unscrewed a ginger ale. The fizz tickled his throat as he gulped it down. Lyn would spend a few minutes feeding her ugly dog. She'd help herself to some healthy snack like hummus and pita bread or a roll-up of spreadable cheese and spinach. She'd take them to the living room and munch while reading. The curtains were open to let in the late afternoon light.

But today Lyn didn't snack. She didn't read. She hunched over something at her kitchen table. Her back was to the window. When she grabbed the paper plates, he knew she'd decided on target practice.

Her aim was worse than usual. Must've been a bad first day back at school. Funny, how she thought a gun would protect her. Or that ugly dog of hers. She rose from the table with her stack of paper plates. The man tried to look away, but saw the curve of her as she stood.

The man, he was hornets and hate and lust and memories, and they had to come out. They refused to quiet. Everything in him rushed out in a silent, ripping, shameful convulsion over which he had no control. He put his hand over his mouth.

He could no longer see her through the bay window, but after a few minutes, he knew where she was because of the rhythmic beat of gunshots.

Chapter 11

THE SNOW HAD MELTED away, but the ground still felt like sponge. Lyn thought she heard steps. Between shots, she was sure someone cleared his throat. She stopped with one practice round unshot.

"You have one round left."

She turned, impressed that he had noticed. But of course he did. A good cop would. "Oh, hi," she said.

"I was in the area, and I thought I'd stop. If it's not a good time..."

"No. It's fine. My fingers have had enough." Lyn began collecting her bullet casings, and Leif crouched down to help. Their faces were inches apart. Leif smiled easily; Lyn moved awkwardly, grasping the casings with finger joints that needed oil and use. All the smoothness in her had died three years ago. Whatever fluidity she possessed had leached into the soil with Jude's blood. Leif's confidence highlighted everything about her that clunked. He poured his casings into her hands, and the feather light touch of his fingers was flame. She shuddered and nearly fumbled the lot of them. He cupped his large hands under hers to catch, and for a second, their hands were sealed. Praying, hers inside his. She leaped back and awkwardly dumped the casings into an old coffee can.

"Rough day back?" he asked.

"You could say that."

"I've been asking around. The rangers have a love-hate relationship with you."

Lyn gestured to her property. "My backyard firing range. I've not practiced much until lately."

"There's no hunting in the park, so each time you pull the trigger they have to make sure it's not someone breaking the law."

"I know it, but the indoor range is crowded, and I'm not a people person." Lyn swept her hair back into a tight ponytail.

"You don't say." Leif's deadpan made it unclear whether or not he joked.

"Years ago, the Park Department filed a complaint against me," Lyn said.

"They told me."

"After Jude died, I wanted to shoot. A lot."

Leif studied her. "You nervous, living alone?"

"Not until recently."

He cleared his throat. "Been quiet around here though—since that day?"

"If you call this quiet." Lyn motioned to her target.

"I'd think an English teacher would love words. But not you."

"Come again?"

"Most people I take statements from are like tubes of caulk. You nick even the tiniest hole, the stuff oozes out all over the place."

The English teacher in Lyn didn't miss the simile. When she was in Leif Andrews' vicinity, her insides turned a little mushy, like he was a therapist type. A nick would be all it took, and she'd be telling him how crazy she was, no couch needed. She would not allow herself to feel Jude's death all over again.

Leif continued, "...And you can't stop the jaw flapping even when you want to, when it's been hours and we've been through the entire family tree all the way back to the potato famine...and you know you've still got reports to write and it's already an hour over your scheduled shift. That's how statements usually go, but not yours."

Lyn gave a forced chuckle. "I prefer to communicate with the written word. The delete button's my best friend."

"Something's bothering me about your statement the other day. Can we run through it again?"

Oh, he was good. She'd give him that. This was him trying to cut open the stubborn tube of caulk. "Your partner didn't want to hear it the first time."

"I'm not my partner."

"No, you're definitely not."

"You didn't tell me everything, Lyn."

"*Everything* would take forever. I'd have to start at the potato famine, and we know you don't want that."

"Touché," he said dryly.

Lyn rose and gathered some stray casings. Leif's radio sounded with numbers and letters and talk she didn't understand, but he glanced at the radio, annoyed.

"You need to get that?" she asked.

He cocked an eyebrow. "I can do my job, thank you."

Lyn made an angry cat sound but didn't look his way. She hoped he'd leave. Her fingers were sore from shooting, and she was bone tired. The day's tension had slipped a lead stole around her shoulders. This man dredged up memories from a crypt she had worked hard to seal. Until the day she saw him on her front door step, Lyn forgot she had bitten him. How could she forget?

The voice on the radio repeated herself.

Leif unclipped the radio but spoke to Lyn. "We'll have patrol cars sticking close for another week, but we don't have any leads."

Lyn's insides quivered like piano strings. "Leads?"

"A dead person missing a bucket of the same type of blood."

He clicked the button, opened his mouth to speak into the radio, and changed his mind. He released the button and sighed, "I know it's been a rough couple of days. That day—Saturday—I didn't want to respond when I heard your address. But a job's a job. It's not personal."

"I'm sorry I bit you...years ago."

He waved off her apology. "Signed up for it."

"No, you didn't."

"I could've gone into other work, been a lawyer or an actuary. And that day...it was...it was bad." He adjusted his hat. It threw shade over his eyes, turning them steel. "I figured it would be hard for you to see me, but you're in my zone, so I came. That's all."

The silence ripened while Lyn studied the ground.

"I could teach you to shoot," he said, "...better. I could teach you to hit the target."

She jutted her chin. "I hit it plenty. But thanks anyway."

"Suit yourself." He turned and strode away, speaking gruffly into his radio.

Lyn listened to his steps and his words but kept her eyes on Jude's pile of wood. She thought he'd try harder to convince her to be his understudy, and she wasn't sure how she felt about his abrupt exit. Maybe he wasn't used to *no*. Well, a *no* every now and then was good for the soul.

Every day of Lyn's life was *no*. No Jude. No joy. No love. No. No. No.

This Leif Andrews could never be a help to Lyn. His offer inadvertently pulled the grenade pin on Lyn's past. His uniform, his belt of resistance gear and tactical shoes, his sidearm and radio that could summon the whole Park Hill police force... all of it brought one terrible moment to mind, brought it crashing into Lyn's body like a wave. She realized she would never look at him or his ilk and see only a man because over the years, every blue-wearing man had become the liminal between her life with Jude and her life without him.

She tensed, worrying he'd appear again and tell her she needed to learn how to shoot.

But the engine roared to life, and Lyn allowed herself to breathe, a great gulp of air. Caesar regarded her with glossy eyes; his wagging tail and open, panting mouth were his opinions.

"What are you wagging about?" She addressed Caesar. "He insulted my shooting." As if she needed his help. What did he take her for? A damsel in distress? A scared rabbit? Just because she missed the mark a time or two didn't mean she wasn't a force to be reckoned with. Just ask her paper plates. She'd turned them to dust with her many shots. She'd compensate for her lack of aim with a faster draw and a devastating volley of bullets.

Chapter 12

For the second time that week, breakfast was a croissant from Bear's Bakery. Lyn had picked up an everything bagel for Silas, too. The high school parking lot was not empty as it had been yesterday when she arrived in the dark. Cars and vans representing the local television channels had stationed themselves at both the main entry doors and the side entrance for teachers. Concerned parents who dropped off their kids stuck around and gathered in clusters, trading bits of gossip.

Lyn smiled (fake as it was) and shook her head at the reporters' questions. They barely parted to make way. If her "artist" was among those who watched her walk into school, she hoped she appeared unafraid.

In his office, Silas was on his phone yelling at someone from the insurance company. "...and WHY—pray tell—wouldn't the drywall be covered? Shall we make walls of straw and mud?" He pressed the end button hard and gave her a grimace meant to be a smile.

She offered him the brown bag, grease spots already blooming on the bottom. "Here. It's not enough for the trouble I caused, but I'm fresh out of brand new days." Why Silas insisted on eating cardboard when there were croissants, she couldn't understand.

"You're the best, Darrow. I don't care what anybody else says." He began to unwrap his bagel like it was Christmas. "Have a seat."

Lyn fell into one of the two plush chairs opposite his desk. "I'm surprised the press wasn't here yesterday."

Silas exhaled forcefully. "They were. You arrived before they did, lucky girl."

"What are people saying...about the room?"

"That Mrs. D has a pissed-off nutcase. Parents are afraid to send their kids. Some don't want you teaching. They're afraid your artist is planning to shoot up the school." As he talked, he scrutinized her.

She took a sip of coffee in the most calm and capable manner possible, chin up, eyes down, like she was Scarlett O'Hara. *Does it look like I give a damn?* She did, though. Give a damn, a total damn, and it bothered her that her friend Silas was having a terrible day because of her.

She dropped the tough act. "I'm sorry, Silas."

"Darrow. I can handle the jacked parents and the school board." He sighed. "Rest assured, things will quiet down and get back to normal. They always do. Quit taking this on yourself. *You* didn't paint the room in blood."

Lyn gave him a dim smile. "How's the kitchen coming?"

Silas had taken a bite of bagel and shook his head. With a pleading hand, he begged her not to bring up the subject.

"That bad, huh?"

"Yellow mustard had sex with a highlighter and the baby is on my kitchen walls."

"You know what they say. All babies are cute. Your kitchen will be—"

"—a mutant. A freak of nature. I want to scream and claw out my eyes every time I grab a bowl of cereal or microwave something. And cooking...that's not happening...hey. You okay? You look like you just walked through my kitchen."

"I'm fine."

"I have something that'll cheer you."

Lyn brightened. "Why didn't you say so?"

Silas gestured with his thumb. "It's in your classroom."

She hesitated.

"Go on," he was gruff, but Lyn knew it was an act.

Still, her heart raced as she recalled the last time she walked from Silas' office to her room, and when she arrived, she nearly dropped her coffee mug a second time.

Someone...students, fellow teachers, maybe Silas or at his bidding—had decorated the room with posters and quotes from Shakespeare, even a banner that said, *Welcome back, Mrs. Darrow!* In blue and yellow—school colors. Fresh pillows and throw blankets were placed on the wooden risers. A new, plush rug adorned the space between her tables and risers, and on her desk was a basket of books. Classics. To replace the ones destroyed. And on her chair, a note.

> *Darrow, Nobody reaches these kids like you. They practical-*
> *ly trampled each other to be involved in the resurrection of*
> *your classroom, to contribute in some way. They love you, as*
> *do I. - Your favorite princiPAL—Silas*

Lyn sat at her desk and took in the room, the little touches from students. They wrote thank you notes on her whiteboard and on the blackboard. They left notes and cards on the window ledge. A box of chocolate croissants adorned the central spot. The lid had a note scribbled on it. *- Something to smile about. L. Andrews.*

Leif.

Leif was part of this too? He helped bring her room back to life? She put her nose into the box and inhaled the velvety chocolate. The kindnesses, they almost made her forget, almost pushed out the image of her whiteboard painted in blood.

She dashed back to Silas' office to thank him, tears shining in her eyes.

"Don't make me cry, Darrow. I have a steely-eyed persona to keep up."

Lyn flanked his desk and gave him a side hug, mushing her cheek into his stubbled one and knocking his bow tie askew. He reached up and patted her cheek.

"Oh, I almost forgot." Silas pulled out an envelope. "In other news, this was in front of the staff door. I should get a pay raise for my heroic willpower in not ripping it open."

Mrs. Darrow was scrawled across the entire face of it in black sharpie.

"Good artist. Used all the available space," Silas mused.

Lyn held out her hand. "I know who this is from."

He passed the envelope. "So do I. Ever wonder why we write the names so small? It's because our habit is to leave room for an address and stamps and a return address, but when the envelope needs only a name, why not write it large?"

"Delaney's got flair," Lyn admitted.

Silas cupped his chin with both hands, expectant.

"Oh. You want me to read it *now*? I have so much grading to catch up on. I was going to take it home—"

"Darrow, if you wait another minute to open that letter, you're fired."

Lyn passed it under her nose and sniffed, enjoying Silas's squirming. He lunged across the desk and playfully went for it. She swiped it out of reach. "You can't afford to fire me. You'd have to teach my class."

"Actually." He took a bite of bagel. "It's the delivery service I'd miss."

Lyn broke open the letter.

Mrs. Darrow, You know I was joking about the toilet paper, but they blamed me for your classroom. How original. I get blamed for everything. I mean, what the fuck? Sorry for fucking swearing, but you get fucked over enough times, you no longer give one. I'm done. It doesn't matter what I do. Everyone sees what they want to see. I have to go someplace where no one sees me at all. I took my copy of Watership Down. Yes, it's technically stealing, but it's your fault for building it up. I can't imagine how a story about rabbits can be as good as you say. Fuck off to everyone but you. -Delaney

P.S. I didn't mess up your room. I didn't actually say that in the letter. You should be proud of me for proofreading.

Silas leaned back in his chair and pillowed his head in his hands. "Delaney Lucas, running from her problems. Should we be surprised? You artsy types tend to eschew life's trials by running off into the sunset—of a book. Or in this case literally running off."

Lyn snorted. "I'm offended."

"But not contradicting," Silas pointed out. "I'm glad it was this way. I didn't want you to hear it from somebody else."

"What do you mean?"

"Apparently, she admitted to rolling your house the other day."

"It was a joke. She was joking. Everyone knew it."

"Right, but bad timing. That oaf of a detective pulled her out of Spanish yesterday. She lost it. But first she called him some choice names, loud enough for everyone to hear. *Fucking Pork Rind* stands out. She is an artist of the expletive—you teach her that? Anyway, we tried to stop her, but you know, we can't touch them." He put both arms up as if to say *no foul*. "And manhandling is definitely out, so she strolled out the front door. I think she's bluffing. Kids always say they're going to run. She's probably holed up in her bedroom, binge-watching Netflix."

"I don't know. Delaney's an old soul. In class she says things that go over everyone's heads. They don't understand her, so they tear her down."

"Where do you think she'll go?"

"I don't know. She's got an older sister living in Colorado. That's where I'd go."

Silas frowned as he studied it. "She won't graduate."

"Mark me, she'll figure it out, get her GED or enroll out there. Delaney Lucas has done what she didn't want to for her whole life, mothering her own mother and all. She'll figure out she needs a diploma. She wrote circles around most everyone in class, and writing wasn't even her thing." Lyn tucked the letter into her purse. "I wish my problems hadn't spilled onto her."

After her students' arrival, their hi-fives, and hugs, Lyn gestured to her room's makeover. "This is the best gift I've ever received. Thank you."

A hand went up in the back.

"Yes, Stephen?"

"We actually, like, wrote something. Together. For you."

Lyn rocked back, hit with the thoughtfulness of her students.

Stephen stood and began to read.

"Mrs. Darrow, We hope you don't mind. We wanted to have this ready on your first day back, but Ryan didn't do his *one job* and order the welcome-back banner—anyway, the two days school was closed we had a sort of *Breakfast Club*—" He interrupted himself. "That's a movie about—"

"—I'm familiar with it." She closed her eyes and smiled.

"—right. And we all contributed a piece. I put the thoughts together, is all. We wanted you to know how much we appreciate you."

He read on. Some students sniffled.

Lyn's eyes drifted to Delaney Lucas' empty seat. Stephen's words were meant to erase the hate that had been left in her classroom. And they did, mostly. Like the grey smudge left after an erasure, an ache remained. She wanted to confess to her students that she wasn't as brave as they thought. Deep down she was a cold and fearful mess. Besides Delaney, none of her students had suffered the death of a parent. And it would be many years, if ever, that any one of them would know the pain of losing a husband or a wife. May they never.

"You make teaching a joy," Lyn managed. "Light will always beat darkness. A match in a dark room, no matter how big, will fend off the dark."

Her students looked at her expectantly. Some were confused at her metaphor, their faces wrinkled in puzzlement. Lyn held up her finger for them to give her a minute and strode out. In the bathroom she blew her nose, gazed into the mirror, and told herself to get it together. She returned, warmly thanked her students, and taught her morning classes.

At lunch, Lyn's room was swarmed, with Buck at the head of a pack of curious teachers and aides. After praising the resurrection of Lyn's classroom, Buck got down to business.

"How about Delaney Lucas? Who runs off, unless they're guilty?"

Lyn's ire was instant. "Ralph. *Lord of the Flies*. Holden Caulfield. *Catcher in the Rye*. Andy Dufresne. *Shawsh—"*

"I mean in life," Buck said.

"Life. Literature. What's the difference? Delaney didn't do it."

"Who, then?" Buck tossed a balled-up napkin toward the trash. He missed. It registered on his face: shock at his missing. Lyn hadn't ever, in all her years, seen Buck miss a shot to the trash can. For a moment the teachers were stunned. It was only a missed shot. But it also wasn't. Lyn's room had gotten under everyone's skin. Even Buck was off kilter.

Too many teachers had memories of how and when they had punished Delaney Lucas. If it wasn't her, every pissed-off student was on the table. As the teachers talked, it became clear Lyn's classroom debacle had an unintended but good effect on the teachers at Park Hill. In the one and a half days since school resumed, they had all become kinder and more forgiving to students. Buck himself had not assigned a single wall-sit.

Everyone needed to believe it was Delaney, and they wanted Lyn to confirm their suspicions and give them peace. But she couldn't. Delaney simply wasn't capable. Just because she was bad in one way didn't make her bad in every way. Lyn tried to explain why Delaney couldn't be to blame, but she could tell by the frowns and shaking heads no one agreed with her. If not Delaney Lucas, then *who?*

Chapter 13

The "Boyfriend"

THE END-OF-DAY BELL RANG. From his vantage point, the man heard the front doors burst open, spilling chatter and laughter into the chilly spring day. He spit into his cupped hand and with his index finger swirled around the yellow glob, breaking it up, losing some clear saliva down the back of his wrist. He didn't notice it drip on the binoculars. Saliva and blood felt almost the same if you closed your eyes and dredged up the smell of pennies. The Park Hill High School lot was steadily emptying of cars. Eventually, the homo principal got into his black BMW. Lyn would be right behind him. He alternated his attention between the staff entrance and her Land Rover.

The memory of his art was so recent, the coppery bouquet still tickled his nose. Playing with his slippery warm saliva, massaging it into his palm and between his fingers, he thought of how it would be with Lyn, face to face, all secrets out.

This wasn't his first time watching Lyn from the picnic table next to the visitor parking lot, but it put him on edge that he'd be seen or recognized. Or someone would ask what he was doing, there, on the edge of high school property. He had to have a story ready. He'd say he was bird watching, that a fellow birder—that was the term they used for themselves—told him a...what was it called? Some stupid, rare woodpecker was seen hammering on the eaves of the school building. That he had to stay a respectable distance away so he wouldn't scare the...thing, and here he could see without disturbing it and take pictures and notes and whatever else birders did. He had a notepad handy, but it wasn't full of birds.

He finished cleaning his hands with a napkin from Whitey's Bar, concentrating on each finger in turn and glancing at the parking lot every so often. Though he hated to be distracted for even an instant, not knowing the name of the woodpecker could make trouble for him. He did an internet search of *rare birds of the northeast* and found it: the ivory-billed woodpecker. That would keep him legit. He considered writing it down, but the notebook was sacred. It was full of his plans, and he wasn't about to slop it up with bird names. Instead, he took a screenshot.

Where was she?

Finally, she emerged from the staff door. He trained the binocs on her face, and she did the strangest thing, almost like she did it at him. She *laughed*. In magnification, her white teeth were enormous. She smiled the whole way across the lot, swaggering like she was somebody and not a pansy-ass school teacher who couldn't even shoot a gun right. The skyward tilt of her head was an insult to him and to his art. Soon, he'd smother that laugh. The smile on her lips would die.

Chapter 14

THE KINDNESS OF HER students buoyed Lyn for the school day, but driving home and being alone made her feel vulnerable and exposed once more. Her hands still ached from the target practice, so after school she made a cup of tea, curled up on the couch, and tucked a blanket around her. Her answer to uncomfortable feelings: a book, of course. *Take a Knee*—the book about Stephen—had started strong.

"The English teacher in you will love this," Nolan had said, and though she thought it would be hard to forget her troubles, the story took her the way a sure dancer takes a partner, glides her around a shiny floor, and spins her till she's breathless. *The English teacher would love this?* Hardly. The part of Lyn that loved this book was less philosophical. She poured all her attention into the words.

> *Stephen and his friends huddled around the cow's corpse, batting flies and acting cool, as if the pathetic bleats of her orbiting calf didn't bother them. The other boys prodded the swollen teats with sticks.*
>
> *"If only girl boobs were this big," Stan said.*
>
> *Stephen averted his eyes, disgusted. He pitied the calf. As the boys bragged about what they'd do with nipples that huge, their hot breath ticked Stephen's ears, and he found himself feeling something unexpected, not as a result of the cow, but in response to the delicious, fervent whispers of his friends. He hoped his blush would be misunderstood.*

It was. Stephen went undiscovered for many years.

In his senior year of high school, after a dramatic lacrosse win, Stephen's team had arms around each other and were sing-shouting "We are the Champions" by Queen—Queen—when he felt a strong grip to his left. Zane smiled and held the gaze overlong. The wink was almost imperceptible. Almost.

Both boys changed slower than everyone else in the locker room, slipping furtive glances and tossing out bunk with the other players as if a current wasn't rushing under their feet, licking up the spires of their legs as they dried off from the showers. At the clang of the metal door on the last teammate, Zane rushed Stephen, and both boys groaned at the slam of their lean and solid bodies against the lockers. Zane tasted like mint and strength.

"Willow Bend." Zane said. And wordlessly they hefted their matching backpacks and got into their separate cars in the mostly-empty parking lot. At the Willow Bend trailhead, they parked their cars deep into the bridle path so they wouldn't be seen by passing motorists. Without a word, Zane led Stephen to a picnic table and spun him around with the roughness of bottled desire. The wood grain against Stephen's palms and cheek stung like a rug burn and complimented the deliciousness of being handled. He was home.

<>

Miss Menly, his twelfth grade English teacher, knew Stephen as a shy student who captured her attention with his prose. Stephen's writing was muscular and adventurous. His talent for describing the human body, of making a landscape out of a shoulder or a neck made his teacher want to know: How could one so young see with eyes so old? She asked him to stay after class and suggested he enter his latest essay into a contest. He blushed, and endeared himself to her even more.

"What books do you read?" The teacher asked.

"Everything I can get my hands on." The brazen intensity with which he looked into her eyes flipped a switch inside the teacher.

She broke eye contact and instead studied his hands, red and raw from something. "Recently, then. What are you reading? You must read beyond what I assign."

He put his backpack down and unzipped it. Out of it he slipped a book. Lady Chatterley's Lover, most erotic of the classics. Banned as pornography until 1960—when pretty much everything was unbanned—the book boiled with sex. It was the teacher's secret favorite.

Lyn closed the book but kept her finger holding the spot. To Caesar she said, "I mentioned Lady Chatterley's Lover to Nikki, at school. And here it is, in this book." She shook her head but read on.

The teacher's face reddened at the thought of a certain scene, but she pressed. "And are you enjoying Lady Chatterley's Lover?"

Stephen's lips parted and his eyes alone smiled. "That would be a funny thing you said, if it was taken out of context, Miss. M. I think it's full of dull and unremarkable characters, but the sex scenes are hot. I've never heard the word cun—"

"Stop." The teacher closed her eyes and put up her hand as if she were directing traffic.

Stephen uttered a husky laugh. "Okay, okay. I've never heard the c-word used with so much flair and...affection." He allowed his eyes to rove over his teacher, to settle on her.

There.

At that, the first wave of heat whipped through her. With a deep blush she excused Stephen and vowed never to ask him to stay after class again.

In the silence of the empty room, the nearly empty school, the teacher mused. Every so often the janitor passed by, carrying a bucket or buffing the floor, or talking on his phone. She'd never spoken to him, though they were often "together" in the building at night. Why? Why did she not make the effort at small talk? Because, what would they possibly have in common? He didn't look like the bookish type, this janitor. But didn't she always say "The cover isn't the book"? Yet here she was, writing him off because he cleaned floors. Writing everyone off, really. Other than with Stephen—her student—she couldn't re-member the last time she had a deep conversation, about anything. She felt the hollowness more acutely than ever before. Because life had stomped on her, kicked her in the teeth, taken what she held dear, she'd stopped engaging with anything but stories.

Her choices had put her in a vulnerable spot. The teacher knew she was full of nothing but fiction.

Lyn looked up, blinked tears that landed on the page, onto the sentence that was too much her:

The teacher knew she was full of nothing but fiction.

Lyn snapped the book shut. An English teacher. *Lady Chatterley.* How many high school English teachers considered that their favorite? The parallels between the book in her hands and her present reality pinched her skin into goose flesh. Lyn hadn't consciously vowed to shun the company of people, especially men. Just, she'd not ventured there. She'd lost the art, if ever she had it. Jude said she had it. He brought her out of her shell and turned her "wild" in the bedroom. His word, *wild.*

"Let the wild rumpus start," was how he initiated lovemaking, turning a beloved children's tale into something else entirely. "I'll eat you up," he'd quote the children's book. And Lyn would giggle, then writhe in delight. At least there was no attractive, gay student named Stephen in any of her classes, there was that. Lyn flipped the pages, going from where the story switched from Stephen's viewpoint to the teacher's, a Miss Menly. So far the book didn't offer a first name. And while the writing wasn't out of the ordinary, the sudden point of view switch was abrupt. Almost as if it was an editing oversight. Nolan's books were of the highest quality, so it had to be intentional, the shift. Lyn mused and gently tapped the book against her chin until the cuckoo clock's ticking reminded her that time didn't stop when she disappeared into a book.

Caesar whined at the door.

She reluctantly set the book down. "Hang on, boy, I need my hiking shoes." In the bedroom, Lyn hesitated at the king bed, all hers for three years. There was one perfect mound of pillow with an unrumpled, un-slept on pillowcase. She sniffed the pillow and wished like crazy it still held Jude's scent.

She shook her head, as if that could dispel the heat in her cheeks—and elsewhere. Why did she feel uncomfortable in her lust? Not because the boys were gay. No. Was it because she felt alive? —over a scene getting inside her head the way only Jude should? Her response was to put her mind as close to Jude's memory as possible. She ran to the closet and buried her face into his coat sleeve.

She cried on it as she had many times before.

Caesar, tired of waiting by the door, trotted to the closet and pushed a wet nose into her hand.

"Why do I see myself in these books?"

Caesar sat still and tall, hoping the walk would ensue.

"Because..." Lyn walked to the foyer where she kept the leash. Caesar spun and pranced in excitement. "Because..." Lyn would not say it out loud.

Caesar, as a last resort, barked for Lyn to get going already. He barked and barked and made it impossible for her to think. She clipped the leash on him and put her pistol in her back pocket. It was best practice (especially for the gun-stupid, so said the clerk at the firearms store) to keep a gun uncocked.

But not today.

She'd take her chances shooting herself in the foot rather than grapple with the action. The bridle trails went deep into the forest, far away from roads and mind-needling car engines. Far away from help, should she need it. For the first time she was ambivalent about the woods. Nature had always been a place of solitude and safety, but lately she felt more like a rabbit with a hunter's site trained on her.

"I see myself in books because that's where I'd prefer to be. And books can be shut. There. I said it. Happy, Caesar?"

Off to the hiking trails they went.

Chapter 15

THE TRAILS WERE GLOSSED with melting snow and half-rotted leaves that made squishing sounds underfoot. Chipmunks, flushed out of hiding by Caesar, skittered in all directions. Not taking Caesar to obedience school was one of Lyn's regrets. He jammed his nose into every hole, every pile of horse manure, and every peed-on tuft of grass, rock, or fallen branch. He jerked the leash and weaved back and forth like a boozed fish. Lyn had tried to solve the problem with longer leashes, but that only allowed him to ramble in larger parabolas and tangle more.

A deafening crack cut through the forest, sending Caesar and Lyn spinning, searching for the cause. More cracking, and the sound of branches splintering. Some twenty feet ahead, the tops of the pine trees quaked. An evergreen tree leaned, leaned, leaned, faster and faster and faster, breaking and pulling down other trees with it onto the trail before them. The ground vibrated. Snow and dead leaves and needles flew in all directions. The tree tore a hole in the ground as it fell. Its torn roots stuck out the bottom like broken bones.

Lyn had never seen a tree fall.

She found herself jealous. Of a pine tree.

Taking Caesar closer, she examined the fallen giant. Eventually, when the weather warmed, mushrooms and ants would do their patient work, turn the tree to sponge and dust until it was swallowed by the forest floor, no memory of it ever having stood. Of course her thoughts went to Jude. One moment he was riding, bicycle tires expertly balanced on the white edge lines of the road, his body sheened and spent but aching the glorious hurt of a thirty-mile trek through the parkway. The next moment he was gone. And if Jude could die, could up and leave her, how could she ever trust this world? No, in the aftermath of Jude's death, she had been right to shun the world. She'd never even read the police report on his accident. Why put herself through it again? She'd heard what happened with her own ears. Saw the aftermath with her own eyes. Jude on the road. Car on the road. And, physics. Terrible, murderous physics. A body in motion stayed in motion until it was acted upon by another force. Like this tree.

Caesar wagged at her and pulled, wanting to move along, but because of the downed tree, they had to detour through the woods.

They were rounding the tree top, some thirty feet from the path when a branch snapped, then another.

Not again.

Surely another tree was not about to fall? Both Caesar and Lyn scanned the area trying to locate the source. Movement deep in the woods drew her eye and caused Caesar to bark. This time it was low to the ground, an animal or a person, off the trail. Lyn's body tensed and her heart did that creep-up-into-her-throat thing. Her hand fumbled the gun holster open and she pulled it out, death-gripping it.

"Hello?"

Why did she do that? Because animals wouldn't answer, but neither would people with bad intentions. Therefore, it was the dumbest thing to say. She felt like a character in a bad horror film when she called out like that. She was the brainless character and deserved whatever she got.

The footsteps in the woods, they were not squirrels, not a dog. They seemed to approach, but it was hard to know for sure because Caesar wouldn't stop barking.

Lyn froze, spun in a circle pointing her gun in all directions. Part of her wished she could just fire it everywhere, all at once, shut down the threat. She didn't have enough bullets. Her aim wasn't great.

"Shhhh...Caesar."

Broken branches, more heavy footfalls sounded from another direction. Had her fear grown legs and barreled through the woods around them?

Enough, Lyn, get a hold of yourself.

Lyn stared at the pistol in her hand. It wouldn't hurt. Everything would stop. Her fear would vanish. She'd know what Jude knew, like reading his books—all of them in an instant.

She threaded her pointer finger through the trigger hole. She held the possibility in her sweating hand and raised it to her temple.

Three deer crashed through the woods.

Caesar watched them, spellbound by shock. Lyn had nearly squeezed the trigger in her fright.

Harmless deer.

Lyn was like those deer, running scared from who-knew-what. That was the problem. She didn't know what pursued her. She only knew she felt hunted. Her books, her home, her work. Someone wanted her to be terrified *everywhere.*

Since she was already in deep misery, why not let L. Andrews teach her to shoot? Could being his student be worse than being alone, afraid, and slightly suicidal? Wasn't it the high road to face your fear and all that? Why not go in search of her enemy? Take the offensive. Get the fight over with already. If the end was going to be the same, Lyn's demise, let it be on her terms.

Lyn pulled out her phone, dialed the number for patrolman Leif Andrews.

"Hello?"

She opened her mouth, but nothing came out.

"Hello? Who's this?" A bit of irritation in his voice. Police officers were probably the brunt of phone pranks. In the background was the sound of rock music and clanging. Leif sounded out-of-breath. And annoyed.

Lyn swallowed. "It's Lyn. Lyn Darrow."

"Lyn." Everything about his voice changed.

Lyn relaxed. "I'm sorry to bother you—"

"No bother."

"—I was wondering if the offer still stands, to teach me to shoot...better?"

"Sure. I'm at the gym now, but I'll be finished soon. And I'm always famished after. We could meet at Whitey's, in an hour?"

"Whitey's?"

"I can't teach you on an empty stomach."

"Some other day, then." Lyn had almost blown her head off, but the idea of eating with the man felt more dangerous than that.

"Are you serious about protecting yourself or not?"

"Er, I am. Serious. I am." Who was she trying to convince?

"See you there. I'll let you pay, if it makes you feel better. Consider it the cost of the lesson."

Lyn wrung the leash in her hand, her palms red from squeezing. Caesar sat obediently at her feet. She'd swear he was smiling.

Chapter 16

WHITEY'S HAD AN INVITING, cave-like darkness. Low conversational buzzing vied for dominance with pub music, and the result was a harmony of sorts. A cast iron wood burner radiated heat into every corner. The bar seats were full, mostly with couples. It was well past the dinner rush, although a few loners watched the screens overhead and munched on chicken wings. Lyn couldn't remember the last time she'd been to Whitey's. They had the best burgers, but eating alone in a bar was unappealing, which was why Lyn hadn't had a *good* burger since Jude died.

She had started with what she hoped was an appropriate question about Leif's work.

He answered without taking his eyes off the menu. "Police work is duller than you'd imagine and punctuated by moments of extreme stress. People are either scared of me or pissed off at me. Rarely are they happy to see me."

"Add to that, bored with you, and you have—to a lesser degree—what it's like to be a high school English teacher."

Leif eyed her over his menu.

Lyn studied the IPAs. "You and your partner seem to have the good cop/bad cop gig down."

"Don't forget the telepathy." Leif winked stonily. "Finn and I have spent so much time together, I know him better than I know myself, and the job, well it's like we're on a trip to Wally World *every* day, only we never get there. We don't have Wally World to look forward to, only a long car ride mercifully punctuated with crime. I pray for crime to break up the monotony."

The server brought Lyn's beer, took their orders, and hustled off.

Leif leaned across the table. "The Chernobyl burger. Interesting choice."

The Chernobyl was the biggest burger on the menu and could not, under any circumstances, be eaten with hands. It was piled with onions, lettuce, chili, cheese, and sour cream. Lyn used to share it with Jude. She ordered without thinking. Her double imperial IPA did quick work on her. She had to take care not to slur. "How long till I'm as good as you? As good as any cop with a gun?"

He put his drink down and folded his hands. She didn't like the wry smile playing at his lips.

"Not like it's a dumb question," she continued. "You went into police school not knowing how to shoot, and you came out knowing. That simple. I want the sped-up version. How long?"

"Academy. It's called the Police Academy," he said.

"Sorry. *Academy*." She could see where Barnfeld got it. *Academy*. She motioned with her hand to encompass their table and the whole bar. "I want to feel...safe. Augh." With several more gulps, she took her beer to empty. "Hate the whiny way that sounds. But I do. Want to. Feel safe."

From the bar, the server asked how Lyn wanted her burger cooked, and Lyn did her best to shout with equal volume that she wanted medium rare. And another beer. Please.

"Go big or go home, right?" She teared up when she thought of sharing it with Jude.

Leif frowned. "Eating the Chernobyl burger is not safe. Don't worry, Lyn Darrow, we'll have you shooting like Annie Oakley in no time." He changed the subject. "You know why cops are always associated with donuts?"

"Because they've never had croissants?"

He laughed. "Actually, back in the day—before 24-hour every-thing—when cops were up all night or had to work the early shift, the only places that were open and served coffee were—"

"Donut shops."

"Exactly. It wasn't even about the donuts, although I know a guy or two who's eating more than his fair share of donuts. There. I gave you a history lesson."

The burgers came. Lyn put an enormous bite in her mouth, then in silence ate her half of her-and-Jude's burger. Around bites, she and Leif exchanged talk about their respective jobs. She wasn't what he expected, he said.

"You expected a cannibal."

"Oh the biting thing. Forget it."

IPA's and her burger filled her belly and warmed her. Leif insisted on paying though he'd said she would pay as compensation for the lesson. A Styrofoam container with Jude's half of the Chernobyl burger would go home with her.

"Shall we?" Lyn asked.

"Shall we what?"

"Go practice."

"Lyn, you drank two beers."

"So?"

He sighed the way out-of-patience parents do, the way Lyn sometimes did at her students.

"I wouldn't have ordered a second beer if I knew..."

"Bah, we can practice tomorrow when you get off work. I'll come to your place."

Unease bubbled up in Lyn, the inclination (figuratively) to shoot first and ask questions later. But this Leif was grinning and twirling his fork in his fingers like it was a miniature baton. Now she'd have to see him again, tomorrow. She had plans tomorrow. Reading. Lots of reading. And walking Caesar. She couldn't—

—her mind went back to a couple of hours ago, to the fallen tree and the fleeing deer. She'd made a commitment to herself to turn on her heel and pursue her pursuer, whatever that looked like. She wasn't prepared for how delicious the beer would be and how much fuzziness it would impart. Of course she couldn't expect to go home and do target practice. Guns and booze, bad combo. Driving, too. Should she drive? Normally, she wouldn't question it, but here she was with a cop.

As if he read her mind, Leif asked, "How are you for driving?"

"I only had two."

"Want to play darts, let it wear off?"

No. "Sure, why not?"

Had she lost her mind? The problem was, being across the table from anyone besides Jude was so disturbing, the beer was reflexive. She was in survival mode.

And she'd survive a few games of darts and the Friday afternoon shooting lesson.

Chapter 17

Caesar bounded into the bed of Leif's truck as if he'd done it a thousand times. It took some convincing for Lyn to agree to let him ride in the open truck bed. He'd never done it before, and Lyn worried he'd leap out to chase a squirrel. Leif ruffled his fur and pronounced Caesar too smart a dog.

Lyn tied his leash to the truck bed in case he wasn't as smart as Leif thought. She had been spending Saturday morning in her usual way—reading about Stephen and Zane and the lonely English teacher—when Leif called. Was she up for shooting lesson number two on this unseasonably warm day? Would Caesar like a hike afterward? Lyn could come too, if she wanted. Leif would tell her everything he knew about self-defense and policing.

"I'm reading," was Lyn's excuse.

"Reading isn't living."

What to say to that? Reading was all the living she'd done for the past three years.

Not only had Lyn survived the Friday afternoon shooting lesson, she had relaxed into her new role as student. Marksmanship couldn't be taught in one or even two lessons, Leif explained. Muscle memory took time to develop. If she was serious about being Annie Oakley, she'd need to be patient. When she balked, Leif said, "You know enough to be dangerous. A few more lessons is all you need."

And a hike, apparently.

What else, besides reading, did she have to do? Leif had asked, once she'd shredded a dozen paper plates, and her hand was a throbbing hell.

And no doubt about it, it was the perfect day for a hike.

Leif's radio played a familiar piano/cello piece Lyn couldn't place, but it made the winding road and scenery outside her window feel majestic and singular. Hanging from the rear view mirror was a lizard made of iridescent beads, hung with a green ribbon to match the eyes. When Lyn mentioned how prettily it threw rainbow shards all over the truck, Leif said it was a Christmas present from forever ago.

He took the park roads at a careful pace. The first warm days of spring nudged everyone into the great outdoors: joggers, dog walkers, and casual bike riders who stuck to the asphalt trail. The road cyclists had trains of cars snaking along behind them. Each helmeted cyclist drew Lyn's eye, as if the past three years could be only a nightmare, and she would recognize one of them as Jude.

No one was Jude.

The trailhead was a turnaround of packed earth and a pit bathroom. A large map encased in plastic showed the mileage and hike options.

"You won't need that." Leif nodded to Lyn's backpack. "I've got everything."

Lyn shouldered the pack anyway. Caesar shook himself out and spun in happy circles, yanking Lyn's arm as he caught this or that scent. The moment they entered the trail, a wall of cool, damp air, insulated by a canopy of evergreens and melted snow, met and enfolded them. After some talk of trail history Lyn already knew but listened to, long patches of comfortable silence stretched between them, punctuated by rhythmic footfalls and calls of spring peepers. The woods were a skeletal brown, their buds not yet big enough to see. Here and there bloodroot and trout lilies studded the barren landscape with white and yellow. They were deep into the woods, cut off from the world. Leif often put out a hand and touched the barks of trees nearest the path. Every so often, he'd stop and inspect a bug or a leaf or the rotted trunk of a tree.

On the northern ridge hill, Lyn struggled.

"Want to rest?" he asked.

Lyn shook her head. "Half marathon, no problem. Wee little hill, forget it."

After several minutes, Leif stopped and put out his hand.

"What?" Lyn gasped. It sounded more like *whaaaa*.

"Your pack. Give it here."

Lyn gulped a few breaths. "I'm good, really." Which came out: *Ah guh, relah.*

"How about I take Caesar's leash?"

Lyn could only shake her head. Caesar was pulling *her* up the hill. She needed him.

"Want to take a rest? I could use one."

He needed a rest like she needed a bee sting. Lyn ignored the question. Answering took too much breath.

After a few minutes of plodding and Lyn gasping like a sprinter, Leif sat on a boulder. "I'm resting."

"You don't need a rest."

"But *you* do."

"You're patronizing me."

"Fitting, since you're being stubborn."

Lyn recoiled. *I beg your pardon.* "Ah be yah pardah."

"You heard me." His tone softened. "You're obviously struggling, and I only offered to take your pack. I didn't ask you to quit your job and be my barefoot wife. Maybe it's those steely man-balls of yours weighing you down."

Lyn was beginning to understand why Leif was single. She trudged on, mentally picking and discarding a retaliatory witticism, wheezing and forcing her legs to go faster. She turned. He was still on the rock, legs crossed.

Lyn would rest at the top, when she was good and ready. Caesar, unhappy at leaving Leif behind, yanked to stop as well, but Lyn coaxed him forward, rolling her eyes at the injustice of now having to pull *him* up the hill. She listened for the crunch of Leif's following footfalls, but they never came. At the summit she bent over, resting palms on her knees, gulping, gulping, trying to push back the spots that threatened her vision. She could run a half marathon. What the actual hell with elevation changes?

"Caesar, you are a bad dog." (See-har...wheeze, wheeze...ooh are a baaa dah.)

The valley was a beautiful bramble of tree tops and evergreens. A few birches flashed white, marking out the creek bed. Lyn glanced behind, but the curved trail obscured everything beyond a few yards. After catching her breath, she addressed Caesar. "Why didn't I let him take the pack? What do I have against chivalry?"

Caesar whimpered. A good romp around the forest was what he wanted.

"What was that he called me? –*stubborn*. I haven't even begun to be stubborn."

A branch cracked, bone loud.

Probably a deer.

Lyn scanned the trail and panned the woods. Caesar wanted to sniff at something over the sheer drop, but no way was Lyn getting close to the edge. As she hunched to secure Caesar to a tree, a shadow loomed.

She spun and caught sight of trees snapping back into place. "Leif?" Now she regretted leaving him behind. She fished around in her pack until she touched the one thing that gave her a sense of security. "There you are."

"Here I am."

A clipped scream escaped Lyn's lips before she could get a hold of herself.

Leif had circumvented the trail and sneaked up behind her—what stealth. But there was that mischievous smile.

"You scared me."

Leif gathered several rocks and juggled them. "I'm not going to apologize. You left me behind."

"You stopped walking."

"And you didn't. That's called leaving someone behind."

"Are you always this annoying?"

"No, I just like you." He winked. "And maybe my social skills are a little rusty. That's what my partner tells me."

"I agree with him."

"Says Miss hasn't-been-out-in-years Congeniality. I'd have made the offer to take the pack if you were a guy, too. Why do women always make it about that?"

"Because it's always about that."

"The other day a woman I pulled over for a speed violation read me the riot act when I referred to her as *ma'am*. Today I try to help with your pack and it's fists-up. I don't get it."

"You're a bit old school."

Leif harrumphed.

Lyn took a panoramic picture of the skyline and captured a shot of Leif, bending down to nuzzle his cheek into Caesar's. The two decided the boulder was a good place to rest. Caesar plunked down to pant in the cool dirt and spongy leaves.

Leif pulled out two beers and arranged plates on a beach towel.

"Tell me a cop story," Lyn said.

Leif was thoughtful as he trawled his cheese through the stone ground mustard. "I've been to the ex-mayor's house a time or two...he calls 911 for a pizza with extra cheese, red onions, and jalapeños. It is an emergency, he insists. He's hungry and his 'tyrannical'—his word—wife keeps stealing his phone. He's the mayor for Pete's sake. You bet it's an emergency."

"*Was* the mayor."

"Perception is reality, Lyn. So apparently the ex-mayor ordered so many pizzas and forgot about them that his 'tyrannical' wife called every pizza shop in the delivery radius and had them flag the phone number. The mayor—ex-mayor—lost his mind...which was when the 911 calls began."

"Now I know who to call the next time I have a pizza emergency."

"For you, I wouldn't mind." The sunlight reflected off his eyes.

Oh, but those playful eyes. Play came hard for Lyn, so she avoided them. "What's the hardest thing you do?"

"Traffic stops."

"No way."

"Yes way. Especially on the night shift. Every time I approach a vehicle, I tell myself what I hope is a lie."

"I don't follow."

"Most cops die on routine traffic stops. It sounds harsh, but I approach every stop as if that driver wants to kill me. I hope I'm wrong, but until they prove otherwise, it's how I stay alive to pull over the next guy."

"How would you know if somebody wanted to kill you?"

"I watch their hands. Hands kill."

Lyn couldn't resist looking at Leif's hands. One rested upon another. He wore no rings.

"I don't understand how a person can choose that life."

"Because of the good days, Lyn. I love the sound of the cruiser door slamming when I've tossed in a drunk." He pointed to his chest. "*I* took him off the road. I've always wanted to catch bad guys. It might sound juvenile to you, but that's what most of us are about. We're not perfect. But we want to make our mark, leave the world better than we found it."

"You deal with terrible things to leave that mark."

"You're thinking of the day we met, days like that. Tragic scenes."

"Yes."

Lyn had done it again. Brought the mood down. She brought Jude and death and awkwardness to their picnic. Leif swished his beer and studied the can.

"I wish I could change that day for you, Lyn, that I could make it not have happened."

Lyn did, too. Jude was there, between them.

Finally, Leif broke the spell. "Your job's dangerous, too. A certain student comes to mind. Delaney Lucas gives us plenty to do. She threatened to kill the principal because he confiscated her cell phone."

"But she wouldn't, really *kill* anybody. Especially Silas. He's had her back more than most teachers." Lyn drew lines in the dirt with her shoes. "Silas and your chief bike together. Not road bikes though. Trails. Silas shows me his bruises and cuts. He calls them *Red Badges of Courage*, which is a ref—"

"What do you take me for? I've read it."

"Sorry. I just...my social skills are rusty, too."

"Don't worry about it." Leif waved away her insult. "I remember a few months ago, the chief was having a full-on midlife crisis, so rather than get a Harley like everybody else, he takes up mountain biking. All the guys said it was a stupid idea. I personally told him he'd break a leg. Turns out it was his arm. And his skull, thick as it is. Your boss happened to be trucking along the trail and found him. Got the chief out of there and took him to the ER."

"I knew Silas had a biking buddy who made Tom a little jealous, but he never told me the hero story."

"Like the chief, I guess your boss isn't the type to brag. They bike together these days in case somebody breaks something. Boy, did the chief take it on the chin for that one. The guys said he switched teams."

"The guys who said that are jerks. I'd be on Silas' team any day. He's got a big heart; he's tough too."

"For the record, I wasn't one of those guys."

Lyn took in the forest around them, the catawampus tree trunks, long-leaning against trunks of the ones still able to reach into the earth and hold on.

Leif picked up a leaf. It was brown and curled. He spun it by its stem. "You suffer from survivor's guilt."

"You're wrong. I suffer from survival, period. I read books to feel close to Jude. I smell his clothes. I think about joining him. I called you because I want to control how I go out. I want to go down like a tree, thunder and dignity. I don't want to be pathetic. The things that happened in my yard and at school—they got me good."

"I'm sure that was the point."

"Now I feel...scared, yes, but also reckless."

Leif responded, "Recklessness never ends well."

"Oh?"

There was a story behind that statement. Lyn was sure of it. But Leif didn't offer it, and Lyn didn't pry.

Leif rose and stretched his arms over his head. In the cathedral hush of forest they packed up their picnic and continued their hike until they reached a spot where they had a panoramic view of the valley. The brown treetops were smudged and softened by distance and cloud blanket. A rock had been smoothed by many a hiker and was a natural seat for viewing. The trees in the vicinity were canvas to scores of lovers and hikers. Hearts and dates and block-lettered names adorned every thick trunk and even some thin ones.

Leif wiped the sweat from his forehead. "Tell me more about Delaney Lucas."

"Delaney's no criminal. Like I told Barnfeld, she's troubled, not trouble."

"Yeah, but hurt people hurt people. The guys at the station call her 'the artist.'"

"The artist. She's definitely that. She's brilliant. I didn't tell the detective because in his mind he's already got the kid behind bars, but Delaney did a rendition of me."

"No kidding?"

Lyn closed her eyes, remembering. "It was last year and looked nothing like the whiteboard. I flunked her for plagiarizing an essay. Her mom called a conference to explain to me that 'intellectual property is a gray area.' When Delaney got her essay back, she argued her mom had already taken care of it, and her grade should be higher. I told Delaney her mom and I held different opinions, and the grade would stand. So, in front of the whole class, Delaney tears the essay into little pieces and says, 'Mrs. Darrow, suck my ass.' I considered correcting her, but *ass* was appropriate since she's a girl— and it was fresh use of language."

Leif couldn't stop the grin playing at his mouth.

"Right?" Lyn nudged some loose stones with her shoe. "I wanted to send her back to middle school. I thought, *How in the hell am I going to reach this one?* I had her spend the remainder of class in the hallway. We had a chat afterwards. I told her the other students would now feel free to tell me to suck their asses, which would make my job significantly harder. Then I told her all the promise I saw in her, how she had more natural ability than the other students, but she had to show up. No cheating. Delaney offered to paint a larger-than-life mural of my face on one of the classroom walls as penance, as if those things are related in any way. We agreed on a written apology. Still, she drew me in charcoal and presented it when she read her apology to the entire class. Kid's got an eye."

"I'd be interested in seeing the drawing she did."

Lyn looked away. That wouldn't be happening.

"It should be analyzed."

"I told you I don't want Barnfeld using it."

"No. I mean *I* want to analyze it, for personal reasons."

Lyn's throat got tight. She was sure she blushed. The trees suddenly fascinated her.

Leif stepped into her line of sight, into what she considered her space. "Would you rather I lie? Look, you're attractive. I'm not going to pretend I'm not standing in front of an attractive woman. I'm a straight shooter, Lyn. That should make you feel better, not worse."

A bevy of explosions went off in her, sensations she'd not experienced for years. His words were stone and the mischief in his eyes was flint and

Lyn could not stop her visceral reaction to them. Her face felt fiery. No way could he not see it.

Caesar let out a shrill bark, startling them both, followed by a long, low growl.

"You smell something?" Leif asked Caesar, who whined, snarled, and barked in fury at something over the cliff. He lunged against the leash and snapped his jaws.

Chapter 18

Leif leapt to his feet and approached the edge of the cliff. "Hello?"

There was no answer, only Caesar going off like a siren. The treetops rattled in the wind.

"Hello? Anybody down there?" Leif had to yell over Caesar. He leaned over the outcropping.

"Don't," Lyn said.

Leif turned to her. "It's okay." He patted his side, and Lyn realized that, like her, he was carrying. Of course he was. He was a police officer. She relaxed, but only a little.

Caesar didn't.

A snapping of branches below said something large and heavy was clawing through the thicket. Leif leaned over farther, and Lyn's heart pounded.

Caesar—he wouldn't stop. He was hysterical, wending back and forth and straining at the leash Lyn held, choking on it, sprays of saliva sparklers going off at every snap of his jaws. Leif craned for a better view over the rock face then took stealthy steps to the other side of the ledge to see from a different angle.

"What is it?" Lyn asked.

He put a finger to his lips to quiet her.

More rustlings. For a moment Caesar silenced, and a guttural breathing manifested below. Caesar started up again and drowned it out with barks.

Leif made a frustrated shrug, unclipped his gun holster and scanned the valley. There must have been another shelf below because Leif dropped down and out of Lyn's sight.

Seconds passed, endless seconds.

Caesar stopped barking. Only the rustle of bare branches keened against each other in the wind. Caesar sat at attention, panting. His fluffy white tail swished in the dirt and leaves. Lyn craned to hear Leif, listening for grunts of climbing or scrapes of his boot against the rock face. Or better yet, a friendly conversation with a fellow hiker along the lines of *sorry about our psycho dog...have a nice day.*

Nothing.

"Leif?" Lyn crawled toward the edge of the rock. The trail below snaked along a twisty brooklet peppered with rocks and boulders and downed trees of all sizes and in all stages of rot. Lyn leaned out a little farther. There was the shelf. Where was—

A head popped up, inches from hers. Lyn screamed and shrank back. Leif wore the devilish grin she alternately liked and hated. Hated, presently.

"*This* time I'll apologize."

Lyn flashed him the arched eyebrow she reserved for miscreant students, but she couldn't hold it long. "What was down there?"

"I don't know, probably a deer or a fox."

"Sounded bigger than a fox."

He jumped up with one spry motion. "Whatever it was, it's gone now. Want to hike the Quarry Loop?"

The Quarry Loop was a varied trail through gulches and open fields that ended at a picturesque sandstone quarry. Though she was a little fuzzy from the beer, Lyn agreed. The day was too gorgeous to quit hiking.

The trail narrowed and he motioned for her to go first. Whatever made Caesar nutty could still be behind them, he said, and she rolled her eyes.

"Not a baby, you know," she said and listened for the soft snap of Leif clipping his holster but didn't hear it. She glanced at Leif to get a read on his level of vigilance, but he was unreadable.

Every time a twig broke, Lyn jerked her head toward the sound, scanning for danger. Caesar, tired of tracking, trundled along at her side. He'd become immune to the forest's occasional outbursts. When the trail widened, the two walked abreast, Caesar in front. The flat terrain allowed Lyn to stop slurping air. A root here or there broke the rhythm, but otherwise their boots struck the trail like synchronized oars. Lyn almost wished Leif would put his arm around her. Almost.

A movement on the ground caught her eye. Black, like a hose. A whipping shadow thrashed in the leaves. With catlike speed, Lyn crouched and reached out for the garter snake. She tweezed it by its round head and held it like a prize fish. Its length went to the ground. A yellow stripe ran down its twisting coils. "Take a picture for Silas, will you?"

Leif backed away and dropped his pack. "You. are. strange." But he did as she asked and paced until he got the best angle.

Lyn wrinkled her nose. "I scared him alright. He stinks."

"How about a smile?" Leif turned the phone vertical.

She shook her head against the funk and forced a smile. "Hurry...I...can't...breathe." She held him out a little farther and Leif took several shots. The snake writhed and froze, writhed and froze. "Want to hold him?"

Leif vigorously shook his head.

"You sure?"

He backed off.

Lyn flicked the serpent so it grazed Leif's arm. Repulsed, he spun away. She flicked it again like a whip and it thumped against his torso. "That's for scaring me, twice."

Leif pocketed his phone and brushed himself off in mock horror.

Lyn released the snake. It bolted, leaves sizzling in its wake. She clasped Leif's hands and was startled at their warmth. Not letting on how the touch affected her, Lyn squeezed and twined her sticky snake-stunk fingers in his, all the while challenging him to stop her. The rank smell bloomed stronger as Lyn's palms filed against his skin and each finger in turn. She massaged snake musk into his hands. With her eyes, she dared him to pull away.

Leif, for once, was speechless.

"*Now* we're even." Lyn said.

At the quarry, Lyn plunged her snake-smelly hands into the frigid water. Leif followed suit. Huge scraps of unusable sandstone broke the blue-green surface. They lay in disarray, like the forgotten playthings of a long-gone giant. Frozen water columns dripped and glistened from rust and sand-colored crags.

"We should come back when it's warm. We could swim," Leif said.

What a thought. Leif in summer. Swimming here. *Lyn, Stop.* "I don't get it," she said.

"Get what?"

She flashed him a smile. "You got eleven toes or something?"

"Something."

When he didn't elaborate, Lyn grabbed a flat stone and skipped it. It jumped three giant arcs.

Leif took an enormous stone and hefted it like a shot put. It went almost as far as Lyn's skipped stone, hitting a jutting sandstone and exploding into dust. He grunted with the effort. "And I have eight fingers, see?" Leif held up his perfect hands. Frightened snake smell still radiated from them.

Lyn wrinkled her nose.

"It's your fault my hands smell." He shot his hand out, waving it under Lyn's nose. To avoid it, she arched back. With a sweep of his foot, he gently swept her left foot, unbalancing her. With his other hand he caught her like a dancer. Cinched in a recline, Lyn's face was inches from his. He put his free hand under her nose again, and she squirmed and giggled and screamed.

"*Now* we're even." And the husky voice and the lips so near hers said they were, in fact, even.

Later, sitting on a boulder and shading their eyes from the dazzling light thrown by the water, Leif took her hand again. He put it to his mouth and kissed it, snake musk and all.

Everything inside of Lyn turned to wax and lava. She was speechless. Her eyes filled. She cried because she wished this man were Jude and because she felt something for a man who wasn't Jude.

"Hey...what's going on in there?" He reached over and gently pointed to her temple. "We're having fun, remember? You're allowed to laugh. Hell, you *need* to laugh. And it's nothing to feel guilty about. We're enjoying a beautiful day like it's meant to be enjoyed. No harm in that."

She could only nod. He used the word, *guilty*. In no time at all, this man pointed out the elephant in the living room of Lyn's soul: to enjoy herself was betrayal to Jude.

"Come on. I want to show you something," he said.

The other side of the quarry was an untraversable swamp, but in the years since Jude died, the park built a narrow boardwalk that allowed hikers a passage deep into it. Red-winged blackbirds screeched from cattails, and American egrets stood out against the brown landscape like angular ghosts. The herons were harder to spot, but they, too, balanced on reedy legs and lightning quick, plunged their beaks into the water. Lyn watched with a macabre fascination as one tossed the writhing silver shard and caught it in an impossibly wide mouth. The waggle of its thin neck gave her the willies as the struggling fish made its final trip into the bird's stomach.

"There." Leif nodded to a tangle of dead trees jutting from the water. Once a verdant copse, the area was choked by standing water, and the swamp became home to a wide variety of birds. The trees still upright were bereft of bark and sported more holes than a pegboard panel. The downed ones crisscrossed in intricate bridges of varying widths. On every water-slicked trunk, trains of turtles sunned themselves, their shells glossed with reflection.

At Lyn and Leif's approach, one shy turtle slipped into the enfolding murk. Only a slight ripple and an open space on the log betrayed its exit. The less graceful frogs made splashy plops.

Leif pointed to an enormous trunk, worn smooth by time and obviously an often-used bird-watching spot. They sat side by side for a while before Leif took her hand in his.

Lyn bit her lip. Leif moved in closer, still holding her hand. She had to crane her neck to meet his eyes. He pulled her hand to his face and swabbed his cheek with it. The slight stubble zapped her. When the back of her hand grazed his lips, she yanked it, but he was undaunted.

"What do you like to do, Lyn Darrow, besides read and shoot paper plates?"

Lyn untangled her hand from his, stood, and distanced herself on the pretense of wanting to balance on another dead trunk. A frown of concentration etched her face. It had been so long since she'd thought of herself as a person who did things. Especially enjoyable things. Hobbies were for other people, people who didn't see their husbands deprived of skin and half a leg.

At the halfway mark, her weight dipped the trunk, throwing her off balance. She wobbled and flung her arms and legs as counterbalances, swinging like a pendulum. Leif yelled her name as if the sound could right her. She bent over double, grabbed the spongy trunk, and found her center again.

"I don't know what I like." She cast Leif a meaningful look. "Yet."

"If there were no books and no students, what would you do?"

"Die."

"I'm serious."

Leif hunched down and ruffled Caesar's ears. "Well, we're going to have to change that. Aren't we, boy? All work and no play makes Lyn—"

A gunshot spooked all of them. Lyn fell into the water, which was only knee deep but muddy and cold. Leif had his gun out before she could take refuge behind the tree, her shoes lost, sucked off by the muck. Caesar snaked around their legs, ears back, tail low. The shots were a few seconds apart but kept coming. It seemed they issued from the densely forested ridge from which she and Leif had come. Leif faced the way of the trail and shielded Lyn against that direction, gun out, panning right and left. Something buzzed by Lyn's ear, and bark exploded from the tree beside them.

"Are they shooting at us?"

Leif didn't answer. His face was drained of humanity. Like a machine, he swept the area around them, strategizing.

"Why aren't you shooting back?!"

No answer.

"Leif!"

"I can't shoot blind into the woods. It could be hunters or... kids."

Dirt exploded near their feet. Leif grabbed her arm and ushered her back into the cold water, toward a large piece of sandstone that would offer protection.

Caesar followed, alternately swimming and getting tangled and yelping.

"Hey!" Leif yelled. "Stop shooting! They're people down here."

Several more shots went off. They made it to the rock and Leif called out again. Bullets whizzed by, sounding like high-pitched insect screams. Two hit the water near Caesar.

Screw this. Lyn ripped open her pack and pulled out her soaking-wet gun. She fired several shots into the trees, screaming machine-gun curses with each trigger pull. Blood flowed down her hand from where the action sliced her knuckle.

Leif yelled her name like it was an obscenity and hurled himself into her. They fell as one and were enveloped by the cold and gelid tongue of water. For a panicked moment, she was pinned under his weight.

He rolled off and she broke the surface. Buffeted by a rank medley of fish, algae, and sulfur, she stumbled to her feet and scrambled for cover behind the boulder, frozen and furious beyond words.

Leif glared right back from out in the open. He slowly and deliberately made his way back, almost daring a bullet to hit him.

"You tackled me!" Lyn grabbed his wet shirt to shake him, but it clung and her hands got no purchase.

Leif ignored her, turning his attention to the reports, which ebbed. Behind the rock the three shivered and waited. Lyn grabbed Caesar's leash with one arm and cradled his midsection in the other. With his fur plastered down, he made a pathetic sight.

Both Leif and Lyn breathed raggedly through blue lips. The shots stopped.

"Idiots with guns...." Leif peeked around the rock.

Lyn wanted to respectfully disagree about his choice of the word *idiot*. An idiot cut you off in traffic. An idiot let the door slam on you. Whoever was shooting deserved a more passionate epithet. *Asshole* came to mind.

"I think we can come out now."

Lyn shook her head. Cold as she was, the idea of coming out did not appeal.

"I'm going."

She grabbed his arm. "Don't. What if they start shooting again?"

"Your Dirty Harry moment scared them off. Or maybe it was your potty-mouth. Both, probably."

"Fuck you, potty mouth."

"You want to stay here and freeze? ...Look at poor Caesar."

It was true. Even with Lyn holding him, Caesar paddled to keep afloat. The water at the rock was up to Lyn's waist. Her right foot stung. She was pretty sure she'd cut it on rocks or on who-knew-what was under the murky water. The turtles had fled the log, their whispered plops into wet oblivion drowned either by gunshots or splashing. Leif had a splotch of wet grasses on his neck.

"I'm just...you think they *happened* to be shooting? In our general direction?"

"I don't think somebody was trying to snipe us."

"Why not? What about the body? My classroom? What about the book?"

"What book?"

"Hmph." Lyn crossed her arms and thrust her chin toward the horizon.

"Cops don't shoot at targets we can't see. Period."

"How chivalrous of you."

"Chivalrous? Killing somebody would've ruined the whole afternoon."

"And getting killed is way more fun."

"Lyn, what if I hit somebody? Somebody innocent? Bye-bye, job. And I don't think whoever was shooting was trying to hit us."

"Why not?"

"Because they didn't *hit* us. It was probably a bunch of kids shooting Dad's rifle into the woods. Most people have no idea how far a bullet'll go."

"You're awfully trusting."

"And you're awfully not. Look, I'm going to step out from behind the rock now. Maybe we should make up, in case I'm wrong and they pull off a kill shot. It could be your last chance." The wink again.

Lyn scoffed. "That was the worst joke I've ever heard."

"I'm trying to make you smile."

"After what happened to Jude?"

"Damn...I wasn't thinking." Leif stepped out of cover. His eyes clouded and he pulled his hat down roughly. Without looking back, he made his way to shore.

After several minutes, Lyn and Caesar followed. The air was uncomfortably quiet, except for the gurgles from their plodding. Leif didn't say *I told you so* when no shots greeted them, and Lyn kept her gaze on the trail.

They'd walked several miles over rock and root-choked trails and were almost to the trailhead when Lyn heard Leif exclaim, "Lyn!"

"What?"

"You're limping. You've no shoes."

She waved him off and took a few steps before she felt a gentle hand on her shoulder.

"Give me Caesar."

Lyn handed him the leash.

In an impossibly swift movement that showed Leif was far stronger than he looked, he swept Lyn off her feet and into the honeymoon carry.

Lyn opened her mouth to protest.

"Don't. Not a word."

Once at the truck, he set her in the bed and scrutinized the bottom of her foot. Pain lanced her as he squeezed.

"Lay back. I'm going to dig." Leif held her foot aloft, her wet clothes chilling her now that she didn't have the heat of his body.

"I don't understand how cops can put up with danger all the time," she said through gritted teeth.

"It's not dangerous all the time."

"But when it is, how do you handle it?"

"Eventually we're all going to die, one way or another." He tweezed a bit of raw flesh trying to get at the splinter.

Lyn gritted her teeth. "Still. That doesn't explain why you're willing to risk your life."

He shook his head and resumed digging in her foot. After a thoughtful pause, he said, "As a cop, I am entrusted with people's safety. People trust me and depend on me to be courageous when shit hits the fan." He frowned at some memory. "I cannot run away from danger. I have to face my fears. It's part of the job. Cops who lack courage should not be in law enforcement. It's that simple."

Lyn could think of no response, and then the icy flow of his bottled water over her foot nearly made her cry out. She clamped her chattering teeth together. Leif stopped and gave her a once-over to see if he could continue. She leaned her head back into the corrugated bed and focused on the bare-branched tree limbs swaying in the breeze. After several more merciless digs into the bottom of her foot, he exclaimed, "Gotcha!" and held up an inch-long splinter. "How you walked as long as you did, I don't know."

Chapter 19

Nolan wasn't at the circulation desk.

After yesterday's hiking debacle, Lyn wanted to lose herself in somebody else's life—more than she wanted target practice or hiking or even chocolate croissants (although she did pick one up since she was already in town). Today Lyn intended to pick her own book because Nolan's last two suggestions were the opposite of escape. The first, *Bookworm*, made her question her sanity, and the one about the English teacher was too close to home. Not that Lyn was in the habit of getting cozy with her students, but so much else of the book was *her*, Lyn. Could she admit to Nolan that she didn't finish the book he recommended? She wasn't sure, but since he wasn't at his desk, maybe she wouldn't have to.

Like an unmoored canoe, Lyn tacked along the aisles slipping out books, re-shelving them absently in the wrong places. Her phone buzzed in her purse. She checked the number before silencing it. *Leif.* Her phone buzzed several times as she paced the aisles.

Nothing held her interest. Had she become too dependent on Nolan's recommendations? She pulled all the books off one of the endcaps and brought them to a table where she could pore over their flaps. Her phone buzzed and buzzed.

No offense, Officer Andrews, I'm ghosting you. This was her, keeping her boundaries. Yes it was. After he pulled the splinter out of her foot, they had almost kissed, but Lyn came to herself before that could hap-pen, and they had a silent, cringey ride home.

Time spent with Leif had shifted something inside her, had thawed parts of her she hadn't known were frozen, and the idea of communi-cating with him felt like playing with fire, which everyone knew was not wise.

She was partway through her pile of books and had made no selections when Nolan slid into the seat in front of her.

"Find anything good?" He had a pink tinge to his cheeks and the crisp, pleasant smell of cold about him. With a few finger combs, he tamed his windblown hair.

"Not really."

After an awkward silence, Nolan said, "Haven't seen you in a while. How'd you like *Take a Knee*?"

Lyn felt her face go hot. She forced herself to meet his eyes. "I didn't finish it."

He blinked, stunned.

"That wasn't from the Jude genre, was it?" she asked.

"No. I just thought you'd like it, being a teacher and all." He was holding in his disappointment. It showed in the flickering muscles of his jaw.

He rose abruptly.

"I'm sorry I didn't finish the book." She willed herself to make eye contact. "I'm always going on about people judging books before fin-ishing. It's been rough at work. A classroom was vandalized, and they closed the school."

"Oh?"

"A classroom was painted in blood. You may have seen it on the news." No need to tell him it was hers.

Nolan rocked back on his heels. "That's awful. I'm sorry."

"Me too. I'm in the middle of one of Dante's lower levels of hell, actually. I need something happy. But not sappy. And not entirely happy. Has to be a little edgy. Happy. Mostly happy."

Nolan glanced at her sideways. "Not a tall order at all. Will you trust me, after I steered you wrong?"

Lyn was glad she'd managed to patch things up. She nodded.

He bounded off and was back in with a book. "Here. This one made me happy." He wagged the book and smiled. "And here. This one has simple language, but the story is to die for. I read it in one night." Nolan handed her a thin book she recognized.

"I read that one. Cadence Sinclair was the first character I ever loved, and I've been loving them ever since."

"One of my favorites as well. Come with me." Nolan re-shelved *We Were Liars*. He touched along several spines as if they were the vertebrae of a woman, caressing them, thinking, moving on. At times he mumbled dismissing adjectives: Amish...violent...yuck...predictable...gorgeous-but-no...He settled on another one and pulled it. "This will make you smile. And it's from the Jude genre."

"Really? Oh, thank you." Without thinking, Lyn did something she'd not done in years. She hugged Nolan.

He stiffened, patted her back in a robotic manner. "Lyn, I know I don't know you well, but I...well...if you ever want to talk books, think of me. How else do you make a friend, besides talking?" His voice cracked. Clearly he was out of his comfort zone.

Librarians were probably the only people as introverted as Lyn. The idea of chatting it up with Nolan was almost as uncomfortable as the idea of being in the company of one Leif Andrews.

She pointed to the books he held. "My friends."

He gulped somewhat adorably. "Maybe you need a friend who's not made of words."

"Aren't you working?" was Lyn's attempt at deflection.

"I'm off today." He took her books and bade her follow him to one of the study rooms walled in glass. "These rooms are soundproof. Can I get you a coffee?"

The idea of coffee washed over Lyn like a warm current. She nodded, watched his lumbering stride through the length of the library until he disappeared into the staff area. The study room was silent, but she could imagine the papery slide of books into shelves, the whoosh of the sliding doors, the feathery whispers of patrons, the gait of a solitary librarian trying not to slosh coffee. Her phone buzzed. She ignored it.

A friend not made of words, he said. Lyn turned the phrase over and over in her mind, thinking of the friends she had, the ones in books. Many of those friends were given to her by Nolan, in a roundabout way. And here he was, suggesting she try another tack. And what was he doing here on his day off, anyway? She would make sure to ask.

She let her mind drift while she awaited his return. She remembered the day she'd met Nolan. It stuck in her mind because it was the night of Jude's presentation at the college. His last presentation. Jude's funeral portrait had been snapped that night, though they hadn't known it at the time: Jude at the podium, achingly brilliant. He had dropped Lyn at the library and gone to pick up his suit from the cleaners. He asked her to pick a book for herself and for him. Lyn was in a way-back, rural aisle of the library. It was so quiet in the depths of non-fiction, so untraveled. For her class, she wanted to quote *The Private Life of the Rabbit,* and had it in her hand when she heard the slight crush of carpet.

Librarians were the kind of folk Lyn could understand. Awkward and shy beyond belief. Nolan—she read the name on his lanyard—shelved a book and tipped his head to her.

"Have you read this?" She held up *The Private Life of the Rabbit*. She passed it to Nolan, who dropped it on her toe. That, she remembered. It wasn't too heavy a book, but the corner was sharp enough to chip a yell out of her. After a slew of whispered *sorry's*, he shook her hand. Sorry, he was caught off guard, he said. Sorry, he was clumsy. Sorry, it was his first week on the job. Sorry—he thought he knew her from somewhere, he said, he was trying to think where. Did she know him? She knew only the pain in her toe. Much later and after Jude died, it became a joke between them that he'd throw books at her if she came to his book club. "You'll be perfectly safe. Wear steel-toed boots. We're discussing a heavy book."

Nolan eventually stopped the banter when Lyn neglected to attend the book clubs. Even so, Nolan gave her books from the Jude genre, had done so these three years. How many books were left?

Nolan returned with a steaming Styrofoam cup. "All we have here is powdered cream, but I figured you'd put up with it, this once."

"Hmm...first books. Now my coffee." Lyn sniffled. "A friend not made of words."

"You look like you could use one."

At that, Lyn started crying. Nolan waited for her to finish, untouched coffee still in his hands.

She confessed she hadn't given up trying to find the part in the book that described Jude's accident, that she went through the book over and over, and the scene wasn't there. How was that possible? Nolan shrugged and offered her the coffee, which she finally took and threw back one gulp, then another, not caring for the burn that followed down her throat.

"Is it possible you fell asleep while reading?" he asked. "I do that, especially if I'm reading in my recliner and drinking bourbon."

"No. It was first thing in the morning. I didn't dream it. The passage was there. And now it's not. And I can't explain it. And that's not all..."

Nolan leaned forward.

"That morning, there was a body in my backyard. I mean, I thought it was a body."

At Nolan's confused frown, she added, "I mean, it got up and walked away, so it wasn't dead. It must have just put the hornets' nest over its face." She shuddered. "And my magnolia tree...it was decorated in toilet paper. When the cops arrived, there was no body, so they thought I was crazy—one of them thought so, anyway—and on Monday somebody painted my classroom in blood. At first I thought it was animal blood. Well, I thought it was paint at first because who would ever..." She shook her head and took a sip. "And now this cop says I need shooting lessons." Lyn broke down again. "Which is kind of him to offer, but I don't know...I'm not used to people."

"Really? He's giving you personal lessons?"

Lyn blew her nose and nodded.

Nolan didn't respond except to point to where Lyn's knuckle was scabbed, where she was clumsy with the action yesterday at the quarry. "And what about this?"

Lyn's phone buzzed. She used it as an excuse to break off the conversation, but it was a number she didn't recognize. "I should go." She stood. "You've always been so helpful, Nolan. Thank you."

"Here...don't forget your books."

At the swish of the sliding glass doors, Lyn realized she had acted rather like Leif's tube of caulk, oozing her problems on Nolan. The frayed ends of her nerves cried out for the silence of her living room, for a bolted door, a coffee with a healthy splash of Bailey's, Caesar at her feet, and a book in which to lose herself. A good one this time.

But in her defense, he'd asked for it when he said she could use "friends not made of words." And…darn. She forgot to ask why he was at work on his day off. Lyn never went into school on holidays, but she supposed that was different since she could (and did) grade papers at home. She found herself getting the same jitters she had over Leif Andrews. She sighed. Interactions with people would be a necessary evil until she sorted out who was behind the recent events. But once she got the answers she needed, back to only-books she'd go. Yay and amen. Books were once her best and trustworthy companions and would be so again. No reason to break up with books. Lyn had a long history with them.

Leif was another story. Nolan, too.

Conflicting thoughts about the two men warred inside her mind, and she could not sort them. The phone had buzzed on and off while she talked with Nolan. As the library doors slid shut behind her, she checked her recent calls and saw the first one was from Leif. The rest were from that local number she didn't recognize.

Chapter 20

LYN'S HONORS ENGLISH CLASS was in deep discussion of the book, *Watership Down*.

Silas knocked and strode over to her. With his back turned to the class, he whispered in her ear that the fat-ass detective was back, and he wanted to question her. "Not like you're busy doing anything here. I told him to come back after school, and he threatened me with obstruction of justice."

Lyn squeezed Silas' arm. "Sorry for the drama."

"I've got this," Silas said, meaning, her classroom.

The students began their own buzz, discussing what the change of guard meant. Lyn reconfigured the PowerPoint to cast from the laptop instead of her phone, and under her breath said, "Good luck."

"Not needed." He straightened and addressed the class. "One of my favorites. *Watership Down* is a sleeper, but has its fans, namely Stephen King..."

Barnfeld had not availed himself of any of the chairs in Silas' office. They were narrow, and the wood was old. Instead, he perched his ample butt on Silas' desk. His legs crossed at the ankles, and his arms over his chest. At Lyn's arrival, he pursed his lips like a duck.

"Need some information from you."

"My students need information from me, too. Unfortunately, they're not getting it."

"Yeah, well…justice works 24/7. And I tried you yesterday a handful of times." He sighed to prove the point: so much to do, so many people to interrogate. "Have a seat, Miss Darrow?"

"I'll stand, thanks."

"Whatever. Seems you're getting chummy with one of ours." He tapped his badge.

Lyn didn't know what this line of questioning had to do with anything. "He's giving me shooting lessons."

Barnfeld scoffed. "Oh, there's been more than lessons. And I heard about you shooting at innocent people."

"Leif told you that?"

Barnfeld whistled. "Recklessly discharging a firearm where guns aren't permitted—same thing. And *you* just confirmed my suspicions. Little trick we detectives play to cut through the garbage and get to the truth."

Lyn shook her head and willed the tears to suck back into her eyeballs. Leif told this guy she shot into the woods? Why would he do that? What good could come of that?

Barnfeld got in her face. "See here, if you hadn't shot your gun blind into the woods, your answer would've been something like, 'What are you talking about, Detective?' or 'I don't understand.' There would be a genuine look of confusion on your face as you tried to process this accusation that to your mind came out of left field. But that's not what happened. You were clearly upset at Patrolman Andrews for tattling on you, which tells me you *did* shoot into the woods without regard for innocent people. I'm a walking lie detector, yes ma'am. And you're welcome for that brief enlightenment into investigative genius."

Lyn rubbed her temples. "What can I do for you, Detective?"

"You can tell me where Delaney Lucas is. You can tell me why she'd want to paint your classroom in blood. You can tell me why you called my officers to your place for that nothingburger of a body."

"It was there. They saw it."

"They saw tracks. And you, in your bathrobe. I bet your boyfriend, Patrolman Andrews, didn't tell you. We got the blood back from forensics. It was purchased."

"Purchased?"

"Online. You can buy just about anything these days, including blood. Admit it, you and your student wanted some attention, and you cooked up this scheme..."

Lyn's mind was only half on Barnfeld and his questions. The other half tried to piece together things that would not fit. Why was this man accusing her?

"—Miss Darrow...Hey. Earth to Miss Darrow."

Lyn was deep in thought and had a revelation. "Wait. I don't have to answer any of these questions."

"Pissing off a cop's never a good idea." He touched his cuffs. "We have the power to take your liberty." He patted his handcuffs.

"Why, that's an awful lot of power." Lyn batted her eyes.

Lyn knew it would not be wise to provoke this arrogant asshole, but she'd had the sort of week that made a person do the opposite of what was in her best interests. Life had slapped her, and the essence of that slap was in the doughy, smug face and cigarette-funked detective who had dared to set his gelatinous ass on Silas' desk. She wanted to—no, she needed to slap his face *figuratively*.

"Get out," she said.

He blinked and his mouth dropped open. "I don't even need probable cause to hold an investigative interview. Maybe what you need is a change of scenery—to jog your memory. I'll take you to the station and we can *do it* there. Or maybe we'll *do it* in my cruiser." He uncinched the cuffs from his belt. "Did you know the police levy didn't pass last year?"

"So?"

"That means we didn't get the body cameras the chief wanted." He crossed the space between them and got in her face. "C'mon. You like cops, you like guns. I got a real big gun."

It was Lyn's turn to be shocked into stupefaction. And rage.

He smiled, all hate, and stepped on her toes. She wore heeled sandals; he, tactical shoes. She bit her lip. He pressed harder, grinding his foot onto her toe.

Lyn clenched her teeth.

Silas came in. Lyn hadn't heard the final bell. "What's going on?" he asked.

Barnfeld didn't bother to answer. He caught Lyn's wrist and cuffed it. "You hire this one? She's not very smart."

Silas didn't bother to answer. Lyn watched him assess the scene. She knew her boss would make quick sense of his desk papers carelessly shoved to the side, Lyn, blinking off pain, Barnfeld's smirk. Silas divined countless half-finished altercations at Park Hill High. A principal knew there were as many versions of a dispute as there were people involved. Over the years he learned to pay more attention to eye contact and hands, to a slouch or a face beaded with sweat. These contradicted the stories that poured out of adolescent mouths with Oscar-worthy passion. All this he had shared with Lyn, so she knew he'd read the scene.

"What did she do?" Silas asked tonelessly.

"None of your business."

"You're in my school. Everything here is my business." Silas pulled out his phone and fixed his eyes on Barnfeld.

"Things escalated. She needed to tone it down."

"Bullshit," Lyn said.

"It's my understanding of the law that you can't haul away one of my teachers for an interview."

"You're right." With unexpected swiftness, Barnfeld spun her and clasped the cuff on her other wrist with enough ferocity to make her cry out. "But I can haul her away for a CCW violation." To Lyn he said, "Didn't think I knew, did you?"

Silas held his thumb over the call button, confused.

"That's having a firearm on school property, in child-speak. It's my job to notice things. And last time I was here, I noticed a purse dropped in the doorway of her classroom. You know what was sticking out?" Barnfeld made his finger into the shape of a gun and pointed it first at Silas, then at Lyn. "Your girl's been carrying a weapon on school property, which as you must know, Mr. My-Understanding-of-the-Law, is a federal offense. Definitely probable cause." With dexterity that surprised both Lyn and Silas, Barnfeld swiped the purse off the desk, and the contents clattered to the floor. "Oops. I'm sorry." He picked up the Ruger. "What have we here?"

Silas reddened and pocketed his phone.

Barnfeld paraded Lyn out the front door, past the train of parked buses. Wide-eyed faces pressed against the bus windows, and clods of students made way, tripping over themselves. Lyn fought the urge to shrivel inside.

On the march to the cruiser, she met the wide, surprised, curious eyes of her students. All those half-grown eyes with so many lessons to learn. Like, how life set down tracks without asking your opinion and you wished desperately for a crane big enough to pluck up the tracks and lay them in another direction. All Lyn could do was hold her head up. Take a step. Take another.

For carrying her gun on school grounds Silas *could* suspend her. Would he? He might have to. He had bosses, too. The superintendent. The school board. She looked up at his window and wasn't surprised to see him standing there.

Chapter 21

At the station, Barnfeld hadn't asked her a single question. He'd wanted to parade her before her students, embarrass her. He made a big show of sending her off with a warning not to carry a weapon on school grounds, bawling her out in front of the pretty receptionist. He made the same speech when Silas came to the station to pick her up.

Good old Silas.

Barnfeld threatened him, too. How would it look, the principal knowing one of his teachers had a handgun in class, and he did nothing to stop it? In the car, Silas had strung together obscenities in ways Lyn had never heard before. It was like a foreign language. He got himself so worked up, he had to roll down the window and stick his head out like Caesar.

By the time they arrived back at the school for Lyn's car, Silas' fury had amplified her own, and even when she got home, rage had her too jacked to do anything but pace the kitchen and have imaginary shouting matches with Barnfeld. And Leif.

Tires screeched against the driveway. Even the slam of the car door sounded angry. Lyn peeked through the sheer curtains. A squad car. Leif's number: 77. His uniform gave him an air of impenetrableness, which for the first time, unnerved her.

He knocked with a heavy hand.

No way would she answer after what he told Barnfeld about her "reckless shooting." Lyn wasn't even sure the detective had seen her gun in her purse. Maybe Leif told him she carried. She crept to the bedroom without making any floorboard creaks so she could watch him from the window.

He stood unmoving in a wide stance, hands on his hips, eyes cast down at her welcome mat. Caesar scratched at the door from the inside and of course, didn't bark. If Caesar could let Leif in, he would.

After several knocks, Leif made his way to the backyard. Caesar followed his route from inside, watching through the low windows, whining. Leif walked the property, searching for who-knew-what, and stopped at Jude's pile-of-wood shrine, running his fingers along the smooth ax handle.

Lyn tensed. He might pick up a piece of Jude's wood, might nudge it with his foot. He didn't know about the wood, that it was off limits.

He stepped over several chunks, half-digested by earth. He checked behind the woodpile and started to wade through the yard, as if his intention was to knock on the sliding glass door, but he seemed to change his mind, turned and retraced his steps back around the house. She heard a car door slam.

She held out a mug of lukewarm coffee to Caesar, which he gratefully slurped. He licked what slops fell onto the hardwood floor, too. "We can't trust him, Caesar."

Caesar licked the coffee from his chops and panted at her.

Lyn tried to lose herself inside a book. There was nothing wrong with the book. It didn't remind her of herself or of Jude, but at the ends of chapters, she found she was pulled back into her own skin, into the fear buzzing inside her like a great and deadly hive. Maybe she should grade papers. Years of grading had given her the ability to tune out a tornado if she had essays due. The Ear essays were full of profound thoughts as her students put themselves in Van Gogh's position and alternately judged him a lunatic or had empathy for his struggle and pain. Van Gogh was a desperate man. Loss made him crazy. Lyn knew what that was like. She grabbed the stack and began grading, but the essays could not hold her attention, not today. Her eyes wandered and took her mind with them. With an absent air she scratched Caesar and let the half-read essay lay against her chest.

The lusty knock zapped her like an electric shock. She hadn't heard a car return.

"I have a warrant," said a voice full of sandpaper.

She jumped up and sent the essays fluttering.

Leif.

Lyn put her fist in her mouth.

More knocking. Rhythmic, like a child playing drums knocking.

Leif stared at the curtains as though he could see right through them. "I know you're in there, Lyn. Don't play games." Leif's knocks became decidedly more frustrated. He obviously wasn't going any-where.

"Talk through the door," Lyn said.

"Are you serious?"

"Did you hear about my classroom?"

"Hear?"

"That somebody bought the blood."

"Doesn't mean you're safe."

"You told Barnfeld...everything."

"What? No, I didn't. What's there to tell?"

Lyn sighed her loudest, most frustrated sigh. "You told him I shot at people. Thanks for that."

"You don't know what you're talking about, Lyn. Open the door and I'll explain."

Caesar whined at the door.

"You know, I'm ticked off that you don't trust me." He gave the doorknob one last savage jiggle and spun on his heel. "Finn said not to get involved with you. Did I listen? No...You know what? Fine. I'm out."

Lyn waited a few minutes. When she heard nothing, she cracked open the door and stepped outside. Caesar followed. The driveway was empty. To Caesar she said, "Finn said that? For him to stay away from me?"

Leif stepped out from behind the house, hands on hips. "Yes."

Lyn staggered back a step. "What the actual hell, Leif?"

He shrugged. "Sorry. Not sorry. I'm used to compliance."

Lyn spun for the door. Caesar took sides, winding around Leif's legs and wagging. "Caesar, come." Lyn demanded.

Leif petted him and looked smug.

From the doorway, Lyn asked, "And why would Finn say that—that you shouldn't be with me?"

"I don't know."

Lyn put her hands on her hips, mimicking his body language. "Finn doesn't know me."

"But he does know *me*." Leif strode in long steps toward the door, taking off his hat and closing the distance till his face was inches from hers. "Did you consider someone might have seen us that day and reported it?"

Lyn hadn't.

"It feels crappy that you don't trust me."

"Well, it's because—"

"—I've given you a reason not to?"

"No, but—"

"Everyone lies to me, Lyn. Did you know that?" He didn't wait for an answer. "Everyone's scared of cops, so they lie." He palmed each of her shoulders. "I'm on your side, you should know that."

"Should I? Know that?" Lyn thought for a moment. "Hold on." She disentangled herself from him and disappeared into the house. In a moment she was back with her Smith & Wesson. She slid the action, readied it for firing. Her finger was on the trigger. Leif's eyes never left her hand.

She lifted the gun and pointed it at the window, closed one eye and sighted. She deliberately panned the front yard, halting before she got to Leif. "I'm wishing I could point this at Barnfeld. Don't want to shoot him, just make him feel powerless, like he did to me."

"You're being unsafe again," he said through clenched teeth.

"Now I know why some people hate cops. Too much power."

"I've seen you shoot. He'd have to be awfully close to do any damage."

"Brave of you to sass me, under these circumstances."

He moved into her, and with a leisurely wipe of his arm, moved the gun aside. "I like that you got under Barnfeld's skin." Leif folded her in his arms and gave her a bear hug. He slipped the gun from her hand and tucked it into his belt. Caesar wound himself around Leif's legs and put his nose on the floor, content.

"You can trust me," he said.

"I did think someone was following us at the park," Lyn admitted. "Caesar knew it, too. He barked his head off."

"It's never right to shoot when you don't know what you're shooting at. Your fear is dangerous, Lyn."

"Why didn't you tell me the blood was purchased?"

"There you go, not trusting me again."

Lyn waited.

Leif rolled his eyes. "I didn't know, okay? I don't get notified every time something happens. And Barnfeld hates me. Listen, I'm not convinced you're out of immediate danger. Just 'cause this whacko painted your room in blood he purchased online, doesn't mean he's harmless."

Lyn dropped into her couch, shaking her head. "I have Caesar. And my…" She flung her hand toward her gun, her thoughts trailing away.

Leif knelt by the couch. "Lyn. Even if you were a dead shot, your gun's not enough against a sick mind. This guy's putting serious thought into terrorizing you. You think he doesn't know you have a gun? Hell, Lyn, the guy probably knows what you eat for breakfast."

Lyn shook her head in denial. "You told Barnfeld I wasn't stable."

"No. I answered his questions truthfully. I told him we were called to your residence on report of a body, and that upon our arrival, there were tracks and no evidence of a body. I told him you were visibly upset. I answered questions on an active investigation that may or may not end up in an affidavit for a future court case."

Lyn wanted to believe Leif had her best interests in mind. But whenever she thought of his uniform, she envisioned Jude, dead in a ditch. Leif did not cause Jude's death, she knew, but being in his presence, allowing herself to trust him—it felt as if she was killing something in herself—her love for Jude? Or perhaps it was that she had resurrected something inside herself that should not be disturbed.

She allowed herself a search of his face.

Her breath caught, and she understood: feelings of any sort were reckless, given what had happened to Jude. Something Leif said kept coming to mind: *Recklessness never ends well.* Maybe that was true and maybe it wasn't. She had no way to know. Protecting herself from the sicko and protecting herself from unwanted feelings for this man were a tangled mess inside her.

Chapter 22

A WEEK PASSED WITHOUT incident: no bodies came calling, no hornets delivered; no weirdness in her books. Delaney Lucas was still missing, and posters had gone up around town. Leif had asked Lyn to target practice twice that week, and afterward they hiked the park trails. He began both of their walks with the question, "So...we carrying today?"

Her response was the same both times, to jut her chin and smile mischievously until he moved in and patted her ribs, her waist, her legs.

"You *are* carrying," he said.

"So arrest me," she countered.

After the walk, Lyn offered, "Eat at my place tonight?" And they did. Seamlessly, they worked together in the kitchen, cooking the egg noodles and preparing the Alfredo sauce. Leif grilled the chicken. Lyn brought him a glass of Chardonnay. They played chess on the stone-topped coffee table, both preferring to sit on the plush rug.

Lyn stared at the board.

Leif yawned. "Your strategy is to bore me to death and win by forfeit."

"I'm thinking of my next move."

"You've had time to think of a hundred moves."

"Give up?"

Leif snorted. "Take your time."

When Lyn went to move her pawn, Caesar's tail swiped the pieces clean away.

"Oh well," Lyn said. "I would have won in a move or two anyway."

"*I* would have won in a move or two."

"I guess we'll never know."

They moved onto the cushioned chairs on Lyn's front porch. The cloudless night sky glittered with stars. A candle burned on the wood crate serving as an end table.

"Is this safe?" Lyn asked.

Leif stared at the candle flame. "Define *safe*."

"I'll be enjoying myself, like right now, and then I wonder if I'm being watched. From the woods. I'm glad you're here, but still...being outside..."

"You've got to live your life."

"I'm doing more living than I have in years."

"Here, here," Leif said, and clinked her wine glass.

"Seems like we'd be safer at your place," she ventured.

He choked on his wine. "I don't think so."

Lyn gave him a sideways glance.

Leif massaged his jaw. "I have this neighbor...She's a piece of work. Trust me, we're safer here."

"She pretty?"

Leif laughed. "Fifty years ago, she was gorgeous." His eyes, Lyn fell into them the way she fell into books. She drank in the mixed scents of cloves and soap and set her glass aside. He kissed her in the same confident, sprawling way he lifted her off the ground that first day in the woods. He took his time. He held back. He had incredible restraint. She didn't. She scrambled into his lap, running her hands along his neck and chest and arms, delighting in the scalloped ridges of muscle. They kissed until not enough air existed to fill Lyn's hungry body. Leif pulled back, shivered, and took a deep breath. "I should go."

"Yes, to my bedroom," Lyn whispered in his ear.

"You're not making this easy."

"I'm making it incredibly easy."

"We've had too many drinks." Leif grabbed Caesar's leash and the two were off, down the path.

"So?" She called after him, breathless.

"Rule of my life," he called over his shoulder. "I'll explain some other time."

Rule of his life? Cops and their rules. Lyn hummed as she washed the dinner dishes and packed her lunch for the next day. Caesar loved Leif so much it was disgusting. An hour later, the two of them appeared on the driveway, Caesar unleashed and bounding happily by his side.

"Wouldn't it be safest if you stayed here?" Lyn tried again.

But Leif hugged her and said goodnight. The next morning, she woke to a text from him.

> He stepped down, trying not to look long at her, as if she were the sun, yet he saw her, like the sun, even without looking.

Tolstoy, Lyn thought, Anna Karenina, again. She recalled the morning in Bear's Bakery. Yes, Tolstoy's novels wandered, but sometimes his language soared. And this, quoted to her? Her? Lyn texted back a Tolstoy quote.

> Nothing enriches the world more than kindness. Thank you.

Lyn sailed into her day at school. She didn't pick up a book all week. There was neither the time nor the inclination, for every free moment was spent with Leif.

At Whitey's on Friday night, Lyn asked if there'd been any breaks on the investigation.

Leif stared into the reflection of his butter knife. "Not sure if there's a connection, but a body was found a few miles from the Seven Baths."

"Where they're doing all the construction?"

"Yeah."

Lyn put her beer down. "I'm listening."

"We're eating." He picked up a fried pickle to prove it.

"I can take it."

"After we eat."

"I can take it."

"You don't want to take it. Trust me."

"I do. I used to hike there all the time before they closed it. What did they find?" Lyn gave him the hardest stare she owned.

"A prostitute. Her body snagged on the water treatment grate."

A pickle stuck in Lyn's throat. "How did she die?"

Leif sighed. "Blunt impact with a narrow object. Coroner believes it was her stiletto heels. After that, she was skewered on a deer hook and hung from a tree. There. Happy?"

Lyn pushed away from the table. Bye bye, appetite.

Leif swirled noodles on his fork. "I'm a fan of ignorance-is-bliss. Now maybe you are, too."

In the restroom, she splashed cool water on her face while her guts decided if they were going to toss up her half-eaten dinner. A few times she felt the sting of acid in the back of her throat, but she swallowed it back down and gulped air. Was it because of the brutality she felt ill? Or because that brutality might be coming in her direction?

When she returned to the table, Leif asked—in a rather smarmy tone—if she was all right.

"Smug much?" Lyn plopped into her seat, regarded her cold fries, and pushed the plate away.

Leif twirled his fork. "Told you."

"Hmph...Another beer?"

"Can your stomach handle it?"

"I didn't throw up, you know."

"No? Points for you. Next time you'll trust me when I say it's not dinner conversation." Leif tipped his stout, letting it roll on his tongue and humming his pleasure. A plate of fried pickles was half gone.

"I can't believe you're still hungry."

"You have to eat pickles with stout. It's the rules."

"And you are a rule-follower."

"Law-abiding citizen. There's a difference. I'd like to think it's a big one." Leif pointed at her with his pickle for emphasis.

Lyn threw up her arms. "How about a game of pool?"

They played two games of pool, both of which Leif won handily. For one tricky shot, she yanked her stick back and heard an "oooof." The end had gone into the side of a man who sat at the bar. He didn't think her apology was enough, since he didn't even turn to acknowledge it.

Leif decided they should finish their drinks at the booth. "You're dangerous," he remarked. "You know...you never finished telling me about the hornets."

Lyn stopped, her beer half-way to her lips. "We're having fun."

"Stories are fun. You love stories."

"Not true ones."

"You already told Barnfeld the whole story, right?"

She hadn't. Detective Barnfeld was a jerk.

"Seriously. Lyn, people can't do their jobs if you don't give them the tools. There may be leads they're not exploring."

"I don't trust him. Besides, that was ancient history."

He checked his watch. "Oh look. History class starts now."

Lyn threw back what remained of her beer. "You're not going to like me anymore if I tell you."

"Did you kill someone?"

"No."

"Then we're good. I'm listening." He signaled for another round of drinks and fixed his attention entirely and uncomfortably on Lyn. "And too late. I already like you."

She didn't want to like him back, but did one choose to slip? No. She had stepped onto the ice when she agreed to let him teach her to shoot. She had waded farther and farther onto the ice with hikes and laughter. She studied him and figured he'd break her heart. It was just a matter of time. She consoled herself that perhaps her confession would drive him away once and for all.

The space around them, Whitey's with its sounds of pool balls whacking each other and the sides of the table, the clink of glasses washing, the low conversation, the flickering light of televisions, all of it sloughed away as Lyn allowed herself to go back in time. Before Jude's accident. Years before she even met Jude. Before she understood that—not only was the world a place of peril—but she herself was a participant in its ugly deeds.

Leif rested his chin in his hands and waited for Lyn to begin her story.

Chapter 23

Nine-year-old Lyn's precious caterpillars were dead.

She had been collecting the caterpillars for what felt like forever. Being only nine, forever was probably a few weeks, but the caterpillars had been her first pets, plucked out of the middle of the road or off the sidewalk. The ones that were safe on trees, she left alone. In the bucket, she arranged a soft bed of leaves and some sticks for them to climb. At her dad's suggestion, she added a piece of wet sponge. Dad said the caterpillars wouldn't spin in there because they knew it wasn't the right place. Dad wasn't for caging things, he said.

"It's a bucket, not a cage."

Her dad had sighed. That's what he did when he wasn't in the mood for winning the argument.

Lyn had to have butterflies.

"Moths." Her dad corrected.

"Fine. Moths." The idea of the fuzzy crawlers the size of her fingers going into hiding and coming out with wings...how could that be? She had to get as close to the magic as possible. The moths were always on her mind, no matter where she was or what she was doing. One day, a few white spools of cottony string appeared. Then more, then all had gone into their secret closet to change into something beautiful. Lyn hadn't gone into such a closet yet. She was a gangly, awkward child. She couldn't wait to watch them break free from the confines of their cocoons. She'd read that the brutal work of escape was how they got the strength to fly. The pushing and the pain made their wings strong and ready. The moths had a lesson to teach: strength was created by hardship.

And then they were dead.

Her orange bucket was filled with water, the moths drowned.

It got back to her that eighteen-year-old Simon bragged about how he'd put the garden hose into Lyn's bucket and drowned them. Bugs had no feelings, according to Simon. Who cared for the stupid things?

In response to Simon's destruction of her moths, a dark incredulity spun its own cocoon around Lyn. What could she do against a boy older and stronger? The helplessness bound her as surely as any spool of steely thread, but eventually she pushed out of her paralytic grief and gained, not wings, not beauty, but a black rage toward the world in general for allowing this injustice, and especially toward Simon for being its main instrument. It consumed her: how she'd get revenge.

The hornets, did she call them to her? She often wondered in the years following that terrible summer. It seemed too great a coincidence. The hornets had never come before, and they never came again. Just one time. For her and for her vengeance.

Hornets' nested in the eave above her second-floor bedroom, their little exoskeletons pinging against her window. They revealed to her a fully-formed plan. Simon had never left her mind. He'd become the image of all things despicable. He was a larger-than-life statue in her consciousness. How stealthy they were, hornets. They could hurt anyone, no matter how big or how strong—and she thought of Simon.

A month later, Simon had surely had forgotten all about Lyn, had written her off as a little stick he played with and broken over his knee.

She knew how she could get back at him. What did he love that she could take away, as he took her caterpillars? That ridiculous car. He even named it. *The Raven.* Now *that* was stupid. Simon didn't even glance Lyn's way when he tooled his stupid car down the street like he was in a parade.

One brave and stupid day, Lyn donned her dad's motorcycle helmet, wrapped scarves around her neck, and duct taped all the seams. Thick rubber gloves cinched to her wrists with rubber bands made it difficult to wiggle her fingers. She waited until dusk and leaned out her window. The hornets' nest was within reach. She put a coffee can over it and slid a butcher knife between the can and the house, shaving the nest from its moorings. As she placed a plastic lid on the can, a lone hornet crawled inside her shirt and stung again and again. At the strikes of pain, she dropped the can from the second story window and tore her shirt off, running around the house as if she could outpace the enemy inside her shirt. Thankfully, no one was home to hear or see her, but the lid popped off the can when it fell. An angry hornet explosion kept her from retrieving her nest that night.

The next morning before the sun or the hornets were up, and sore from her stings, Lyn carefully replaced the lid on the coffee can. Lyn had her weapon. She had a plan.

Things never go according to plan.

The next night, Lyn overheard her mother on the phone organizing meals for a family. Meal train moms helped down-and-out families while at the same time being in *the know.* No second-hand gossip for meal train moms. They got the details. Small town. Everybody knew everybody's business. Naturally, Lyn was curious, but when she asked her mother who the meatloaf was for, the answer changed her life forever and was likely the cause of all her trouble, even today.

Chapter 24

In the booth at Whitey's, grateful for the dim lights, but wishing for pitch blackness in which to hide herself, Lyn hung her head and swallowed. She took a minute to compose herself and continued, "The meal train was for Simon's mom. She..." Lyn's throat clenched. So many years since the incident and still, she couldn't make the words come out.

"What happened to Simon's mom?" Leif coaxed.

Lyn did not want to say what happened. Rather, she asked the question she had asked herself over and over through the years: "Simon was eighteen years old—he couldn't get his own oil changed?"

"No." Leif said.

"Simon's mom crashed into a telephone pole. I put the hornets in *his* car, and his mom drove it."

Leif's eyes widened. His horror was a mirror, one Lyn had never wanted to gaze into.

"Right. That's why I don't like to tell this story."

Leif rolled his glass between his palms, deep in thought. "You did something terrible. You were just a kid..."

Lyn picked up her tale, "...a kid who lost her mind. After hearing about Simon's mom, I didn't have the energy to get out of bed. I said I was sick. I refused dinner when Mom brought it to me, the meatloaf. She'd made one for Simon's mom and one for us. It was like my body had been emptied of blood and guts, and cement had been poured inside. I remember thinking my mattress springs would bend because of how heavy I was. This went on for a day, then two, then a week, then two weeks. Food was mud in my mouth. I'd eat half a bite and shove the rest into my heating vent beside my bed. The longer I stayed in bed, the more impossible the thought of ever getting out became. Simon's mom was all I could think about, but of course I couldn't tell anyone. Everyone who entered my room wore the same worried frown. Dad tried to enlist my help in building a rabbit hutch, which was drastic action for him because Dad was not for caging things. It was a kind gesture, though. And Mom would throw open the bedroom door, shatter the silence and ask, was I up for a movie? Shopping for school clothes? School was weeks away.

Nope. Not up for it.

Mom would deflate, sigh, and pat my leg. 'I know you're working through something, Lyn. You don't have to do it alone.'

Oh, but I did. No one would forgive what I did to Simon's mom.

The putrid food scraps in the heating register reached some zenith of decay that caused Mom to pucker her face.

'You smell that?' she asked.

I shook my head but kept my eyes on her blanket, my hands twining a piece of wayward yarn.

Mom sniffed and lunged around the room to find the source. Over the heating vent she stopped and studied the rot behind the metal slits. 'Lyn...oh, Lyn!' Mom threw back the sheets and gasped. I guess I'd lost some weight. Well, a lot of weight.

'What have you done? This has to stop.' That afternoon, Mom packed me into the car and took me to the hospital. They admitted me to the psychiatric unit of Sacred Heart Hospital.

The wing had been recently renovated, which was why it still smelled of new plastic, paint, and freshly cut drywall. The modular chairs were chunky and clean and upholstered in wipeable faux leather. The wall murals brought childlike energy to every space and depicted simple scenes of mountains, forests, wetlands, and oceans. The mountains were triangles; the birds were black silhouettes; the fish were all the same shape, like colorful stamps.

Nothing too realistic. This was a safe place.

I lost all sense of time in Sacred Heart Hospital, couldn't tell you whether I had been there for hours or days. I have a memory of someone shaking me and demanding I go to lunch. A nurse. Her viselike grip plucked me out of my daydream and into pitch blackness. I took my 'free time' in the orange chunky chair, staring at the mountain scene. A lone butterfly flitted over the flower fields. I had been piloting that butterfly in my imagination, traveling the picture, thanks to some powerful meds. At the nurse's harsh shake, a chair materialized under me, and I was plunked back into reality, but I was blind.

'I can't see,' I said, but the nurse either didn't hear or didn't care.

The doors swished open and the harsh voice carried down the hall. 'Lunch!...Lunch time!...Don't you people know how to tell time? Lunch...' The voice became softer as the person retreated. Doors opened and closed and the lace-less sneakers squeaked against the floor: kids going to lunch.

'Hey...guys, I can't see,' I called out.

Thanks to mood-enhancing drugs, the blindness didn't concern me too much. What did bother me was that absence from lunch would earn me extra one-on-one time with the bug-eyed psychiatrist, Dr. X, who was the stare-down champion of the free world and generally made me squirm with his eternal silences and his *lay off thises* and *lay off thats*. His name was too hard for anyone to say, so everyone called him *Dr. X.* He never said what I *should* do, just what I *shouldn't.* I shouldn't daydream, shouldn't stay in bed all day, shouldn't stop my pills, shouldn't skip meals...

I stretched my arms out like a zombie and staggered toward the doors, feeling with my feet against the tile. If I bent almost in half, I could see my hospital socks through a small slit. The socks were the kind with rubber grips in a pattern of paw prints, and the no-slips had twisted to the top of my foot, which was good for sliding a toe along the floor in front of me. When I brought my head up, I was blind again.

After nodding my head several times, I realized I wasn't blind. It was my eyelids that weren't working. They were stuck on down, and no matter how hard I tried, I couldn't get them to open. Through the little slit where my eyelids didn't seal, I could see a sliver of world, thin as a chip. In this way I pushed my lunch tray along the silver track, in a back-breaking limbo move trying to make sure to pick turkey, not ham, and build a respectable sandwich.

Dr. X said the dosage of my meds had been too high; that's what happened to my eyelids. He lowered the dose and after that, no matter how hard I stared at the butterfly picture, I never had the wonderful hallucination of being a butterfly again. A dog-eared copy of *We Were Liars* had been left on the end table. Out of boredom and desperation, I grabbed the slight book and flipped to the first page.

And fell headlong into the unbalanced life of Cadence Sinclair. For a while I forgot the picture, the psych unit, and the socked feet that shuffled by every now and again. Eventually a nurse came and asked if I'd been to lunch. I took the book to the cafeteria. Thanks to my 'blind' experience, I could walk fine with my head in a book and, because the story so engrossed me, I barely noticed when I grabbed a slice of ham instead of turkey.

I devoured Cadence for six hours straight. At lights-out I moved into the bathroom and read until the toilet seat put my legs to sleep. I used a towel to cushion my butt against the tile floor. It was after two in the morning when I finished the book. I was a slow reader then. I grieved the loss of Cadence when the book ended, but grieving for someone besides Simon's mom was refreshing. I fell asleep thinking of Cadence and the awful, tragic, disastrous thing that happened in the book *We Were Liars*. See, I wasn't the only horrible one. That I wasn't the only girl in the world who had done something terrible was a life-giving thought. Even if the other terrible person was a character in a book.

It took a few failures to realize not all books were created equal. I thought I could pick up anything with a spine and get lost for a few hours. Not so. I learned to distrust any book on whose cover a man and a woman were embracing or that featured a shirtless, muscled man.

I had to find an expert on books, and I knew exactly where to find one.

My fellow inmates, Stripes and Athena, leaned over a book, heads touching, giggling and arguing about this or that turn of phrase. I knocked and timidly asked for a book recommendation, and Stripes told me to get lost.

But I wouldn't be flicked away. I poked at their backs until Athena hurled a fistful of pens and pencils like mini-javelins, and I continued to poke with regularity until Athena roared a swear word at the ceiling and tossed me a dog-eared copy of *The Lord of the Flies*.

I slunk away, mollified.

Dr. X noticed I had become more animated in our one-on-ones, especially over characters in my books.

'*Dr. Jekyll and Mr. Hyde* is a classic,' he remarked nonchalantly, scribbling away on my chart.

'What's that mean, a classic?'

'A book smart people read. But they're a little beyond you. You won't get it.'

That decided it. I had never heard the phrase *reverse psychology*. I floundered through *Dr. Jekyll and Mr. Hyde* on pride and little understanding, and I didn't accept any more suggestions from Dr. X. Still, the book whetted my taste for horror, which became my brain food.

It was me who brought up Stripes to Dr. X.

'Stay away from him *and* Stephen King.' Dr. X mumbled it as he jotted notes.

'Why?'

Dr. X shot me a scowl over his readers.

I shrugged. 'What?'

'He's unwell, Lyn.'

'So am I.'

That provoked the eternal stare-down from Dr. X.

I shrugged. 'What?'

'Stay away from Stripes.'

The session was done and Dr. X waved to the door, indicating I could join the others.

Stripes was older than me but a foot shorter, which made him dwarf of the ward. He moved his considerable mass with the stealth of a Cheshire cat and had a stash of King under each of his dresser drawers, secreted in the space between the metal tracks.

He not only loved King. He believed he *was* King. The Stephen King out there was an impostor who had stolen Stripes' body, his mind, and all his stories too. Stephen King was famous and making billions of dollars selling Stripes' stories. The thing was, Stripes was so fat I wondered if he had swallowed Stephen King, whole. That, I kept to myself.

Stripes could prove he was Stephen King, he said, and he wrote every day, on napkins, on the Scrabble board, on the back of Monopoly money. All this because Dr. X wouldn't give him any paper of his own. Everybody else was given reams of paper, whole legal pads to write their feelings down. Only Stripes was banned. I didn't know what his real name was because everybody called him Stripes for the striped pants he never took off. He didn't seem to mind or notice no one called him *Stephen* or *Mr. King*. The nurses had to bribe him with paper and a Twix bar to let them wash his pajama pants once a week while he waited under his sheets. The fabric had to cool before he'd slip the striped flannel back on.

Stripes' best friend was the black-haired Athena, whose scarred forearms looked like Freddy Kruger and Edward Scissorhands had a fight over them. She was always picking her scabs and chewing on them. Thin trickles of blood ran consistently down some part of her arms, stopping nurses short and throwing them into hygienic fits. But Athena knew her King. And she knew when to keep her mouth shut about delusional disorders. At least once every day Athena handed Stripes a black Sharpie she'd scored from the nurses' station.

'Can I have your autograph?'

Stripes would scrawl *Stephen King* in huge letters that used all the space on Athena's back or arm or who-knew-what-other-body-part.

They were inseparable.

Until Athena was released. Poof. No warning. Stripes spent the day screaming and banging his head on anything hard. Every time he convinced the nurses to let him out of bed, he'd go straight to the nearest wall and bang his head. They sedated him to the point of blindness. I knew that feeling. Stripes' eyelids were stuck on down, and he cried in terror that he was blind. I went to his bedside and explained his meds made his lids too heavy, and it would pass. He wasn't blind.

'Good,' he sniffed. 'I don't know how I'd write if I went blind.'

Stripes said I could be his fan because he had a recent opening for a fan.

'You mean Athena.'

'Don't say that name, ever.'

'She got discharged.'

'She left me to rot.'

'She's probably got parents who miss her. And she can't stay forever. This isn't the Waldorf Astoria.'

Stripes laughed, but it was hollow and full of bitterness. He pulled out a copy of *Carrie*. 'I wrote this for her, and the bitch left me.'

'That's harsh, Stripes. ...Can I read it?'

Stripes said not to let Dr. X know whose book it was because Stripes was to lay off the writing, and this was indisputable proof he wasn't listening. Stripes lent me his first successful novel, *Carrie*, then *Cujo*, then *It*. Reading became a secret. It was even more fun when it was forbidden.

Stripes was writing *The Great American Horror Novel* for me, he said. And working feverishly. The napkins disappeared in bulk. Stripes asked for subplots. I gave him a kid who killed my moths.

'That's boring,' said Stripes.

'But then someone puts a hornets' nest in his car...'

'Stupid.'

'His mom gets stung over and over and crashes it?'

'Now we're talking. Wait. His mom?'

I choked out some details but could not go on, so Stripes helped.

'Ryn—which is you—I have to change the name to protect myself from the bloodsucker lawyers who'll sue me for slander if we use your real name. Ryn, has the key to the pet cemetery and lures the moth-killer into the cemetery and disables his car with—what? Ninja throwing stars thrown with one-hundred percent accuracy. Ryn, who is like the horse whisperer but with dead pets from *the* cemetery, stands outside the broken-down car and gives a great speech about not killing things, with a finger on the unlock button on the fob. She pushes *unlock* at the height of her speech, and a flow of zombie pets dashes into the car, hungry—no, *ravenous* for the flesh of...'

There was no face. Stripes made one up.

Stripes and I were in the process of naming and describing the dead pets when I was released from Sacred Heart Hospital."

Chapter 25

SOMETHING SHATTERED IN THE kitchen at Whitey's, pulling Lyn from her reverie. "And that's my origin story haha."

"Here you are…" The server set down another round of drinks, her face registering the seriousness of the conversation. She hustled to the bar and called over her shoulder, "Let me know if you need anything."

The basketball game was heating up, and the cheers and heckles joined "Hotel California" playing in the background.

Lyn took a long pull at her beer and leaned in closer. "Even in the hospital, Mom kept me apprised about Simon's mom. She had no idea it was my fault, of course. Simon's mom was the ongoing saga on everyone's lips, and Mom couldn't possibly know what it did to me to hear about her. For a few months, it looked like she wouldn't survive. Surgery took the pressure off her skull, but the extent of the damage couldn't be known until she woke from the coma, which wasn't happening, and the doctors couldn't figure out why. I kept wondering if the police were going to show up at the psych ward to take me away. Or if Simon knew about the coffee can, if he would find out and kill me, with hornets. Or maybe his car. The jaws of life were used to get his mom out. I prayed the coffee can got mangled enough to not be obvious."

Leif was thoughtful. "I'm sure detectives searched the car. They rebuild the moments before a crash to see what caused it."

"I know that now, but I didn't know then. It was a hot day, and Simon's mom had the windows down. My best guess is the can flew out of the car when it crashed."

"Why do you think that?"

"Because Simon didn't kill me." Lyn shook her head. "A ramp had to be built for his mom."

"She was paralyzed?"

"Eventually she walked, but it took a long time. She never lost the limp, as far as I know." Lyn took a cold pickle.

"I don't know what to say," Leif murmured.

"See why I didn't want to tell?"

"Lyn, we all make mistakes. I hope I'm not judged by the worst decision I ever made." He stared into his glass. "I don't judge you by yours."

"I think Jude's accident could have been revenge for what I did to Simon's mom. I always thought God was angry with me, but now, because of what's happened lately, I wonder if Simon is the one...you know...because of the hornets...that he's getting revenge." Lyn dashed away the tears at her eyes. "Jude's books were my escape after he died. I come up for air every now and again. I can teach on autopilot, do whatever chores or errands that way, too. Because I've done a terrible thing, I can empathize with people who do terrible things."

Leif leaned forward. "We've *all* done terrible things, Lyn. You know that, don't you?"

She cleared her throat, unable to speak. Yes, she knew everyone technically did terrible things, but Lyn had a hierarchy of terrible, and her act set her apart.

He reached across the table and took both her hands in his. "I'll tell you my terrible thing next time. You'll see. You're not so bad."

The ice in his eyes made her believe him.

As they pulled into Lyn's driveway, the headlights threw twin bands of harsh illumination. "The front light's out," Lyn said.

"After so many hours, they do that."

"I know. I'm paranoid."

"You're with me, so relax. Cops go looking for trouble. Not the other way around." Leif rounded the car and circled her waist, drawing her to him. The night air was moist and heavy and blanketed them in silk. Lyn's lips brushed the shadowed depression where his collarbones met. She inhaled his scent and the hint of malt on his breath.

With a handful of her hair, he drew her face toward his. A current of desire ripped through her; she felt the sparks tossed by their climb toward one another in the dark space.

Then from somewhere, a vibration needled. It came again and again.

Leif put both hands in her hair and kissed her neck and around the back of her ear. She shivered.

A moan, half annoyed, half ecstasy, escaped Leif. "I better see who's calling."

"Don't."

But he had already accepted the call. A rude light cast his face in shadow and brilliance. "Hello? ...Oh hey, Finn. I didn't recognize the nu—"

The voice on the other end interrupted. Leif stepped a few paces away and grabbed the lamp post as if it would support him. Lyn strained to hear, but the voice was garbled and frantic. "I'm sorry, man. I'll be right there. I'm at Lyn's. Go. I'll meet you."

"What was that?" Lyn asked.

"Finn. Says he has a family emergency."

"Did he say anything else?"

Leif shook his head. His eyes had a far-off, glazed look, as if he were trying to piece his partner's troubles together. "Finn asked to stay at my place tonight, but I need to let him in." He traced the landscape of her eyebrow, her cheek, let his fingertips journey down her neck with erotic stealth. "I'll be back."

In the pitch blackness, Leif missed the keyhole several times and swore. Finally, he got it. Lyn pushed open the door and flipped on the light. He pulled her in for one last kiss before releasing her. "Lock up." He pulled the door closed.

"I know, I know." Lyn slid the bolt into place and listened for the cheerless sound of Leif's truck pulling away. She stood in the middle of the living room swaying like a buoy. *Great timing, Finn.* Caesar wound around her legs, and she knelt and buried her face in his thick fur. It still smelled of coconut from his grooming.

"What could be wrong with Finn?" She asked Caesar.

If he had to sleep at Leif's place, maybe they had a fire at his house? But Leif didn't say *they*. Leif said *he*, Finn, needed a place to stay, and Lyn was pretty sure Finn was married. Leif seemed to know more than he let on, but she could wait until tomorrow to hear about Finn's troubles. Right now, only one thing interested her, and he had just left. Lyn had an emergency, too. She paced the living room, trying to leave her desire behind. She was unsuccessful.

Eleven o'clock.

Two eternal hours passed since she had confessed her life's regret to Leif Andrews. Only one other person knew the story. Simon. How long had it been since she had thought of him, let alone said his name out loud. Even when she recalled the body and the hornets, she suppressed thoughts of Simon. In the quiet, in the retreating alcohol buzz, a cold nakedness stole over her, and she wondered if she had said too much. Leif wasn't her priest, but when he listened, when he leaned in and his eyes bore into her, she spilled everything. It was like he threw open a door she'd locked, not a crack, but wide open, and all the things she'd kept put away came out. It was both relieving and terrifying. Lyn needed him to come back. There would be little, if any, sleeping when Leif returned. Lyn undressed down to her underwear and a spaghetti strap tank and lay on the couch to wait.

Waking on the couch surprised Lyn. She checked her room. There was no sign of him. His truck wasn't in the driveway. Lyn texted, but he didn't answer. Surely he wasn't still with Finn? He said he'd be right back.

A book lay on the floor beside the couch. It faintly called to her.

Lyn tugged on a pair of flannel pajama pants. She started the water heating and ground the dark, oily beans, letting the sharp aroma and high whine of the steel blades wake her. While the coffee steeped in the French press, she texted Leif. Then twice again while she pressed down the filter. She let Caesar out through the sliding back door where he romped off and sniffed the rhododendron at the woods' edge. Through the curtains, she surveyed the yard. Jude's shrine didn't hitch her breath like it used to every time she glanced at it. Spring breeze sheared the tiny white petals from the dogwood trees and set them aloft in waves and swirls. The magnolia had pink child hands, half open. In a few days the flowers would splay fully. In a few more months, they would fall. The circle of life and death.

Death.

That did it. She took the next step and called Leif.

No answer.

The stove timer said the coffee was done. Lyn turned off her burner plate as she walked by, a clockwork she performed thoughtlessly. With her coffee and phone beside her, Lyn turned to a book. The book was solid in her hands. She opened it, then snapped it shut before reading a word.

She didn't want a book.

For the first time, a book would not do.

Lyn dialed the non-emergency police number. Was Officer Andrews available?

No.

Had he been at the station last night?

The receptionist couldn't say. She just came on her shift.

Would Lyn like to be transferred to his voicemail?

No.

Chapter 26

At the knock, Caesar padded over to the front door and sat at attention. Lyn was both relieved and furious. She'd prepared some choice words for Leif.

As she passed the curtain, the silhouette struck her as unfamiliar, shorter, and shifting weight from foot to foot.

Not Leif.

Lyn hopped over the back of her couch with an adrenaline surge, thankful her curtains were closed. Who would be knocking at 8 a.m.? She padded to the closet and plucked the gun from her purse, set it on the windowsill, and peeked around the curtains.

Nolan stood on her porch—with a handful of books—smiling a goofy, brilliant smile. When he saw Lyn peeking, he waved, nearly losing the tower of books in his other hand. He righted them, but not before one slipped off the top. He bent to retrieve it, shaking his head.

Lyn opened the door. "Nolan, you brought me books?"

An enigmatic smile was his response.

A mountain bike was parked in the walkway behind him. It had a steel basket on the back and an empty canvas bag for carrying things, like books. A sheen of sweat and ruddiness graced his cheeks. But it was strange, the librarian here, on her porch. He wore a pair of athletic shorts and a nylon shirt, his sunglasses perched on his head.

Lyn leaned half in, half out the door.

Nolan looked first at what a bra should be covering, then his eyes furtively skipped beyond her into the house. He held out a stack of books. "I know it's not customary, but you haven't been to the library in a while, and after how you were that day...well, I worried. I picked some books and waited for you to come by. When you didn't, I got your address from the database. Don't tell the other patrons or I'll be delivering books for everyone." His eyes were everywhere except on her shirt.

"How kind." Lyn crossed her arms over her chest. "I'm doing better now. I'm sorry for dumping my problems on you. I don't make it a habit."

"I didn't mind at all. I enjoyed it, actually. I missed you at the library...You been reading?"

"I did start one."

"Which?"

"The one..." She couldn't even supply one sentence about the book. Had she actually read any of it?

A smile played on Nolan's lips but didn't land. His parlous stack of books shifted. Before it could tumble, he set it straight and peered beyond her, into the living room.

From behind her, Caesar whimpered. Lyn opened the door. "Would you like to come in?"

Nolan accepted, set her books on the end table, and looked around, awed. "You practically have a library right here." He motioned toward the floor-to-ceiling bookshelves lining three of the four dining room walls.

"I'll be right back." Lyn went to the bedroom and threw on a bra. She talked through the crack in the door. "I was having a cup of coffee, but you probably want some water after riding all the way here. I'm not as ambitious...still in my pajamas." She emerged from the bedroom, piling her hair into a nesty bun and feeling only slightly less ridiculous now that she had a bra on. "Where'd you park?"

"I rode from home."

"Oh. Where do you live?"

"Off 83, beyond the trailhead parking ."

"Wow. I didn't know we're practically neighbors."

"I think of 'neighbors' as being a little closer. We're in the middle of nowhere here. Does that ever bother you? I mean, especially after what happened to your classroom."

"I'm learning how to live with fear," Lyn said. "Until recently, I wasn't afraid. I enjoy the seclusion of park property...ice water?" Lyn texted Leif while she got Nolan's water. Had Nolan answered for water? She texted Leif again with a worried emoji and slipped the phone in her pajama pocket. Nolan strolled along her book-lined walls in much the same way he did at the library, fingers tapping the spines.

She offered him the water, and he ran the cold glass along his forehead. Lyn patted her phone. Had she turned up the volume? Or was it on vibrate? What if she'd turned *off* the vibrate? Maybe he'd already texted back. A quick check to make sure the vibrate was on wouldn't be too rude, would it?

"...don't you think?"

Lyn blinked stupidly. "I'm sorry. What did you say?"

"I said, a room without books is like a body without a soul."

"Oh...yes. Cicero. That quote finds its way to my classroom often enough. I teach simile with it, among other things."

"Love of books...no greater lesson." Nolan relaxed in his favorite subject. For a while, Lyn half listened until he brought up the book she didn't finish, *Take a Knee.* All she heard was the title, not what he had said about it.

So she feigned attention and said, "I'm not sure what the character Stephen saw in his English teacher. He's not even straight. He's young; she's old...in relation to him. All she's done is praise his writing. What reason could Stephen possibly have for seducing his high school English teacher?"

Nolan smiled mischievously. "Boys—and men—enjoy a power difference."

"So he falls for his teacher because she gives him an A? I'm not buying that."

"He falls for her because she sees him. No one else has. And she reminds me of you. That's why I picked it."

Lyn's blush dived into the lower parts of her. "I didn't see any similarities (*big, fat lie*), but then again, I didn't finish it."

"Maybe young Stephen is more devious than you imagine. Maybe he wants to ensure the *A.* Or force it." He traced his glass with his finger.

They discussed other books, and Lyn could not believe Nolan was sitting on her couch, that all this time he lived down the road. The partitions of her life were splitting. Nolan had great taste in books—usually—and his banter passed the time. It was somewhat of a distraction against *where-the-hell-was-Leif?* Why had he not called? WHY? Lyn slipped out her phone and pressed the home button. Still no call. No text. What could be keeping him? And he couldn't call to let her know? It was *that* uninterruptible? Lyn hadn't been hearing Nolan, and his talk veered off books and into some other subject, a subject she couldn't access because she was paying zero attention. *Again.* She hoped he'd give a clue, and she could pick up the thread of his conversation without having to admit she wasn't listening. He didn't. Nolan looked at her expectantly.

"I'm sorry. Can you repeat that last part?"

"Forget it. I was trying to tell you something in a roundabout, obtuse way, when what I should do is spit it out, right?" Nolan's chin trembled. He gazed around the room at the pictures of her and Jude on the walls, at the cuckoo clock, the floor, Caesar. He glanced out the bay window with its view of the magnolia tree and the bluff across the road. "I've been thinking about you."

"Oh?"

"Not about books, what books I can find for you. Um...since the day at the library, I've had trouble *not* thinking about you."

Lyn's heart began to canter. "It was wrong of me to unload on you like that."

"No. It's fine—I liked it. Just, you don't strike me as an off sort of person, and that got me thinking. To paint your room in blood is pretty extreme. Why would anyone want to hurt *you*?"

The confession she had made to Leif came to mind, but she shrugged. "Why does anyone want to hurt anyone?"

Nolan's face became unreadable. After a moment, he held up his glass. "Mind if I get more?"

"I'll do it," Lyn said.

But he was up and in the kitchen before she could stop him. The ice tumbled into his glass, then water. On his way back, he spotted the gun on the windowsill and blinked in surprise. "Is that...?" He set his glass down. A shadow passed over his face and disappeared. He ran a finger along the barrel the way he did with book spines. He palmed it. "Is this real?"

Lyn stood and oriented herself away from the barrel. "Real enough to not want it pointed my way."

Nolan turned, and the barrel faced her again. In his palm it couldn't discharge, but still. Lyn didn't like the barrel's black throat facing her. Was Nolan really so gun-stupid? She moved again. So did he. Like they were dancing. Nolan threaded his finger through the trigger hole, studied the gun, and asked what kind it was and how many bullets and did it have a safety?

She forced a carefree lilt into her voice. "A bit late to ask that question, since it's pointed at me." She used the palm of her hand to move it aside.

"Is it? Too late?" With a surprising deftness, Nolan turned over his hand, caught the gun trigger in his middle finger and held it expertly in an outstretched arm. "This doesn't sight well."

So he *did* know guns. "It's my up-close gun," Lyn admitted.

"Do you always keep a gun on the windowsill, or were you thinking we'd get up close?" He spoke while sighting down the barrel. The muscles in his neck flexed as he pivoted first one way, then the other.

Before Lyn could think of an answer, Nolan deftly re-engaged the safety.

He held her gun out, handle toward her this time. His question remained on his face, the question of *were they going to get up close.*

Lyn's deer-in-the-headlights eyes were her only answer. She placed the gun back on the window ledge. Nolan had a boyish innocence that clashed with what she'd just seen.

"You pretended not to know guns," Lyn whispered.

"You pretended not to have one. I saw it when I came in. Guns spook people."

That's it? *Guns* spooked people? *People* spooked people.

"This guy will keep you safe." He patted Caesar's cottony head.

"Caesar's so friendly. I'm not sure—"

A harsh knock interrupted them. Nolan seemed annoyed.

Lief?!

Her heart fell when she opened the door to Finn, in uniform. "Hey, Lyn. Sorry to bother you, but is Leif around? He didn't show up for work, and I can't get him on his phone."

Lyn let the door and her jaw open. Caesar pushed by her and sniffed at Finn's hand, then his crotch.

"Oh...didn't know you had company." Finn frowned and steered Caesar's nose away. He looked confused as he processed Lyn in her pajamas and Nolan, there. "Leif here?"

"He left last night," Lyn whispered. "Right after you called."

Finn shook his head. "I haven't talked to Leif since our shift ended yesterday."

"He said you had an emergency."

"What emergency?"

"Family. He said you had a family emergency."

"Well, I can tell you I don't have an emergency, except the one where my partner doesn't show for his shift. Maybe you heard the name wrong or it was a different Finn. I'm going to his place. I figured I'd try here first, since he's always *here*." He threw a meaningful glare to Nolan before striding back to his cruiser.

"Wait...Finn." Lyn followed him. "It was you. I'm sure of it. Leif wasn't scheduled to work today, that's why we went to Whitey's and—"

"Lyn. Don't you think I know whether or not my partner is scheduled to work? Look. I don't know what's going on between you two, and I don't care so long as Leif does his job. Until today, he has. It's probably none of my business, but who's the bloke?"

"A friend."

Suspicion flashed across Finn's face.

"He works at the library."

"He makes house calls?"

Lyn exhaled her exasperation. "He lives down the road. He recommends books, and he came by this morning because I haven't been to the library in a while."

"Sounds like he's more than a friend."

"Then you need a hearing aid." Lyn spoke more softly. "Finn. I *heard* you on the phone last night." Maybe Finn was too embarrassed to admit he called. He didn't want people to know he had problems.

"I'm not saying you didn't hear somebody, but it wasn't me." Finn pulled out his phone. "Look, see? No outbound call to Leif. I'm trying him again."

"Why would Leif lie?"

Finn shrugged his shoulders and frowned, phone to his ear.

Lyn glanced beyond her to see if Nolan was close by, but she couldn't see him. Perhaps he used the restroom or distanced himself to give her privacy.

"No answer. I'll call you when I get to his house." Concern settled on Finn's face. "He's probably asleep on the couch with a dead phone battery. And when I get there, I'm going to kill him."

"Tell him to call me."

Finn narrowed his eyes and gave a curt nod. He slammed the door and made his tires squeal against the blacktop.

Inside, Nolan was on the couch flipping through one of the books he brought over. When Lyn entered, he looked up. "Everything alright?"

"Meh, I don't want to dump on you again. I'm not company material right now."

"Your friend, he a police officer?"

She nodded.

"I think he came by the library yesterday. Big guy. Dark hair. He was asking about you. He has a strange, forgettable name. Lem or Lionel."

"Leif."

"That's it. *Leif.* He was asking how long I've known you, what sort of books you request. He got irate when I refused to share your checkout history, but that's private information. You'd think he'd know that, being in law enforcement."

"Leif was at the library?"

"Lyn, I don't want to pry, but I overheard you and that officer, and if you're involved with the same cop who came around yesterday, he was...well, I wasn't entirely up front with you when I said I happened by."

"What do you mean?"

"I got worried. You haven't been to the library, and a cop shows up acting like he owns you. I wanted to make sure you're okay. People see a uniform and they assume: hero. Any loser can cover up with blue polyester and a shiny badge. Some of the most insecure men—well, you know..." The flush in Nolan's cheeks brought out the chisel of his features as he stepped close, closer to Lyn than they'd ever been in the library. "I don't live far, and if you need anything...I can be here faster than anyone."

"So long as you don't ride your bike." Lyn tried for levity and stepped back a few paces. "It was thoughtful of you to come and check. But I'm fine. Really. And it's nice to know you're just down the road. Next time I see you, I won't be wearing my pajamas."

Why the hell did she say it that way?

"People wear them everywhere these days. I don't think you can wear something...uncomplimentary."

Deer in the headlights again. Lyn extended a hand. "Thanks for coming."

Nolan took her hand and gave a gentle shake, a bit long. "When you feel like company material, I hope you'll let me know what you think of *Take a Knee*."

Lyn didn't follow.

"You left your bookmark in it. I saw where you left off, so I brought it back in case I could persuade you to give it another chance."

"Oh, the boys." Lyn's hand rose to her neckline at the thought of the scene she'd read, the one that turned her insides to lava.

"What do you think it takes to write a scene like that?" Nolan moved closer.

"Either experience or imagination. Both, likely." Lyn's face heated.

"I can imagine myself anywhere." He said it with the same double entendre Stephen used on the teacher.

As they moved toward the door, she shot him a glance over her shoulder, but she couldn't get a read. His smile was innocuous.

Something that shouldn't have been in the middle of the floor caught her foot, something large and soft but immovable. Caesar. He was sprawled out and she was about to land right on top of him. He lifted his face to watch Lyn throw herself to the side and knee-first, roll out on the wood with bone-whacking clunks. She hadn't seen her ceiling in a long time. But there it was, along with some shafts of agony in her knee and palm and elbow. Nolan was beside her, crouched.

"Wow. That was impressive. You fell perfectly. No thanks to your dog."

Nolan leaned over her, his face inches from hers. He put his arm around her waist to help her stand.

She didn't need help, and knew he knew she didn't need help, but the moment allowed him to touch her and he took it. Nolan turned a corner. Lyn knew the way you know what's coming next in a book. Like she knew what was next for Stephen and Zane, she knew what was coming next from Nolan. *Want* radiated from him like a bonfire, like the books and their burning scenes. A blaze from which she would turn away, but it would still throw heat everywhere. Nolan knew her thoughts, knew her tastes in books better than she did. *I can imagine myself anywhere.*

This wasn't happening.

A blow torch went off behind Lyn's cheeks. "I'm fine." She jumped out of Nolan's touch.

"You sure? You whacked your head pretty good."

"Nope. I'm..." She backed into Caesar and almost toppled again.

Nolan grasped her and guided her to the couch. "You'll have to try harder to trip over Caesar a third time, but I have faith that if anyone can do it, you can."

Lyn was grateful for the tone shift. "I'm perfect."

"Okay, if you're sure."

"Yes." She made her face a blank page.

Nolan hesitated, then made his way to the door. Over his shoulder he called, "Remember, I'm right here if you need anything."

Chapter 27

About a half an hour later, there was a third knock on Lyn's door.

Finally. Relief flooded Lyn.

Only to be replaced by abject annoyance. Barnfeld stood, hands on hips, smoking a cigarette. He chucked it into her flowerbeds when she opened the door. Caesar barked half heartedly but approached the detective when he held out his hand with a treat.

"Miss Darrow, I'm investigating an incident involving your fuck buddy, aka Patrolman Andrews, and I need to ask you some questions."

"Where is he?" The words flew out.

Barnfeld scowled and scribbled in his notepad.

"Well? Is he okay? Is he hurt?"

"I'm asking the questions here." He pointed to his badge. "Says *detective*. That makes me smarter than Patrolman Andrews."

"And modest, too."

"I have to dig—that's what I do, dig."

Lyn couldn't speak. Leif's gaze swam in her mind. His focus, his smile. The way it felt to have his hand hold hers, the ease with which he carried her off the trail when her foot was hurt.

"I need everything you know about Patrolman Andrews. When you were together, when you weren't. Leave nothing out. If he went to take a leak and you weren't right there holding it for him, I need to know."

Fear for Leif made her brave. "I'm not telling you anything until you tell me where he is."

Red splotches appeared on Barnfeld's neck and cheeks. He squeezed the pen in his hand and seemed to hold his breath before releasing it in a spirit of forfeit. "His neighbor made a call, okay? His partner thinks something's wrong. The guy's been hanging around you, the very unlucky Lyn Darrow."

"So no one's seen him since last night?"

"That's why I'm here. He's an adult, so normally we wouldn't give a fuck. If a guy wants to disappear, it's a free country. But like I said, he's got fans. Maybe there's some foul play I don't know about, yet."

She opened her door and Barnfeld installed himself at Lyn's kitchen table, the same seat Leif used forever ago. He grilled her on the events of the past weeks, from the moment she met Leif to the day he disappeared.

Lyn gave him the basic timeline.

"Were you intimate?"

"I don't see why that's relevant."

"Were you?"

"No." She eyed him. *And I regret it.*

"Why would he disappear?" He asked.

"How should I know?"

Barnfeld slapped his palms against the table. The candles in their crystal holders made soft, woody music, then settled. His smile reminded her of a demented cartoon cat's. "I sure hope I don't feel my life is in danger. You *are* known to shoot first and ask questions later. I'd hate to have to defend myself."

Lyn narrowed her eyes. "Whoever painted my room, have you found him? No. And now Leif's missing? I don't think that's a coincidence. Your envy of Leif keeps you from drawing the right conclusions."

"I was mining you for info. Don't kid yourself, Miss Darrow, you're not worth all this trouble."

"What about the call from Finn?"

"You obviously heard wrong."

No, she had not heard wrong. One of them, either Leif or Finn, was lying. How to explain that?

She couldn't.

Chapter 28

After Detective Barnfeld left, Lyn tried to rouse Caesar for his breakfast, but he wanted only to lay on his back and have his belly rubbed. Even brandishing his favorite toy got barely a wag out of him. She searched *dog suddenly lazy* and found several possibilities that worried her, including heart disease, tick bites, and botulism. The park was redolent with ticks, but Caesar was treated. Still, it wasn't foolproof. If he got into some animal carcass, who knew what disease he could have picked up? He wasn't paralyzed, just tired. Lazy. He'd take a few steps and lay back down. Maybe he missed Leif, too.

Finn called. His tone told Lyn it wasn't good news. "He's not here. I had to break in...Lyn, I have to tell you, I think it's best you find another place to stay for a while."

"Why?"

"I found some things at Leif's house. I can't go into it now, but it doesn't make sense, and...maybe the overly cautious thing would be for you to disappear."

"I teach tomorrow."

"Got any vacation time?"

"Yeah. All summer. Too bad it's April."

"A couple sick days, then. You have anybody you can stay with?"

"Finn, what is it?"

Finn didn't answer.

"Finn. *What* did you find?"

"I can't tell you till I go to the chief."

"Wait, I can come right now."

"No...that's a bad idea. I've got to talk to the chief. If Leif calls you, call me right away...If you see him—Jesus, Lyn, I don't know what to tell you if you see him. Stay in crowded places. Lock your door."

Dread unfurled in her stomach. "Barnfeld was just here. Did you send him?"

He had already hung up.

Fine. The next person inside Leif's house would be Lyn. Whatever was in there, she deserved to see it. It involved her. Finn made it sound like Leif was a danger to her, but she wasn't sure she trusted Finn. When she wasn't sure who to trust, she trusted her gut. Her gut was maybe too close to her heart muscle. And her heart wanted to get in the car and go straight to Leif's and rifle through his possessions. Knowing what Leif Andrews was all about had just become more necessary than air.

Leif's home was situated on a raised lot at the corner of two county roads. Framed in weathered post and rail fencing, the Cape Cod backed into a strip of woods. In the front yard, tall untended grasses poked through the fence, and slender green ribbons, the new grass of spring, pried through the yellow field.

The gravel driveway popped and sputtered no matter how slowly she took it. There were no cars in the driveway or parked along the road shoulder. No one was around. Finn must have left already. Lyn had hoped he would still be there because she didn't know how she'd get inside but hoped an open window would make things easy. Depending on what kind of lock he had, she could try the credit card trick she'd seen demonstrated on YouTube. At this point she was desperate enough to use her wood ax on the front door and buy him a new door later. The ax was a last-minute decision and was in her trunk. What if he had security cameras? She didn't care.

The front door was vintage with a frosted glass pane. The handle was one of those old deals with a keyhole fit only for a skeleton key. No way could she harm the exquisite door. She tried opening it, but of course, it was locked, so she made her way around back. An unfinished deck infused the air with the scent of freshly-cut-wood. Lyn cupped her hands to the sliding glass doors and peeked inside. That was when she noticed the aluminum door was dinged around the lock. Finn? He had said he broke in.

The room was decorated in grays and whites with an accent of orange and was as inviting as it was utilitarian. It said: bachelor who cares about beauty. A little. The wall behind the sofa displayed three pictures that, when looked at as a whole, were of a life-sized white horse. A sectional couch had one bowed cushion. Leif's spot, no doubt. And in the center of the room was an orange accent rug in the shape of an enormous cat, face down. Hanging from the ceiling fan was another of those hand-made bead lizards, like the one on Leif's rearview mirror. It swayed slightly with the motion of the fan, which went in lazy circles. One book was on the end table. Lyn couldn't make it out.

What was amiss? Nothing. Lyn tried the sliding door. Locked. A window fronted the deck as well, with small panes of bubbly glass and trim painted and splintered and re-painted—probably original. Lyn pushed, but it didn't budge, either. The sound of a car on the road made her bristle. Did she look like a criminal, standing on Leif's deck trying the living room window? Maybe a passerby would call the police. That'd be rich.

Lyn had never seen Leif's bedroom. To be fair, he'd never seen hers either. It was an unspoken boundary. Last night, though, Lyn decided to hell with the boundary. She'd been in a desert too long and could choose to leave it. More than anything, she wanted Leif closer. Could he tell?

Lyn sat on the deck steps and ran her hand along the smooth pine. Leif built this. She imagined him sanding the wood, blowing the dust away, wiping the sweat from his brow with an equally sweaty arm. He was careful in touching her, and the lines of paint said he was careful, period. He wasn't prone to mistakes. The porch was half-way to beautiful. The deck, unstained.

A motorcycle sped by with its belchy engine and Pat Benatar's voice, crisp and adamant calling out that love was a battlefield.

Lyn decided to check every window in case one was open.

No luck.

The patio door, the one that had already been damaged was the obvious choice. The back of the property was hidden from the road, flanked by woods. A circular brick fire pit caught her eye. A heap of unburned sticks were piled high, ready to be burned, and ash and blackened sticks studded the ring. One Adirondack chair faced the fire, and Lyn thought of her single coffee cup. A single, blackened metal skewer rested against the brick.

She imagined Leif sitting by the fire, tried to conjure the expression on his face as he watched the flickering flames morph into glowing embers. Sure, Leif would be mad at her for breaking his door, but she was mad, too. And a new door didn't cost much. She'd pay for it.

What would Finn say? Or Barnfeld? Lyn shrugged. She didn't care. Lyn had it with being the victim. Victims waited. Victims stayed in crowded places. Hell, victims called the police. Lyn had a gun and—thanks to Leif—she knew how to use it. She could take care of herself.

A rustle of twigs and leaves startled her. At the edge of the woods lurked a stooped and deeply wrinkled woman. She wore red rubber boots, the kind with handles, and a trench coat, though it was a warm day. Her frizzy hair framed her face in a cloud.

"What're ya doin here? You a solister?" The woman asked.

"A what? Uh, no. I'm a friend. I was looking for Leif."

She stepped out from the brush and swung a rifle onto her shoulder, though she didn't appear strong enough to hold a stick. She squeezed one eye shut and sighted Lyn with the other. "You was doin' more'n lookin'."

The neighbor. Lyn's mouth went dry. Her tongue tried to run down her throat. "Uh...I've been trying to get a hold of Leif. He won't answer his phone. I came to make sure he's okay." She splayed her hands. "You can put that away."

The old woman ambled closer and reluctantly pulled her eye from the gun sight but kept it trained on Lyn. At a couple feet, the barrel almost touched Lyn's chest. The woman surveyed the entirety of her features as if she were considering a purchase. "Hmph. You must be *her*. He's helpin' out a 'friend,' he said. I could tell it warn't no friend, but I thought you'd be more a looker, t' be honest." She screwed up her face and tilted her head to Lyn, still training the rifle on her. Did she expect a response? *Sorry, I'm underwhelming. You're not exactly Elizabeth Taylor.*

She let the barrel drop to the ground, where it made a divot in the earth. "Leff helps me out here an there. I got webs all over the place, and bats as big as you." She waved dismissively at Lyn. "I cain't reach the high ones, so he gits 'em for me."

No wonder Leif chose Lyn's house. "You don't happen to have a key?"

"Nah. I'm too old for such foolishness, but in my day, I coulda had a slew a keys. Why buy the pig when all you want's a sausage? Leff tole me how you need protectin' and he don't mind none." She shot a scornful glance and shook her head. "I bet he don't."

"Okay. This conversation is over." Lyn mumbled under her breath and turned toward her car, only slightly concerned she would get a large hole blown into her back from the rifle. She waved cheerily as she reversed down the drive.

Leif's neighbor didn't return the gesture, but slunk back into the woods, dragging the rifle on the ground behind her.

Chapter 29

WHEN LYN RETURNED HOME from her unsuccessful attempt at breaking into Leif's place, she found Caesar on the kitchen floor.

"Caesar?"

He didn't lift his head.

Oh God, no. She dropped her purse and knelt beside her best friend. Not dead. But not very alive, either. His eyes were closed. If she pried them, they closed again. He breathed though. He breathed.

Her vet's office was closed for the weekend. The answering service put her in touch with an emergency clinic, open for another hour. If she could get there right away, they'd see Caesar. Lyn hung up. She'd have to get her 85 lb. dog into her Land Rover. It was easy when all she had to do was open the door and he bounded in.

Lyn dragged Caesar across the floor, but hesitated to lug him over the threshold. And down the steps? That would hurt. At some point she'd have to get him into the car. She tried a blanket, figuring she'd wrap him in it and heft it over her shoulder.

Fat chance, that.

She cursed and wished harder for Leif. How easily he'd slung her into his arms. Fury and concern mixed inside her. She tried his number. It rang and rang, which meant it was on, somewhere, and he hadn't dismissed it, hadn't broken the phone or powered it off, else her call would've been immediately put into voicemail. The familiar voice told her to leave a message. She plunked down beside Caesar and rubbed his ears. This wasn't an insurmountable problem. Money fixed everything, didn't it? She'd call the vet and pay him to come to her. Whatever it took, any price.

But when she got through, the secretary explained the vet did not make house calls. Not ever. Park Hill did have one traveling farm vet. The receptionist put Lyn on hold and returned with the bad news that he was assisting with a goat birth and would likely not be available until tomorrow. Couldn't she get someone to help her lift Caesar into the car? A neighbor?

A neighbor. She *did* have a neighbor. An odd librarian who made her uncomfortable, but he would have to do.

Nolan said his house was on the corner. Right away she knew the one. A cedar A-frame, windowed from floor to peak and nestled cozily in the woods. Why had she never seen him in the yard? Because she didn't pay attention.

He lay on a hammock strung between two trees, a book in his hands, one leg draped over the hammock cloth, lazily rocking it. She beeped and pulled to the shoulder.

"Nolan, you're not going to believe this, but I already need a favor. Can you come with me? It'll only take a minute."

Nolan dumped himself out of the hammock. He was shirtless and shoeless. "Sure. Let me grab my shoes."

"No time. You won't need them." Lyn explained about Caesar and how she needed a second pair of arms to get him into the car. As they pulled into her driveway, a patrol car passed them.

Finn's. And his scowl was unmistakable.

Shirtless Nolan sneered and mock saluted.

Lyn gritted her teeth. Getting Caesar to the vet was all that mattered. When they returned to the house, Caesar's condition hadn't changed.

"Do you think, when you tripped over him...?" Nolan did not finish the sentence, but Lyn got the implication. She might have kicked him so hard he had an internal injury.

"He's always underfoot and I've tripped over him before. But this...he's not right. I hope I'm not too late."

The two of them eased Caesar into the back of the Land Rover. When Lyn got in, Nolan didn't.

"I'll walk home," he said.

"But you don't have shoes. Don't worry. It only takes a second to drop you off."

He looked at his own feet and smiled. "Oh. I forgot."

As Lyn pulled into his driveway, she thanked him and was relieved that he jumped right out. Every second felt like an eternity that could mean the difference between life and death for Caesar.

Once she got back on the road, she tried Leif one more time, and this time she left a message. She did her best to keep her voice even, but as soon as she said *Caesar,* she choked, and the rest of the message was sobs that ended with, "Where are you?"

She pulled into the emergency vet clinic, a building that was once a farmhouse. The outbuildings had been converted to kennel space, and a gravel trail wound around the property. The roofs of new subdivision homes could just be seen over the grassy hill. Lyn wiped her tears on her arm, opened the back hatch, and bolted through the door. "Can someone help me get my dog out of the car?"

Three hours later, Lyn shuffled out of the clinic without Caesar and with a heavy heart. The vet promised to call as soon as he had news to share.

Hours later and after Lyn had checked her phone a dozen times in case she missed the vet's call, a sedan pulled into her driveway. Lyn had been passing the time weeding in the dark with a headlamp because she didn't know what else to do. Ripping things out of the ground didn't numb her nearly enough, but the sound of roots torn from their comfortable berths felt right. She shielded her eyes from the glare of the headlights, and once her eyes adjusted, could see it was Nolan stepping out of the car wearing jeans and a t-shirt.

Lyn held a bouquet of weeds in each hand.

"Those for me? Aw, you shouldn't have?"

Irritation at his ill-timed levity must have flashed across her face because he quickly continued, "How's Caesar? I would've called, but I don't have your number."

"They kept him for tests."

"I brought you a book." He held out *Cujo*, by Stephen King.

Lyn arched one eyebrow, a look she usually gave to students who behaved in nonsensical, unintelligent ways.

"Fear is a great distraction," Nolan said. "This dog can keep you company while Caesar is away. I'm sure he'll be home in no time."

Strange logic, but whatever.

"Can we exchange numbers? I don't want to keep dropping by, unannounced."

"Right," Lyn said with more enthusiasm than she intended. Preventing Nolan's spontaneous visits sounded good to her. She pulled the headlamp off and in the process smeared dirt all over her face.

Inside, as they wrote their phone numbers for each other, Nolan was both awkward and childishly sad over Caesar. The paper with her phone number had brown fingerprints.

"So...I guess I'll go." He set *Cujo* on the couch.

"Thanks again for your help with Caesar."

Nolan shut the door quietly behind him. Lyn reached a grimy hand to bolt the door when it opened again. "Hey." Nolan flashed his baby-boy smile. "You've finished weeding, right? You need cheering. I have just the thing."

No. She didn't have the energy to fight him off. She sighed. "If it's not bourbon, it's not the thing."

"I love bourbon," he said. "Can I borrow a cup of bourbon, neighbor?"

Lyn did not invite him in but left the door open. From the cupboard above the stove, she fetched the bourbon, intending to hand him a small mason jar and send him on his way. Glasses clinked at the back of the cabinet as she felt around, and in her haste, she grabbed the wrong bottle, Buffalo Trace. Jude's bourbon. She'd been saving it. For what? For his return from the dead? Something inside her sagged. The company of this idiosyncratic man was better than being alone right now.

"Drink?" She put an amber slosh into her glass and threw it back. The burn felt good.

"Take it easy, big guy," Nolan patted Lyn's back. "I'm sure Caesar's going to be alright."

"It's not just Caesar."

After a two-drink silence, Lyn told Nolan how Leif had not called or texted since last night. "I can't decide if I'm worried sick or mad as hell. He's a police officer, so I know he can take care of himself. This isn't like him." She held up her tumbler. "I was saving this. It is—*was*—Jude's."

"Jude-your-husband?"

"Jude-my-husband-who-left me." Lyn nodded and threw back the remainder of a glass.

"I hate when people leave me." Nolan mumbled, almost inaudibly.

Did Nolan know the sting of death? It would explain his generosity with Jude's checkout list.

"Can I show you something?" Nolan asked. "It's a short drive. You can bring the bourbon, and we won't be long, I promise."

Nolan took a left at Sandstone Road and headed toward the center of town. He parked in front of the library. Darkness had fallen, and the retail shops were closed. Lyn never drove through town at this time and was surprised to find it deserted.

Nolan's keys jingled in the door lock. Once inside, he punched a code into the glowing green keypad. "Close your eyes and put your hand on my shoulder so you don't trip."

She did. The smell of books and industrial cleaners put her at ease. She heard the click of an electrical switch.

"Keep them closed." He walked in front of her so she wouldn't smack into the myriad of library tables and armchairs. It seemed they walked the entire length of the library, but it was hard to say, shuffling as she was. There came a whooshing sound and light appeared behind her closed lids. Nolan put his hands on her shoulders and guided her into a chair.

"Okay, open."

The gas fireplace lit up the otherwise dark library and bathed the room in shimmering gold. Even the trees outside the window were audience to its mellow light until Nolan closed the shades. The books flickered with magic; and the world shrunk down, down, down, till it felt like nothing existed besides this lovely place of books. Lyn was a character. Nolan, too.

"This isn't allowed," Nolan whispered, though there was no need, since they were alone.

"Neither is open container." Lyn swished her drink.

Nolan hummed. "A little law-bending now and again is good for the soul, don't you think?"

Nolan's reference to law-bending brought Leif to mind, who would not agree that law-bending was good for the soul. As for Lyn, she wasn't sure, so she said, "Do you come here often? At night, I mean."

"I come here to write."

"What do you write?"

Nolan stared out at the trees, through them and possibly into the world of a story. "It's a hobby." From a small slit between the fireplace and chimney rock, he slipped out a book. "I don't read my own work to anyone. But I had hoped to read *this*." He waved a hard-backed book with a peeling, aged cover. "To you."

Lyn gulped. Years of solitude and emotional starvation and now...what was going on?

His face was gilded from beneath and shadowed, creating stark lines and an unreadable expression. "May I?"

She finished the rest of Jude's bourbon.

Nolan took her silence for assent and began. Almost immediately Lyn recognized the book. *Lady Chatterley's Lover*. His lips easily took the words and played them for her. It was hypnotic, how he kissed the language, how he passed it through himself, through his voice, the way his eyes moved along the page, as if he had a long journey but every step was joy. It wasn't a chore or a quest, but the sweet steps into sunset. His rich voice filled the room to its darkest corners, yet was never loud. It was intimate.

Too intimate. Suddenly Lyn didn't want books. Or words. They were touching her in ways that chafed. And Nolan's voice was not the one she wanted. It wasn't fair to use him as a distraction; it sent the wrong message.

Lyn put up her hand and Nolan stopped, regarding her with an unreadable scrutiny and a flash of hurt. Then it was gone. Poof. She knew why he'd chosen that book. It appeared in the book he'd just recommended about the English teacher. *An English teacher...reminds me of you...*

The silence brought Lyn back to Leif. Everything brought her back to Leif. To the question: Who was Leif?

"I'm Nolan, not Leif."

Lyn didn't realize she'd said Leif's name out loud. "Sorry. The bourbon. You read well."

"Apparently not well enough."

"You were distracting me from Caesar."

"I'm distracting you from everything."

Lyn looked at him sideways. "I don't know if I was ghosted or..."

"Men are pigs."

Lyn raised her eyebrows.

"Seriously. Do you really know this Leif? What do you know about his family? His past? Have you seen how he deals with stress?"

"He's a cop. I'm pretty sure he can handle stress."

"But in relationships? When it's personal?"

"Someone shot at us while we were hiking—by accident according to him—I'm not so sure. I lost my mind, but he handled it like Yoda."

Nolan blinked. "So he keeps his cool. The guy broke his word to you. He said he'd call and he hasn't. Is that the sort of guy you want?"

"I felt safe."

"I'm right around the corner." Nolan reminded her.

The effect of the bourbon and his words, *I'm right around the corner*, took on a sinister tone. All Lyn wanted was to be home. With Caesar. With Lief. But home alone would suffice.

"I need to get going," she said, and even in the darkness, she could see his crestfallen expression. Nolan trudged ahead of her and would have forgotten to turn off the fireplace, but Lyn reminded him.

They left the library, and the cool night blew away the drugged, fantastical moment where fiction and reality blurred. As they pulled away, Lyn's phone went off.

It was the vet. Caesar's blood showed Clonazepam, an anti-anxiety medication. The vet assumed Caesar got into Lyn's medicine, and she didn't correct him. But she had no Clonazepam, hadn't been on medication for anxiety since, well, since she was in the psych unit as a kid. Was it possible someone dropped it near the trail? That Caesar gobbled it up during a walk? No. Lyn hadn't walked Caesar this morning. He'd gone out as usual, like he did every morning. Somebody deliberately put the drug in her backyard, pressed into something Caesar wouldn't be able to resist. Somebody did it the same night Leif left or the next morning. Somebody—

"Hey." Nolan frowned. "Is the news bad?"

"He ate something that made him sick." Lyn stared out the window as she spoke, the phone resting in her hand.

"At least it wasn't you, kicking him."

But that means it was somebody else. Who? Nolan, Finn, and Barnfeld had all been to her home that morning. Each had interacted with Caesar.

That didn't mean one of them poisoned her dog. Someone else could have planted something in her yard while she was out with Leif.

Leif.

An empty house waited for her. The vet wanted to keep him overnight to be on the safe side.

Nolan respected the leaden silence as they drove. For that, she was grateful. She waved tiredly as he pulled out of her driveway. At that moment a car passed, a patrol car. Didn't Finn have anything better to do than to watch her house? She called the number he had called her from. "Where is he?" she asked.

"I don't know."

"You're watching my house."

"At Leif's request. I'm honoring it, even though he's not here. Friends do that."

"My dog was poisoned."

"Aw shit, Lyn. I'm sorry. Is he...?"

"He's not dead. Hopefully he'll be okay. If anything happens overnight, they'll call me. Oh, and Finn. I went to Leif's today."

"You didn't."

"I couldn't get in."

Finn released a breath. "So you met Frankenstein's bride?"

"Yeah."

"I'll get you in, tomorrow. Assuming Leif doesn't show up. Don't go in if he's there and you arrive before me. And call us if he shows up."

Us. As in, the cops. Like Leif was a criminal. Finn thought Leif might show up at Lyn's place. *Why hadn't he?* There was still a zombie-load of bourbon left. Lyn drained it, and in the time it took to check her closets, her locks, even the space under her kitchen sink for monsters, the bourbon worked its alchemy, turning her body to silk. She stumbled to her bedroom, and fell asleep in her clothes on top of the comforter.

Chapter 30

Sunday morning Lyn arrived at Leif's place to find Finn pacing the front porch. The front door stood open a crack. Lyn checked her desire to push past him and dash in. As if prophesying that scenario, Finn put his body in the way of the door. "Have you heard from him?"

"Nothing."

"Me neither. No one has. Listen, were you guys fighting?"

"No. The opposite." Lyn wouldn't meet his eye.

Finn pulled out his phone and scrutinized it. "See, that's what I don't get. You said Leif got a call from me Friday night, but I was with Shayla and the kids all night. We put the kids to bed and watched a movie. So either someone pretended to be me or Leif wasn't telling the truth about that, see?"

"I could swear I heard you, on the phone."

He shook his head. "I'm telling you, it wasn't me. And it's not like Leif to bail, either. He hasn't called in sick once since he's been my partner."

"Is that why you involved Barnfeld?"

"What? No." Finn rolled his eyes. "He likes you."

Lyn arched an eyebrow. "Man's a piece of work, doesn't deserve that badge." Lyn edged toward the open door, eyes hungrily crossing the threshold through the crack. Barnfeld's assholery took a backseat to her concern for Leif.

Finn barred her way with a freckled arm. "See, why I'm telling you this is because you have to know the kind of guy Leif is." He thumbed inside the house. "I had to get the chief's okay to bring you here. Because of your classroom, he says maybe you can help with information. Me, I'm not so sure."

Lyn slipped a hand beyond him and pushed open the door. "May I?" Without waiting for an answer, she continued into the foyer.

"Hey." He hooked her arm in his and gently spun her. "You've been through a lot. You don't have to go in there. Some things get into your head and you can't get them out."

"You know how my husband died, right?"

"I read the report."

"Then you know I've seen the worst." She shouldered by him.

The living room invited her into its warmth, the three-horse picture even more stunning from inside. The cat rug made her smile. She ran her fingers through the plush "fur."

One thing she noticed. "There was a book on this table yesterday."

Finn shrugged.

"I saw it through the window."

Finn stood over her, thumbs in his belt loops, thinking.

"What do you think happened?" she asked.

"I don't know," He opened and closed end-table drawers, searching for who-knew-what. "Policing has taught me not to be surprised. Even so...Leif surprised me."

"What do you mean?"

Finn nodded toward the bedroom. "Don't say I didn't warn you."

Lyn opened the door, and the air was sucked from her lungs. Her eyes could not believe it. She blinked. And again. And still, the scene was there. The first thing that stood out was a familiar and terrible sight:

Loops and arcs and slashes of crimson. Lyn, done in blood contrast, like in her classroom. Her hair, piled in the chignon, rendered in long worms and splatters. It took her breath away.

Finn whistled in mock appreciation. "Mona Lisa's got nothing on you."

Worse, beneath the art was a collage of pictures, newspaper copies, and police reports about Jude's death. There were articles dating back to when Lyn was young, to Simon's mom and the accident. There were aerial shots of the Park Hill Conservatory, Google maps of the trails around the property, and the roads. A shot of Lyn, eating at her table. Even the fork in her hand was clear, the book next to her, discernible. A scarlet splotch covered some of the letters in the title, but not enough. There was Lyn walking Caesar, Lyn at Bear's Bakery.

Finn stepped back and hooked his fingers in his belt. "Not enough we have one at the station. Leif's got his own personal crime board here."

"Is that what this is? A crime board?"

"It's a bloody soup sandwich, is what it is."

Lyn sniffed and reached a finger toward the wall, and Finn yelled, "No—" But before he could stop her, she dipped her finger in the bright red and put it to her nose.

"Ketchup." She stepped back to get more perspective, absently wiping the ketchup on her leg. "Real blood would be darker, like my classroom."

"Now *your* prints are here, too," Finn plucked a photo of Lyn. It was a close-up of her during target practice. She had one eye closed, sighting down the barrel, her lips slightly parted in concentration and steadying breath. Finn stabbed a finger at the picture. "See, I shouldn't have brought you. Chief's already having a squirrel over the fact that Leif was involved with you."

"It's none of his business."

"Sure, sure. Except it becomes his business when an officer disappears after spending an evening with you."

"You think I had something to do with his disappearance?"

"The chief would like an investigatory interview. That's reasonable, since you were the last to see him." Finn gave her a heavy look. "Anything you say here's between us."

Finn was the last to see him.

He paced the room. "Here's what I can't figure out, though," Finn waved his arms at the ketchup. "This...this is definitely not rational."

Lyn crumbled onto Leif's bed and held her head in her hands. "Maybe someone else did this."

Finn cleared his throat, but didn't offer any ideas.

Leif had been watching her? Taking pictures? Gathering information on her past? Lyn became aware she was shaking her head in denial when Finn uttered something about never knowing a person, about how he was his partner. She bit her lip and forced herself to scan the room, to take in all she could.

"Why would Leif do this?"

Finn opened his mouth to answer, when the creak of the front door interrupted, followed by the dull thud of it hitting the wall. Finn was out of the bedroom, gun drawn. Lyn followed, but he put his arm out to ward her off.

"Leif? That you?"

No answer.

"Hello?"

Just the slight creak of floorboards

"Answer me, motherfucker!"

A crackly voice. "What you doin' in Leff's house?"

"Aww, Jesus, Miss Betty. Put that thing down. I could've shot you."

Lyn peeked over Finn's shoulder at a scowling Miss Betty. Her rifle clattered on the tile foyer.

"You's trespassing, potty-mouth."

"It's not trespassing if we're the police."

"You got a warrint?"

"Miss Betty, I know you're doing right by Leif, and he'll be glad to hear how you watched his place for him, but we're here to help. We're his friends."

She narrowed her eyes. "Where'd Leff get to?"

"If we knew, we wouldn't be here. Now you go home and we'll let Leff—Leif—know you called, okay, luv?" He patted her shoulder.

"My webs...who's gonna...?" She fizzled and turned to go.

"That's a good girl." They watched Miss Betty's dejected retreat across the yard. She never looked back.

"She takes block watch to a whole new level," Finn whispered.

"She's sure loyal to Leif. She see anybody around—besides us?"

"I don't know."

"You mean you didn't question her?"

"She's a whack job." Finn holstered his gun and plowed freckled fingers through his hair. "It's impossible to get anything coherent out of her."

"That..." Lyn motioned toward the room. "...Leif couldn't have done that. Did you show Betty the ketchup to get a read on her reaction? Maybe she did it?"

"Are you kidding me? Her? There's no evidence of a break in. What was Leif doing a week ago?"

She squeezed tufts of hair. "He was with *me*...mostly. Someone else could've done this."

"Not with Miss Betty around."

"But it doesn't make sense."

"Criminal behavior's senseless...until it isn't. Some people are masters at deception. Like magicians. While your focus is on one arm, they're stabbing somebody with the other."

"What are you saying?"

"People go bad, Lyn. Judges go bad. Politicians—hell, *angels* went bad. What makes you think Leif's exempt?"

"He was *your partner*."

"Yeah, no one's more surprised than me."

"How can you say that?"

"Do you think I *like* saying it? Look, the badge bunnies fall all over Leif, and what does he do? He takes my—he picks you. After you, he didn't want to hang out anymore, to work out, or have drinks after work, and I called him out on it. He told me to shut up and mind my own business. So I did. To each his own, as long as you're doing your job, I told him. And he *was* doing his job. Until two days ago."

Chapter 31

Leif, two days ago

Leif didn't mind the twisty roads. They gave him a thrill. At this time of night, the parkway was deserted, most people opting for the well-lit and straighter routes, especially since the Seven Baths Road had been washed away by flooding last year. He used his high beams and kept an eye out for deer or other darting animals. Anything could be poised in the black growth hedging the road.

But damn, he missed Lyn already.

Finn sounded desperate and…off. Almost like he'd been drinking. Finn getting sauced would make sense if Shayla kicked him out. Leif winced. Why would Shayla kick him out? A memory lanced him before he shoved it off the shelf of his mind. He and Shayla had ended things. It was a mistake, the greatest personal failure of Leif's life. He'd had too much to drink at the chief's welcome back party. Shayla, too. Finn was out of town for an in-service training, and Leif offered to share an Uber. It began in the back seat when a hard turn brought her leg into contact with his. She wore a silky skirt that had hiked erotically up, and the contact set his starved body on fire. They awoke horrified, and agreed to keep the secret. Shayla said telling would crush Finn and destroy Leif's career. They would never let it happen again. Telling was the cruel thing, Shayla said.

But it ate away at Leif, the secret. The night at Whitey's, he had almost told Lyn about Shayla as a your-greatest-failure/my-greatest-failure quid pro quo, but he had promised Shayla he wouldn't tell. Did he need to keep that promise? Maybe it didn't matter anymore.

Finn's voice had sounded flat and garbled—like a bad actor. None of this washed over him until he was alone in his car and had a moment to think, to disentangle himself from Lyn. Lyn thought him an empathetic soul. Would she think so if she knew everything?

Cresting the hill by the Climber's Bath always made his stomach flip, like a roller coaster, and he sped up to get maximum inertia. His body lifted off the seat for a second, then fell back into place. Little pleasures.

The downhill gave a view of the road. Far ahead, a car was stopped askew, hazards blinking, blocking both lanes. Must've hit a deer. A man wearing a ballcap flagged Leif down.

He didn't have time for this, but he couldn't blow by without helping. He pulled off to the shoulder, and the man approached. Beyond the shadow of his hat a relieved smile radiated.

Ever wary and unable to escape his training, Leif unclasped the snap on his holster and rested his right hand on the gun. He opened the car door and had one foot out when the man made a burst of speed and with a hard shove, slammed the door into Leif's knee. The pain made him see stars, but he had the presence of mind to pull his weapon. It was barely out of the holster when fifty-thousand volts ripped through his neck, convulsing him. His grip tightened with the current. He was in too much agony to be thankful he'd not put his finger on the trigger. Once the current cut off, the gun slipped from his slack hand. He groaned and attempted to search the seat for it.

"Too slow."

Leif's brain barely registered the words as a second bolt of electricity crashed into his temple. It held him rigid until he pissed himself and collapsed into unconsciousness.

A jolt woke Leif. He opened his eyes to green, green, everywhere. Pine needles clawed and jabbed at his neck. He took a breath and noted citrus and the smell of river mud—and almost sucked a pine needle into his mouth. Something was wrong. He was paralyzed. No. Bound. With duct tape. His head was bound to the driver's seat of his truck, his torso too. He was inside the cab of his truck and so was—unbelievably—an evergreen tree, or some of it, anyway. There was enough duct tape to go around him many times. He was a duct tape mummy, which allowed him only shallow breaths. The fingernail of a moon reflected light splinters off the bubbling creek. His toes were cold and wet, and all he could see out the front window were cracks in the glass, broken tree branches, and needles. He blinked at the sharp branch inches from his face. It had gone through the glass and was suspended by the front and rear windows. *Had the branch gone through a few inches to the left...*

The passenger window allowed him a narrow, branch-obscured view to a shale-stocked creek bed and its rough-hewn sides. The driver's window was unobscured, and Leif could make out a leafless tree, bowing to the water, its roots exposed by the ever-widening scour of current. Beyond that, more water. Probably. It was difficult to tell.

Leif was accustomed to fear. It was part of his job. But this fear was not only for himself, it was for the woman he left behind. It was no coincidence, Leif knew. He'd been handled. Gotten out of the way.

As the night gave way to day, sun glinted off the creek and allowed him to discern his truck was nose down in the Last Bath. Had to be, because that was where he was when he saw the disabled vehicle. He thought he recognized some features of the landscape. He'd hiked it enough to know.

Leif yelled and listened, called out and held his breath. He roared until he became hoarse. With how remote he was and the Seven Baths being closed to hikers and cars alike, it might be impossible for anyone to hear him. The horn was close, inches from his hands and face, but he could neither reach a finger nor bow his head to depress it.

As the hours went by, he continued to strain against the tape, though it became clear his struggle was useless. The more he shouted and pulled at the tape, the more exhaustion and thirst he felt. How could he let this happen? But that's what you did when people were in trouble; you stopped and helped. That was how he lived his life, how he landed on Lyn Darrow's doorstep. And how she was on a course to land in his heart.

He recalled the moments right before he was tased. The man wore a ballcap and his face was hidden by shadows. Why hadn't he killed Leif the simple and efficient way, with a gun or a knife? Why go to all this trouble?

Whoever did this wanted Leif out of the way, but also, whoever did this didn't mind if Leif died of exposure because his truck was in a remote area of the Seven Baths. The lower access road was closed, and the Seven Baths Trail was impassible because of flood damage. No one was allowed to drive or hike east of the Seven Baths Road until the land was cleared by engineers. That would happen when things dried out. Was that when they'd find him? May? Leif let fly a volcanic and helpless roar of rage until his throat was raw, though it was pointless. No one would hear.

Chapter 32

Delaney

DELANEY LUCAS WONDERED WHY she'd waited so long to break up with the world. Running away had been easy. Life at Park Hill High School was a white-knuckled grip on a sheer rock face. She had to hang on, said the counselors, the teachers, the social workers. Hang on and things would get better. Well, bullshit. What Delaney had to do was let go. She couldn't fall much farther.

After a hot extract two weeks ago—military speak for getting the fuck out—away from the assholes of Park Hill High School and the king asshole, Detective Barnfeld, Delaney went home. Walked the four miles through yards and along the drainage concrete of I-86. Her mother was passed out in front of the television. Shocker. Maybe this time she'd die. It wasn't that Delaney wished death on the human brick sprawled on the couch. It was a protective measure, not to feel for her mom who seemed bent on killing herself. Fentanyl, Narcan. Fentanyl, Narcan. Fentanyl... Mom acted like a person who wanted to die.

Delaney tore a sheet of paper out of her spiral and scrawled with her Sharpie in large letters. *DNR*. Do not resuscitate. She set it on her mother's chest. The message was for her mother, *if* she woke up. Delaney's way of saying goodbye.

She searched the house for money, but figuring it was running through her mother's veins, didn't expect to find any. With a sigh, she packed all the camping equipment she'd collected over the years. Before they closed the trail, it had been her only escape, the walk-in campsites at the Seven Baths. They were free. All she had to do was sign up. They required a license plate number, but some campers wrote *N/A*, so Delaney did too.

Shortly after her mother had become a student of opioids, Delaney became a student of the wilderness, reading Bear Grylls' autobiography and *How to Stay Alive in the Woods* and *Bushcraft 101*. She'd read them over and over and referred to them on her camp outs. She decided to walk the Appalachian Trail as soon as she turned eighteen. Maybe she'd move up the date. Start sooner. Why not? For now, she wanted to escape Park Hill. The only things she would miss were Miss Pam's cupcakes and Mrs. D. (But not her assignments.)

After leaving her "mother" for what she hoped was the last time, Delaney headed to Walmart, where she stole canned chili, soups, dried fruit, and protein bars. She had some iodine tablets to clean her water, but she needed more. Luckily, the camping section had everything, even the hundred-pack of iodine tablets that fit in her purse.

The biggest challenge was stealing the bottle of Cuervo Margarita Mix from the liquor section of the grocery store. She had to knock over an end cap of red wine bottles as a distraction. How long Delaney would be in the woods, she wasn't sure. Too long to go without liquid happiness. The tiniest cramp hit her conscience each time she walked out of the stores with stolen merchandise, but she saw no other way. When she was grown, she'd perform kind acts to balance the scale. For now, she was her own Robin Hood because she had to be.

Camping had its challenges, as her raw ass and blistered feet would agree, but Mother Nature didn't call her names or accuse her of crimes she didn't commit. Delaney slept a peaceful, dreamless sleep, exhausted by the day's hikes, lulled by the music of owls and other night creatures. She'd secreted a one-man tent under the exposed, cage like roots of a fallen tree and and felt nearly invisible. Sunshine woke her when it found its way through the thick lattice of roots.

No one was allowed beyond the Seven Baths overhead pass, and she'd made camp well into the restricted area. In the peaceful mornings, Delaney lay in her cozy sleeping bag thinking how she was supposedly taking her life into her hands by the mere act of being in the Seven Baths Park area. All the signs read: CAUTION UNSTABLE GROUND.

Bah. That phrase described her life.

The Seven Baths as her place of refuge had been a revelation after Detective Barnfeld's "questioning." It wasn't that he was any worse than any of the other pervs. Just, Barnfeld's groping was the last straw. It was the thought: *Was this how it would go for her—forever? Guilty, until proven innocent?* She considered killing herself for half a second before she got the grand idea to live recklessly, to take her chances with the Seven Baths.

Why not chase a thrill? Here for a good time, not a long time.

The cold of nature had been her first surprise. Late spring nights could get below freezing. The sun became her god. It only took a couple days without a house and heat and insulation for her to understand why ancient civilizations worshiped the sun.

Delaney reinvented herself while roaming the treacherous trails of the Seven Baths, by bathing in the frigid, pristine water of each and every circular depression. Seven "baths" of varying depth and diameter had been carved into the sandstone by time. When she had hiked too far off the familiar trail, Delaney got lost. Reinvention. When she was thirsty and forgot her iodine tablets. Reinvention. Stomach cramps that squeezed her like a python. Reinvention. Diarrhea in the woods, fever. Reinvention. Even when climbing a sheer rock face, a root tore out and Delaney had fallen what looked like nine feet (but felt like more). Reinvention. Luckily, the jagged stone at the base had hit her calf, not her head.

Out in the wilderness, she could fall, sure, but she could also get back up. Life was so good, she almost wanted to thank her mother for sucking at motherhood. The Seven Baths taught her she *did* want to live. With no one to tell her she was ugly or strange or didn't belong, she saw the world as worthwhile. She'd been playing Bear Grylls for almost two weeks and was only now running low on supplies.

In the middle of the night she woke to an alien sound, one she hadn't heard since coming to her forest refuge. She'd gotten a feel for what belonged and what didn't.

The yelling didn't belong.

Leaving her tent while it was still dark would be a fool's errand. There wasn't anything scarier about the forest at night, but she'd tripped enough times and almost walked off an outcropping that would have dropped her twenty feet. Maybe what she heard was people playing jokes or sound carrying from very, very far away. She told herself that and tried to believe it.

On waking, her first thought was that she could no longer hear the screams. She had thought of them as yells in the night, but in the clarity of morning she was pretty sure the sound was too raw and spine-chilling to be anything but someone's radio, a joke, people scaring each other. Sound traveled in crazy ways in the valley.

But in case she wasn't alone, she kept her ears open.

It was just after lunchtime. She had "bathed" in the creek and made herself as presentable as possible for her trip into town for supplies when she heard a car making its way along what had to be the bridle trail, bottoming out where the ruts went deep. Who would disregard the warning signs, break through the wire fencing, and take a chance on the unstable area in a car?

It didn't take long for her to find the answer. A tree had fallen into the bridle trail, preventing the sporty black sedan from going further. Where the mud and dust didn't reach, the car was shiny. She approached, hidden by evergreens, and was relieved to see no one inside.

From somewhere in the distance, Delaney picked up more of the same yelling she'd heard in the night, as well as a faint but human voice, and only when the breeze brought it. She perked up her ears and moved stealthily in the direction of the sounds, treading on tiptoe, pulling aside the saplings and not allowing them to snap back. The sounds led her in the general direction of the main road where it hugged the creek gorge.

As she homed in, she could tell the voices were men—one of them was, anyway. His words didn't reach her, but the tone had a hardness, like he was mocking. Delaney too often was on the other end of a voice like that. The gurgle of the nearby stream kept snatching away the words. If she backtracked and crossed the stream, she could come at the scene from the other side. She slipped off her sneakers and socks and tossed them into her bag. The cool water flowed over her feet and shot urgency into her stride. Shafts of sunlight cut through the stream bed, gilded the wet stones and reflected off the few winged things swirling in the rays. She was careful on the rocks, smiling when she kept her balance.

As she rounded a bend in the stream, her smile faded.

A pile of junk.

No, a car.

Actually, a truck. It was nose-down in the creek bed. The front was accordioned, its grill broken like rib bones, engine guts bursting out. Stuck in the mucky soil of the stream bed, its rear end was balanced against a haphazardly thatched wall of fallen evergreen trees.

A man stood next to the driver's side window, leaning in, talking. He was casual, like they were parked in front of the post office. The man wore a ballcap, jeans, and a nylon sports shirt. He spit. Delaney saw the way he jerked his head with it.

But that truck.

Rubber shreds framed the tire rims, which were half-sunk. The tires must've exploded. A trail of snapped tree limbs snaked up the ravine showing the path the truck had taken. A tree or large piece of one was jammed in the truck's front window, its needled branches enveloped the passenger side.

The truck shuddered at movement inside.

The man in the ballcap wasn't helping. No, he seemed to be enjoying himself.

Delaney put her hands over her mouth. She looked down at her gray athletic pants and black hoodie. Though she was across the stream, behind a tree trunk flanked in thick saplings, she didn't feel camouflaged enough. An invisibility cloak would hardly be camouflage enough. Instead, she shut her eyes. Like when she played hide-and-seek as a child.

The man went on and on about this person, Lyn. Sometimes from inside the cab, she heard a groan or the sound of something smacking glass. When she dared peer around the trunk, she saw a blood-caked face. Yes, it was a head banging into the glass. Short hair. Broad shoulders. A man. Desperate or frustrated or both. Why was he doing that, banging his head into the window?

The sounds coming from the cab were the saddest, most animal-like Delaney had ever heard. She grabbed the tree and dug her nails into the bark. Checking out had come in handy when the kids at school had taunted her, when her dad died of cancer, when Mom was temporarily dead in meth. "Sorry, honey; it's hard," was the excuse Mom gave for checking out. Some nights for dinner, Delaney ate mustard out of the bottle. Or she made tomato soup with ketchup and hot water and a dash of salt. Delaney thought she had it so tough. She had done more than her share of suffering. Listening to this guy in the car, she realized she didn't know the first thing about pain.

To her utter surprise, the man standing outside the wreck turned and left. The other man's head leaned against the window, until he realized he was being abandoned. Then he banged his head against it in what appeared to be begging. The car man's face was obscured by his ballcap, but he didn't look particularly evil or misshapen or monstrous. Yet, to leave somebody like that...

Delaney stayed hidden until she heard the engine start, the pop of tires on stones, the bottoming out, and the high revving on the main road over the gorge—till she was sure the man in the car was long gone. Though she felt she had little choice, approaching the yelling man felt dangerous, too. She was afraid to help and afraid to stay where she was. How alike he and Delaney were. No one ever came for her, either. Her water bottle was half full. She could afford to share. She stepped out of hiding and waded across the stream.

The smell doubled her over.

Chapter 33

Delaney

LAST YEAR, DELANEY'S KITCHEN sink had clogged. Because they didn't have money for a plumber, Mom squeezed into the crawl space and unhooked the pipes, inadvertently allowing black sludge to pour onto the concrete at Delaney's knees as she helped with the plumbing snake. The putrid, oil-like substance caused Delaney to drop the snake and bolt outside, where she lost her guts in the grass, where she could still hear her mom cursing her out. The same wind of vomit and diarrhea and death hit her now. She took off her shirt and balled it against her face so she could get closer. In the midday sunshine, her sports bra was cover enough.

Upon seeing her, the man's eyes went wide. He beat his head against the back glass. A piece of silver duct tape hung from his hair. More silver around his chest. With cautious scans up the ravine and constant surveillance of the creek in both directions, Delaney approached the wreck, stepping on rocks or in shallow places where the stones were smooth. The duct tape was why the man made no move. It was wrapped around the driver's seat down to his navel.

Oh, the flies. A smattering of maggots twitched on the man's jeans.

Delaney mashed her shirt against her nose forcefully. At the sight of her water bottle, the man's eyes went wide. She held it over his open mouth and poured gently, stopping every few seconds.

"More." He croaked. "More. More."

But Delaney shook her head. "You'll barf."

After a few gulps, Delaney put up the one-minute finger and stomped away from the truck. She bent over and slurped some beautiful, clean air. The same air that had gagged her on the way *to* the truck. Her inability to overcome the smell made her feel small and unheroic.

He watched her every move.

The few singular layers of duct tape easily gave way, but where it was thick, it was nearly impossible to tear. The man who didn't help, had he done this? Delaney ran away again to get fresh air. Her eyes constantly skipped to the ledge above, for every forest noise became the car man. His footsteps. Him pushing aside a branch. Him coming to finish the man off. Him seeing—*shut up, Delaney.*

She pulled out her knife and repositioned her balled-up shirt. It was hard to work the knife one-handed. A trickle of blood sprung from between the tape where she'd had to push it under the layers.

"Sorry," Delaney said.

The man didn't flinch.

In frustration, she tucked her shirt under her arm and held her breath. With two hands, she was able to cut the tape. She sliced a few inches before she tore back into the creek and splashed icy water into her face. The man made a grumbly, frustrated sound. She was his ticket to freedom, and she yawed and tacked across the creek bed each time the stink hit her, stomping her feet at the unfairness of it. His eyes were hungry and angry, weak but not without flint, and they seemed to say *C'mon little girl, up your level of give-o-fuck and get me outta here. A little stink never killed anyone.* Or maybe the voice was in Delaney's head. The man knocked his head against the back window a few times, was all.

A few more cuts and she'd freed his hand. Not his arm, only his fingers. He wiggled them and gazed, as if moving were the most wonderful act. To get the scissors between his arm and his side, she had to drop the shirt. It fell in the water. Before it floated off, she swiped it, threw it over her shoulder, and commenced cutting.

"That a girl," he managed.

It almost stopped Delaney cold, being praised. But she focused and pressed on. The care it took to not dig the point into his skin kept her attention off the smell. And the knife could've been sharper. Or the tape not so damn thick. She had to lean into the window and had terrible leverage. To cut, she had to break that rule so harshly hammered into little kids. Never cut toward yourself. If the knife went a flyin', Delaney would bury it in her forehead. She had to exert the most even, precise pull. Up and out. Then slip it in a little farther. Up and out. The slick blood helped slide the knife between his skin and the tape.

With the hand she'd freed, the man took up the task. When he rested, Delaney handed him the water bottle. His Adam's apple hitched and slid at the flood of water. Gratefulness radiated from him.

Which made it all the harder to swipe it out of his hand.

"You'll barf."

He narrowed his eyes but didn't argue. "I can cut now."

Grateful for the respite, she plopped onto a boulder near the opposite bank and watched him "cut."

It was pitiful. He had no strength. At this rate he'd be free by next week.

"Here. Let me."

He sighed and allowed her to continue. As she cut the tape that bound his chest to the seat, he began to cough. A spray of fresh red speckled his front.

"I think you broke some ribs."

"I'm fine." As the last of the tape freed him from the seat, he slumped sideways, but caught himself with a grunt. He waved her off.

He didn't need to ask her twice. Some delicious, fresh air waited for her across the stream.

The cab door wouldn't open, accordioned into the ground as it was. He would have to crawl out the back window and off the truck bed. He had one leg and one arm over the side of the bed and fell the rest of the way with a splash. His scream lashed against Delaney's nerves, and she scrambled to help.

"Don't come. I'm fine."

Men were always "fine." Like her dad. Till he wasn't. He never admitted it either. Dad was *fine* until he was dead. But Delaney obeyed. The man could move on his own.

Seeing he was bathing in the stream, she turned the other way. After a period of extended silence, she glanced over to make sure he hadn't drowned. For an old man, he was ripped, like the statues from art class. Water diamonds cast him in a bath of stars and stole her breath. He bunched and waved his clothes in the rushing water to clean them and caught her staring. How embarrassing. She turned away, cheeks ablaze.

On his way across the creek, he slipped on a mossy rock and fell, cursing and thrashing. Blood made a craggy trail on his face. He rinsed it with cupped hands and swore at the murky water, like it had purposely done him wrong. A light flow of blood still wended its way down his jawline, but she could at least stand the smell of the disheveled, unshaven, and soaking wet man. Gone was the trapped animal, the pitiful man.

"Thank you." He'd only taken a few steps onto land when his eyes rolled back into his head. Delaney knew what was about to happen but was powerless to stop it. Like a tree, the man went down.

Dehydration and starvation were strong opponents—not to mention the alarming bruise she'd spotted on his torso. He might look and smell better, but he was wrecked. When he didn't immediately wake, Delaney decided to search the truck. She bunched up her wet shirt to plug her nostrils because, even without him in the cab, it reeked. Displaced maggots wiggled on the seat and footwell. But there, a pile of beads. Children's beads. They were stuck where the mirror and dashboard met. She carefully placed her hands and knees on clean spots and reached for them. They came away as a whole, and she held a silver bead lizard with emerald eyes. She shoved it in her pocket.

The glove compartment was open. It must've sprung in the crash. Papers, napkins, extra light bulbs, flares, and—most unsettling—a police badge were scattered in the passenger footwell. Delaney's brow furrowed.

A cop?

She swished around in the compartment. Sure enough, she was rewarded with a wallet. *Leif Andrews.*

But he wasn't the cop who blamed her for Mrs. Darrow's room, she reminded herself. Mrs. Darrow would say Delaney needed to be open to each police officer as a new possibility. That she should treat others as she wanted to be treated. Mrs. Darrow said it was a simple-minded *dolt*—she'd had to look up the word—who judged Delaney because of her mother and because of her past. "A person can become new, any time," Mrs. Darrow said. "A decision. A tragedy. A challenge. A moment you overcome." And the class read about such moments in the lives of characters. Mrs. Darrow tried to prove to Delaney: It wasn't fair to judge a person today by her yesterday. That was why it cut so much that people blamed her for vandalizing the room. And, over the days spent curled up with her book in the solemn woods, Delaney learned Mrs. Darrow had been right about another thing, too. Delaney was a survivor. Not a victim. A survivor.

Shoved behind the gas pedal was something useful, though not in Delaney's hands. Delaney pulled and twisted and worried she'd accidentally fire it, but eventually she worked the pistol out. With her index finger and thumb she tweezed the heavier-than-expected weapon and carried it to where the officer lay. The air was cooler with the sun setting. The night would be cold.

With new eyes, she beheld him. He slept, one arm slung across his chest, the other outstretched. She debated the pros and cons of abandoning him. Would he make her go home? He would. That's what cops did. He could walk, couldn't he? Barely. Leaving now would be cruel. And she could always run later, when she got him to the road. With a jolt, Delaney realized what it was about this Leif that drew her to him. All twisted, ropey arms and legs, untamed, unstarched. This downed officer was Delaney's dad on the couch, before his body was eaten from the inside out by cancer. But she didn't have to stand by and watch this man suffer. This one she could help. Because of the steadily graying sky and pink horizon, Delaney decided to wake him. Poking his shoulder seemed kindest, but it was like poking a tree.

"Dude. Wake up. It's getting dark."

Nothing.

She grabbed his shoulder and gave it a lusty shake.

He moaned, fluttered his eyes, and asked for her phone.

"I don't have one."

"What—how?"

"I did have a phone, but they're not much good without a wall socket. No wall socket, no juice. No juice, no phone. Believe me, I'm as surprised as you."

He laughed without joy, a little insane-sounding noise. It morphed into tears. He laughed again and wiped them away. "Of course. And he's got my phone."

"Who?"

"I don't know."

Delaney opened a granola bar. "Did that man...um..."

"I think so. All I remember is...a stranded motorist—him I think—tased me. I came to at the bottom of the ravine. He feels familiar, but he stayed just out of my line of sight."

"I hope he doesn't come back." She offered the opened granola bar. "Here."

"I have to warn her. How about your car—is it far? I'm not sure about my legs, but if it's not—"

"I don't have a car."

The harsh laugh again.

"Sorry I don't have a command center at my disposal. We're in the middle of the Seven Baths Ravine, in case you hadn't noticed. Not really supposed to be here. This is where people go to disappear."

He fell back into the leaves, gray-faced. "What's your name?"

"Jane Doe."

He managed a smile. "Why are you here, Jane Doe?"

"I ran away."

"How long ago?"

"Not long enough."

"What..." He struggled to breathe, closed his eyes, "...are you running from?"

Delaney didn't answer.

Leif closed his eyes.

"You're a cop." She didn't mean for it to come out as an accusation, but she hoped he'd expound, give her an idea of how he ended up crashed in the ravine wrapped in tape. When he didn't say anything, she held up his gun. "I found this."

He opened his eyes and brightened. "Finally, something good."

Chapter 34

Delaney

Delaney watched as the cop tried to rise to his feet, but something was terribly wrong with his left leg. A purple-black bruise had bloomed beneath his knee, like a baseball under his skin. Sweat beaded on his forehead, and he swore at "the fucking dark" like it had no business coming. The talking led to coughing, and for that he had to lean against a tree.

"My tent's about a twenty-minute walk, but I think I can find it in the moonlight," she offered.

He made a despairing sound.

"It's a one-man tent, but I have food."

"Go. Sleep in your tent and bring back food in the morning."

Delaney waffled. It felt wrong to leave him, cop or no. But what was the sense of both of them freezing? And her dry, soft sleeping bag sounded so good right now. Besides, she'd have to go back for food anyway.

He got stern. Made it easy. "Go on. We'll get lost trying to get to the road in the dark. Besides, my leg's messed up. A little rest is all I need."

"You need a lot of hospital." She left him quickly and didn't look back. She picked a slow path through the deepening darkness, afraid she'd pass her tent and more afraid she'd pass that other man. Would she recognize him if she saw him? Any man in the Seven Baths at this hour would be suspect. Delaney kept an ear out, and when she honed in on a beautiful sound, she breathed easier: the slight flapping of the outer layer of nylon. In her haste she hadn't tied it back to the screen. Had she zipped the screen? If not, she'd be sleeping with spiders.

She reached for it.

Whew. Zipped.

Delaney settled into her bag and pulled it tight around her. Until tonight, the darkness hadn't bothered her. Delaney, who wasn't in the habit of nighttime praying, turned her eyes to the top of her tent and held out her fear as an offering.

She prayed the cop would be all right, prayed she'd be able to fall asleep. She thanked God for hearing the car, for finding the cop. Delaney even thanked God for fat asshole cops and vandalized classrooms, without which she wouldn't have been in that place at that time. God's ways were mysterious. Maybe she'd take up praying again.

She, Delaney Lucas, rescued a cop. Well, not yet.

Delaney hoped the officer would be able to sleep blanket-less, under the stars peeking through the tree canopy, sharing a bed with dirt-loving spiders and centipedes. Thankfully, it was still too cold for mosquitos. She didn't think she'd be able to sleep in the open, but then again...yes, she would if she had to. You do what you have to do when you don't have a choice. Besides, he was better off than he had been when she found him.

Birdsong woke Delaney. She popped up and scrambled around for food and water, and took off, retracing her steps from yesterday, praying she'd find a man and not a corpse. What she found wasn't encouraging.

He slumped against a tree.

"Did you sleep?"

"Oh. Hi. I don't know." He scanned the area as if taking in his surroundings for the first time. "Have you seen my phone?"

"It's gone, remember?"

His words slurred. He apologized over and over. But not to Delaney. To someone else, to his friend, Lyn. He kept saying he'd carry the backpack. What backpack?

Delaney crouched and got in his face. She surveyed him as she opened the water bottle. He looked worse, not better. "Here." She held out the bottle. He took it with shaking hands. The bottle slipped and sloshed water into his lap. She put it back. The leg was worse, too. The swelling reached his thigh. His toes were worse, like they would explode.

"You look very bad," she said.

"Lyn!" The name ripped from his throat, hurled toward the tree tops. "Lyn!" He slouched into the earth, crushing pine needles and releasing their aroma. "Don't answer it..." He squeezed his eyes shut and grit his teeth as pain wracked him. Delaney wondered if he had internal bleeding from the crash. The duct tape kept him immobile. In freeing him, Delaney may have hastened his death. Or the exposure to the cold was too much. Whatever was wrong with him was worse this morning than yesterday.

"There's no way you're going to make it out of here on foot."

His eyes rolled into the back of his head and he groaned.

Delaney was seventeen. She knew invoking her age was the beginning of a pity party, but she didn't care. Why was this cop's life falling to her—*on* her. Like a piano falling out of the clear, blue sky. And yet, she thought of her mom and how she hadn't done much momming, how it was Delaney who called the electric company and begged them for more time. It was Delaney who taught herself how to make "tomato" soup out of ketchup, salt, and pepper packets when there they had run out of everything, including condiments. If her shitty life had taught her one thing, it was how to be resourceful. When she stole the Cuervo, she made a promise to herself that she would make up for her theft with acts of kindness. Here, Kindness Number One.

"I'll go for help. The road's not far."

"No. I have to get out of here." The words took all his energy.

"Dude, you can't help her if you're dead. And you look closer to it than yesterday, and yesterday you looked like shit. I'm going to leave my food here. And all the water I have."

He tried to get up and a soft cracking sound issued from his leg, then a forest-shattering scream. He fell and squeezed his blue-black swollen thigh.

"Right. No moving." Delaney placed the food in easy reach and bunched her windbreaker up as a pillow behind him.

He grabbed her with a quickness that startled her. "Here. In case you run into the guy who did this to me. It's ready to go. Don't squeeze the trigger unless you mean it." He handed her his gun.

"I don't know how to..."

"You point it at the bad guy. The closer he is, the better. Put it in your back pocket."

Delaney stared dubiously at the gun.

"Don't sit on it...Jane."

"Jane's not my name. I'm Delaney."

"Delaney Lucas?" His eyes widened.

She nodded.

"You're the student," he managed a chuckle. "Small world."

"I didn't do it."

He patted her hand and his eyes rolled back into his head.

"Hey." She shook him roughly by the shoulders. "Do you keep a blanket in your truck?" She wasn't sure, but she thought he nodded and his lips parted. It was worth the time to try. One thing she remembered about shock from all the movies: Blankets. Very important.

By the time she returned with what looked like a tablecloth, he was asleep. She doubled the cloth and covered him, tucking in the fabric gently on his unhurt leg.

She took off, the gun in her back pocket pressed against her back. Did she have the guts to use it? A few seconds later when a tree branch cracked, she had the weapon out and poised so fast it surprised her.

Chapter 35

LYN PICKED UP CAESAR on her way home from Leif's. Finn got a call and had to leave Leif's place abruptly, which was fine with Lyn. She'd seen more than enough to disturb her, and the state of Leif's home led her to more questions and no answers.

Once Caesar was with her again, safe in the car, she put her head on the steering wheel and allowed herself a cry. During the drive home, she pushed the dial on Leif's number and listened as her call went to voicemail. At his cheerful greeting, she canceled the call.

She did this many times.

Was it only two days ago Leif had kissed her? He had listened to her, raptly in Whitey's as she confessed her Secret, capital *S*. He was a friend, and now he was gone. Poof. And Lyn didn't know what to make of it. It's not like he left only *her*. He left his job, his home, his friends, his partner. People didn't do that. Or if they did, they wrote notes; they packed bags; emptied the savings account. People who left, left a trail. Even if they died, they left a trail. All that Leif left was confusion. The ketchup on Leif's wall and the pictures of Lyn didn't match with the Leif Andrews she experienced. She was careful not to think she knew him, but to consider how the Leif she had experienced matched up with what she saw at his house. It was Finn's voice she swore she heard on the other end of the phone. Yet she didn't feel insincerity from Finn, either. He said he didn't call, and she found herself believing him.

When Lyn pulled into her driveway and saw Leif's car not there, she sagged. Behind her, Caesar whined, as if he, too, shared her sadness. The silence and emptiness of her living room caused her to shiver as if she'd opened the freezer and not her front door. Caesar hobbled to his doggie bed and sighed into it.

Leif, who had shown Lyn what friendship could look like after years of isolation, left her with nothing to hang onto. A lingering kiss, a sigh. He had seemed reluctant to leave when Finn called. Was that a lie? What could be trusted in this world? Books? No, not even those could be trusted. Every handhold she reached for was being systematically removed, with the result that she finally opened her eyes to the horrible day Jude died. She let in the memory and allowed it to run her down as she lay curled up on her living room floor. Eventually, her mind cleared and she felt...not dead anymore, but alive. And enraged.

Lyn rolled onto her back and ran hands through her hair then gave a savage wipe to the tears on her face. She took a deep breath and pushed herself sitting.

"Close your little doggie ears, Caesar, I need to shoot something." She crawled to his dog bed and petted him before stomping to the kitchen and grabbing her Smith & Wesson. She tore the whole drawer out of the dresser. The gun and all the contents spilled onto the floor. She didn't bother picking anything up except the gun.

She didn't even bother with ear protection or paper plates. As the reports hit her ears and recoil bruised her shoulders, that pain took away the other pains. Before she knew it, Lyn used up all of her practice rounds. She rested on the picnic table bench, realizing that the last time she had sat there was when Jude lived, when they had sat there together.

Caesar pawed at the glass, begging to come out. Lyn sighed and opened the door, then grabbed a stick for him and sat down, watched him mulch his prize with less than his usual gusto. He was almost through with it when she realized: she had swiped the wood from Jude's shrine. A stab of pain pushed into her throat. Sharp. Hot. For a second she couldn't pull in air. Did she just *forget* Jude? With a resolute shake of her head, she led Caesar back inside and loaded the magazines with hollow points. The silence felt wrong after so much thunder, and she wasn't done with thunder.

When her paper plate was more confetti than plate, she turned and took the shots she thought she'd never take. Chips and splinters flew off the pile of wood Jude had left uncut when he died. The pile avalanched. Shots hit the ax head with a resounding ping. She'd even managed to ding the wooden handle. Dusk had come, and the sensor lights turned on and bathed the yard in icy light, revealing how she'd destroyed the pile of Jude's wood, his monument.

Why had she done it—saved the woodpile in exactly the way Jude had left it? Did she think Jude was coming back to finish chopping? She shot a few more times before switching to her cute gun. She extended her arms, exhaled, and was about to pull the trigger.

Steps. Behind her. Barely masked by the reports. She turned. Her heart leapt. Wasn't it always Leif who rounded the side of the house during her target practice? *Leif?*

"Don't shoot." Nolan put his hands in the air playfully, like it was a stick-up. "I didn't bother knocking because I can hear you all the way to my house. I always wondered who was doing that."

"I'm not in a good mood, Nolan."

"Okay." He put his hands up like no foul but didn't leave.

Lyn wished he would. She wanted to shoot things, and yell. Lyn emptied the rest of her magazine into the trees.

"You don't seem like the gun type," Nolan said when she had to reload. He cast a long shadow across her path.

"Women want equality." Lyn held up the gun. "Here it is."

"I pity the guy who tries to mess with you."

"I'm being messed with plenty." Lyn nodded to Caesar. "I'm afraid to let him out alone. Maybe he'll get into more of whatever got him before."

"You think he was poisoned?"

"I know it." Lyn set the gun on the picnic table and picked up her shells. Nolan stooped to help. Everything was déjà vu. This was how she and Leif began, with him picking up her used shells... She held the box to Nolan and thanked him, a bit colder than she intended. "You can wash the lead off your hands inside." She opened the back slider and offered the kitchen sink. Caesar eyed them.

"Caesar looks better," Nolan said. "You're not reading much, are you?"

Hands on hips, she answered with more venom than she intended. "I'd love to escape into one of your books, but right now I need to shoot something."

Nolan wore his hurt front and center. "Well, I'll leave you to it then." He left without washing his hands, and Lyn didn't try to stop him.

Chapter 36

Delaney

THE EXERTION OF HIKING and the rising sun warmed Delaney, but it worried her, too. Hiking out of the baths had taken longer than she remembered, most of the day, in fact. She tied her hoodie around her waist, which hid the bulge of Leif's gun. It felt safer to conceal it now that she was on the road beyond the roadblock where she might flag a car. No sense alarming people. She was glad she hadn't needed it, but oh, how malevolent—Mrs. D would like that word— the forest could sound.

An hour passed with no cars, reminding her of her reason for picking the Seven Baths Ravine: no company. Cars were not allowed past the Seven Baths. The road hadn't seemed so long when she first arrived two weeks ago. But then a man wasn't dying in the woods, waiting for help. As soon as she saw a car approaching, she waved it down, getting more and more desperate as it approached, but the driver didn't stop. The woman driver frowned at Delaney and sped by.

Seriously?

Next came a motorcycle. She wasn't able to make it stop, either. As the next car passed, she tried the tack of walking more casually, but it was difficult hiding her panic. Time was slipping away for the cop, Leif. How would they get him out if it was dark? She vowed that the next car would stop. She'd stand in the middle of the road like one of those airplane marshals and make them stop.

Finally, another car.

She stood on the yellow lines and alternately waved her hands in the air and put them forward. The car, a convertible, slowed to a stop. The woman had long blond hair and wore an elegant, floppy hat. The driver sported a ballcap. Both looked concerned.

"Do you have a cell phone? It's an emergency."

"Oh darlin', what's wrong?" the woman asked. She had warm, kind eyes.

Thank God. Delaney quickly told her made-up story about her friend had been hurt in a hiking accident and their only phone had been in his pocket and was damaged and unusable. She had to leave him to get help, but he was very bad off, and could they call an ambulance?

They wasted no time. The man called 911, and the woman hopped out of the car, put a motherly arm around Delaney, and ushered her into the back seat.

"Here," The woman handed a green bottle over the seat. "I'm Maria."

Delaney held the smallish bottle, not knowing what it was and not wanting to give up her own name. Her parched mouth regretted giving all her water to Leif.

"It's Pellegrino," the woman, Maria said, misinterpreting Delaney's hesitation. "Sorry we don't have any regular water."

Delaney tried it, not expecting the fizz. Her nose wrinkled and she coughed.

Maria pulled her sunglasses down and whispered, "You're the girl who went missing."

Delaney looked at her sideways. Had she thought she could do a good deed for this cop and go unpunished? She didn't respond, but everything in her, every selfish thing, screamed at her to run away. They'd find him eventually. Why she stayed put in the back seat, she didn't know, except something about the couple put her at ease. She sort of wished she could ride off with them, go wherever they were going.

A park ranger arrived first. Delaney couldn't explain how to get to Leif. She had to lead him, she said.

"Then we better wait for the squad." He asked a lot of questions. Like, why wasn't she in school? Delaney could tell he recognized her.

"Let her alone," Maria said. "She's obviously shaken up."

The park ranger stalked a few feet away and called someone. Delaney couldn't hear what he said, but "cuff her" and "uncooperative" stuck out. It wasn't too late. She could bolt.

"You can go now," the ranger said to the couple. Maria, patted Delaney's hand and whispered, "You'll be okay."

It was the most motherly thing that had happened to Delaney, maybe ever. She waved as they drove away.

Not long afterward, a police cruiser, lights ablaze and going far too fast, slammed on the brakes and skidded in the gravel. A red-headed patrolman bounded out of the car and demanded, "Where is he?"

"We're waiting on the squad," the park ranger answered. "She knows his location." He nodded toward Delaney.

"What are *you* doing here?"

Recognized again. Delaney didn't like how everyone seemed to know her all of a sudden. She chose not to answer the cop. She knew her rights.

All the other questions were fired at her again. What was Leif's condition? Did she see his vehicle? How was he acting—delirious? The arriving patrolman, Finn O'Malley, wrote furiously in a little spiral notebook. When she couldn't recall exactly what time it was when she found his truck, he squeezed Delaney's arm and told her this was a matter of life or death.

"You think I don't know that?" Delaney shook her arm free. "Why do you think I'm here?"

The freckled officer stopped writing and gazed at her. "You say you were camping...here, when you found Leif?"

"Yes."

"By yourself?"

She spread out her hands as in, *do you see anybody else here?*

He left off questioning her when the ambulance arrived, its sirens wailing.

"Took you guys long enough. It'll be dark soon." He turned his back and had a quick, low-volume conversation with the paramedic before waving Delaney forward, clearly itching to get moving.

The officers and paramedic picked their way through the woods with a stretcher and backpacks full of who-knew-what. There was no trail. Delaney stopped at one point and chewed her lip.

"Well, lassie? Which way? We're not on holiday."

He was getting on her nerves.

"I'm thinking."

"Think faster."

Was it left at the trailhead? Or right? She considered flipping a coin but didn't think the impatient officer would appreciate blitheness. She *did* care, but she'd been so worried about her own problems, about getting taken back to Park Hill, she hadn't been as diligent with her trail markers as she should've been. On her way to the road, she'd been rehearsing her story, a story that would do her no good now because her face was known. *My car broke down and I thought I'd cut through the Seven Baths...got lost...found this dude...*

When they came upon a rock formation shaped like a horse head, she knew she'd chosen the right way. O'Malley rolled his eyes and shook his head at the sigh of relief she didn't mean to make so obvious.

Once they got to the stream, Delaney pointed off in the direction of Leif's downed truck. The two officers peeled off and went that way. O'Malley stuck with her and the paramedic.

"What were you doing here? This area is closed to hikers," he asked.

"Not obeying the law, obviously. You going to arrest me?"

He snorted. "You like to paint?"

"Go to hell."

He raised his eyebrows. She expected him to get angry. He told her it was not a "very girly" thing to do, camping in the valley, and she rolled her eyes.

"I can't imagine a girl your age lasting five minutes after sundown. You weren't scared?" he asked.

"Not till I found the cop." Delaney pointed. "There he is."

O'Malley's gaze followed Delaney's finger, and when he found Leif, he said, "Jesus, what the hell happened?" And high-tailed it to Leif. Delaney and the paramedic followed.

Leif dropped his head against the tree trunk in utter relief. "Finn, Lyn's in trouble."

Finn O'Malley crouched down. The authoritative bark he'd used on Delaney was gone, but the Irish cop's voice had an edge. "Lyn Darrow is fine. *You're* in trouble."

Delaney had done her duty. Whatever was going on here was none of her business, *not her work*, as her mom would say, back when she said mommish things. With careful steps backward, Delaney began her escape, while they focused on the cop. She decided she would hike around Vista Road and double back to her tent under the cover of darkness.

She didn't want to have to steal another one. And there was her copy of *Watership Down*. She didn't want to leave it.

A strong arm gripped her from behind. A husky, no-nonsense female voice, the paramedic. She spoke low so only Delaney could hear. "Girl, where you think you're going?"

Delaney pleaded with her eyes at the tattooed paramedic, a cross between a beauty queen and a muscled pirate. She shook her head and hoped the woman, who clearly had known her own share of trouble, or at least came from the wrong side of the tracks like Delaney, would understand a runaway's need to...well, run away.

Please... said Delaney's eyes.

"Where you gonna go?" She spoke low.

"I got help, like I promised him. Now I have to go."

"You in trouble?" She released her grip on Delaney's arm.

"Only if I stick around. Tell him..." Delaney didn't know what message she wanted to convey to the cop.

The stunning paramedic looked squarely at Delaney, through her. Delaney knew she looked like a derelict. A week in the forest did that to a person. Her dyed black hair was still in the ropelike braid from three days ago, but it had lost its hold on the shorter hair surrounding her face, and Delaney had been failing at keeping it tucked behind her ears. Her black t-shirt and jeans were so dirty they could practically walk themselves. Her nails were bitten to the quick.

The sweep of the paramedic's gaze didn't bring the usual pursed lips and judgment, but a gentle recognition. She tossed her head in the direction Delaney should take.

"I got you, girl," she said. "You did good, gettin' us here."

The paramedic engaged the officer in conversation, so he would not notice Delaney slip into the darkening woods.

Chapter 37

Lyn mechanically ate her dinner. She thought of how Nolan left—dejected—and felt a twinge of guilt. She couldn't help it that she wasn't into books right now. Or into him. She was exhausted from target practice, from "breaking into" Leif's place with Finn, and from picking up Caesar from the vet. Hearing how close she'd come to losing her dog turned the hummus to sawdust on her tongue, and the barely-chewed cracker scratched her throat as she swallowed. In the three years since Jude died, Lyn had allowed her mind to revisit that awful day in bits and pieces. When her thoughts began to drift to the day Jude died, she pushed the memory down and replaced it with a scene from one of Jude's books. In this way, she kept her husband both close and far. And she kept her sanity. Now confused and lonely and traumatized by Caesar's poisoning, something new and subterranean broke apart inside her. Her losses rose to the surface of her consciousness like a great tidal wave, and she cried and swore and shoved aside her food. Too miserable even to get up, she sat slouched with her head on the kitchen table.

Something began to needle her mind. Something was wrong. Besides everything. Something else. Something else was wrong, and she picked her head up to listen.

The silence.

That was it. A silence that shouldn't be there because the *ha ha ha* of dog breath should be there. The *ha ha ha* should be punctuated by the click of claws against the hardwood. The *ha ha ha* and the papery scrapes of paw pads were always, always there, beginning at sunrise and culminating with a lick to her neck when he could wait no longer for her to get up and let him out.

Caesar's white furry back was to her. His rib cage looked...deflated. Horror lapped at the edges of Lyn's consciousness as she struggled to piece it together. Caesar. Not moving. Not...

Across the room she scrambled, screaming his name. She couldn't detect a rise or fall, only an alien coldness when she touched his head. She rubbed his nose the way he loved her to. She ruffled his ears. She gave a harsh shake, but his eyes were wide open, unseeing.

"Caesar!" Lyn placed her forehead on his cold nose. She rubbed the sides of his face, down his back. She touched his claws and rubbed the sandpaper of his foot pads. A second, savage shake to his rib cage still got no response. "Please...wake up."

Lyn picked up the half-empty food bowl. It looked normal. She sniffed and winced at the strong garlic smell.

Arsenic.

She hurled the bowl across the kitchen, her scream of grief and denial louder than the crash of it hitting the refrigerator. The tainted food exploded in brownish confetti. She scrambled to a stand, punched the fridge door, kicked down the dining room chairs, swiped everything off the dining room table, not hearing the glass when the candle globe shattered. She stomped around the living room and slammed her fists against every hard surface. She ground her face into the couch cushions and screamed. Even the books weren't spared, but were swiped from the shelves, landing on the hardwood in chaotic piles.

Caesar. Beautiful Caesar.

When Lyn spent her rage, she crumbled beside her dog and slung an arm around him, shuddering at how cold and unyielding he'd already become.

Why?

Why?

Why Caesar? He loved everyone. Who would do this to a dog?

She lay there, unable to move. All she could do was plow her hands through his velvet white fur over and over as she murmured sweet words, the words she always said. She closed her eyes and remembered how he looked when he wanted a walk, how he sat still and waited for her to open the front door, how he wound around Leif's legs and furred up his uniform. Lyn's tears made watermark constellations on the hardwood floor, which she absently traced with her finger. The sun's pale arms reached in through the curtain slits but did not warm her. On the contrary, the dull light brought out how gone Caesar was. The tainted dog food got mushy in her palm. She couldn't bring herself to do what she knew she had to. Each time she thought of burying her boy, fresh tears came. But she had to do it. She wanted him here, in the backyard. Next to the wood pile. All her sadness should be in the same spot.

Lyn told Caesar stories, stroked his fur, and downed a third of the cheap whiskey she found behind the cooking wine. She couldn't see through her tears to remove his collar and name tag, and her hands shook and couldn't manipulate the clasp. Could she not even do this one, little thing? In the end, she took scissors to the Teflon collar. She rolled him in the plush accent rug he had died on, hating to cover his sweet face, knowing he no longer breathed, but still hating it all the same.

Caesar's grave would go behind what was left of Jude's firewood shrine. She'd see it through the kitchen window, and seeing, would think of them both. Caesar was gone. Jude was gone. What was gone had to be buried.

The topsoil was easy to shovel because of the rotting wood. After a foot or so, it became dense and heavy clay. Sweat got in her eyes and stung. She let it. The world shrunk down to a shovelful of dirt, to jumping on the spade, using her arms to push through the stubborn earth that seemed to not want to accept Caesar. Another shovelful, fire in her back and arms...another...another.

She talked to him, like always. Her last conversation with Caesar was about love. She'd do it all again. Caesar was worth it. So was Jude.

"What's it like, being dead?" She was used to one-way conversations with Caesar, but now separation and mystery inhabited the silence. Behind his unseeing eyes was a liminal over which she had not yet stepped.

The hole was so deep, she had trouble climbing out. Her boots slipped on the earth, and when she tried to get purchase, hefting herself up by her arms, she raked last year's leaves and dirt down into the trench with her. Finally, she muscled her way out and stood over the hole, one big enough for Caesar.

When she attempted to pull the rug and Caesar into the grave, it unfurled, dumping him. No way would Lyn put a dirty rug on top of him, but the clods of dirt on his white fur nearly drove her mad. At first she tried reaching into the hole to clean them off. She couldn't bear to think of the cottony tufts covered in loam, rained on, snowed upon, trampled over by forest critters, couldn't bear the idea of the dirt terrestrials swarming him.

What was she to do? Leave him in the hole, unburied?

A sob ripped from her throat as she pushed a pile of dirt into the hole. She squeezed her eyes shut and pushed more and more dirt in until only white fur showed here and there. She couldn't bear to push dirt onto his head. Could she crawl in there with him and pull dirt onto the both of them? Could she? Lyn removed her muddy shirt and arranged it over Caesar's head so the mud would fall on that. She wore a sports bra, and for the first time considered the person who killed Caesar could be watching from the woods. She put up her middle finger and panned it all around, just in case. The sun was low in the sky. She'd been digging for hours.

If her gun were in her pocket, she'd have shot the woods full of holes. Shoot first. Ask questions later. Leif had been wrong about that. Whoever wanted to torture Lyn, well, Caesar was safe from him, now. Lyn sifted her fingers through the dirt. Her gun barrel could be pointed *in* as well as out. She could press it against her temple, right here in her backyard. With Caesar. She'd go down easy. Safe. It was an achievable step to go grab her gun and bring it back. The light from the living room lamp threw softness out the sliding doors.

"Be right back, boy."

Lyn ambled toward the light, slapping muddy hands on her jeans. She tripped over one of Jude's hewn logs.

Inside the house, she halted. She ran her arm along her face to clear the tears and dirt.

What was she seeing? *What happened here?*

Chapter 38
Tawny

Tawny let the kid go. She could add it to her list of poorly-thought-out decisions, but she had a sense about people. Delaney Lucas was like a battered sailboat in a storm. Forces much bigger than Delaney and far more capricious were sending the troubled teen all over the place, Tawny knew (she kept up on her police gossip), and no matter what the girl did, the winds would be contrary. Kid needed a break; Tawny gave it to her. Besides, she did save Leif. She could've run off, left him for dead. In Tawny's experience, people were neither good nor bad. They were sometimes good and sometimes bad. In fact, the same person could be very good and very bad. Like Tawny. She'd do whatever it took to save a stranger's life, but under the right circumstances, would kill a person. She'd kick the ass of anybody who gave her even a whiff of belittlement. Sometimes she imagined bitch-slapping men who reminded her of a certain uncle who had trespassed against her when she was small. But the worst evil, to Tawny's mind, was people who were shitty to animals. Tawny could probably rip out the fingernails of any person who abused animals.

She pulled her mind into focus because a life depended on it. She gave the left leg several light, exploratory touches (raising a scream from Leif) and pronounced the bone broken. Usually she didn't reveal her findings, but Leif was a friend. And her friend had delusions about getting in a squad car and going to his lady-friend's house. That was not happening; he needed to know.

She cut away his shirt. Where his skin was not smeared with mud or blood, it was the color of dust. His sunken eyes were glazed and fiery. His lips were cracked and bleeding.

As Tawny and Finn each took an end of the stretcher, Leif gritted his teeth. Every movement looked to be agony for him.

"Only place you going is a hospital," she said, slipping on a mildewed rock.

Leif's moan coincided with her fumbling the stretcher. She took stock of him and did the Vegas thing where she asked herself, if she were the house—and the house always won—what would she bet on for Leif—life or death? Although he looked awful, he was young and strong and had motivation for making it out alive: Lyn Darrow.

"Finn, send a car to Lyn's," he choked out.

"I already did."

Tawny knew Finn lied. People in shock, you told them what they wanted to hear. Still, Leif was a cop. She would have given his request more weight than the regular Joe's.

"Well?" Leif asked.

"We knocked. No answer," Finn lied again.

"So break down the door!" Leif ordered.

"You know we can't do that."

"It's a fucking welfare check. We *can* do it." Leif grabbed Tawny's arm. He shook it so hard, she almost dropped her side of the stretcher. "Tawny. We're friends. I need you to put me down so I can beat the shit out of Finn."

Tawny stopped walking, out of breath. "Finn, give the guy a break, will ya? What if it was Shayla in trouble? What would you want *him* to do, hmmm?"

Finn turned on her, narrowed his eyes. "What did you say?"

"I asked what would you want Leif to do for Shayla?"

Finn's face screwed up. He articulated each word carefully. "Interesting question. Leif, what *would* you do to Shayla?"

Tawny noted each man. Leif's eyes widened, and Finn shook his head and double-timed it up the hill. The yank on the stretcher and Finn's bold pace made it so Tawny had to nearly run. At a narrow place in the trail, Finn slipped and almost took Tawny and Leif's stretcher down the side of a ravine.

"Watch it, Finn. We almost bought the farm." Tawny was used to keeping her shit tucked squarely inside her iron guts, and she was a whiz at reading people. Some bad shit was going on between Finn and Leif. Leif had fallen silent about checking on Lyn. Finn was not himself.

Suddenly, the stretcher wrenched sideways. Tawny barely kept a hold of her end, and both she and Leif slid down the gorge. Pain shot through her leg when she hit something, a rock or a downed tree. A sickening whack told her Leif hit something, too. Hopefully not his head.

"Sorry, I tripped." Finn called from the trail some twenty feet above them.

She cursed Finn's clumsiness.

"Give me your phone, Tawny. I need to call Lyn." At least that's what Tawny thought Leif said.

She tried to strap an oxygen mask over Leif's mouth, but he swatted her away. "Finn, he's not cooperating."

Finn scrambled down the ravine to where they'd landed, stopped by a ledge of rock.

Leif tried to say something, but Tawny affixed the mask. "No talking."

"What's that, Leif? You want to confess? It's a little late," Finn said.

Tawny put a gloved hand on Finn's chest. "Whatever's going on between you two needs to pause. I got a job to do." Tawny shot Finn a challenging glare over Leif's body. "I met the lady friend he's concerned about. Got to see the blood in her classroom, too. I say, call in the welfare check, Finn." She nodded to Leif. "Put the man at ease."

"A man like him doesn't deserve to be at ease," Finn said.

Leif mumbled into his oxygen mask, and Finn didn't respond. He seemed more intent on surveying the area.

"Wait. Where'd the girl go?" Finn asked.

"Delaney?" Leif craned his neck to see the trail above.

Tawny shrugged. "She been gone a while, ran off. What'd you expect? ...Hey, you okay, Finn?"

Finn swore under his breath.

Tawny arched an eyebrow. "We need to—"

The bullet was through her shoulder before she could finish her sentence. Sharp fragments of Tawny's clavicle lodged in Leif's face, neck and chest, and blood splatter mixed with his own superficial lacerations. A shard of Tawny's bone went through his eye as she spun and dropped from the force of the bullet. Years of street life had taught her: *Stay down. Play dead.* She wanted to be a hero; she did. But heroes lived to fight another day.

Her ears rang and her blood pounded, but she heard Finn's chilling words.

"I *know,* you son of a bitch, about you and Shayla. I couldn't figure out why my wife was acting like the world was over when you finally got yourself a girlfriend." A few interminable seconds before another gunshot. Finn sobbed. "How could you? How could you do it, Leif?"

Tawny tasted dirt between her gritted teeth and waited to feel a kill shot tear through her.

Chapter 39

Delaney

DELANEY STARTLED AT THE sound of a gunshot. As she hunched over and listened, another followed a few seconds later. Hunters? What were the chances? Hunting was illegal in parks. This area was closed off. That was what made it so attractive. Now, every step felt loud and screamy. Delaney slowed her pace so she could be sure no one was anywhere nearby. She halted every few paces and listened for the sound of breaking branches, crunching leaves, steps on the packed earth, cars, or voices. She tip-toed through the woods and made herself blend into a tree, crouching beneath an evergreen with her knees pulled into her chest, listening. Listening.

Eventually, someone crashed through the foliage, shattering her nerves. The only safe place was up, so she scurried up the tree, not caring a wit about the sap all over her palms. Little branches cut and scratched her face and hands and every exposed part of her. Just in time, she'd climbed the tree. The freckled cop appeared in the woods below.

Delaney knew Mrs. D was part of this. She hadn't realized the *Lyn* was Mrs. D until the cop arrived and said "Lyn Darrow." The idea of Mrs. D—the one person who had been nice to her—in danger made her eyes sting with tears, and she wanted to do something, to help, but Delaney was a realist. She didn't know where Mrs. D lived. She had no phone.

She was a truant and wanted by the law. Only in books and movies could someone like her save the day.

Mrs. D, she *lived* in her books and for her books, but now, it seemed, her life had taken a dangerous turn, and Delaney hoped her teacher would be safe, just like in the movies where the woman survived. In the real world, all Delaney could do was pray for Mrs. D, pray and take care of herself.

Hours later, Delaney sneaked into her own house on tiptoe. As expected, her mother was sprawled on the couch. The coffee table was so stacked with spoons and food wrappers, cigarette butts and pipes, it was hard to find her mother's cell phone. The DNR note had several watermarks on it. What had "Mom" thought about that? Delaney accidentally knocked over a liter of Sprite trying to pick up the note, but when her mother didn't stir, Delaney relaxed. She lit the note on fire with her mom's lighter and used Mom's phone to call the person who, ironically, could help Delaney—Mom's drug dealer. Delaney arranged to meet him in the Walmart parking lot. There, she traded Leif's gun for cash. She doubted the cop would understand, but the gun was no longer needed. Money to start over was what she needed to survive. Surely the cop would want her to survive.

On the red eye bus ride to Atlanta, Delaney couldn't sleep, so she read *Watership Down*, also stolen. Surely Mrs. D would want her to be reading.

Chapter 40

While she was out back burying Caesar, someone had put Lyn's home to rights. The books were where they belonged. The food bits and glass had been swept. She blinked to make sure she was seeing straight. How could this be? From her backyard she had heard no car, nothing. Yet everything was in place.

With one addition.

Bookworm was on her coffee table.

Before the strength could vanish from her legs, Lyn barreled into the bedroom, swiped the comforter off the bed and both guns from her drawer, and fled back outside, to the grave where she sat with her back against a tree, a gun in each hand, fingers on the triggers.

Wrapped in her comforter with her guns, Lyn watched the sun go down. She lay beside the turned earth, her fingers browned and gritty. Calling the police was the "right" thing to do when someone broke into your home, but what to say? Someone broke in and fixed all the stuff she'd broken. Sounded crazy even in her mind. Besides, she didn't exactly trust the police right now. Lyn wanted to be outside, close to Caesar. She tipped the whiskey bottle back and let the warmth flood her mouth. Looking up at the leafless trees and the pines, seeing the darkening sky become one with the tree silhouettes, Lyn's tears tracked down the sides of her face. She whispered to the sky, to God, to grant her vengeance for Caesar's death.

She woke to light between the trees, the empty whiskey bottle resting against her leg, guns one on either side of her.

Monday. She hadn't called herself in as absent. Silas...he'd wonder. He had probably called, but her phone was inside. Did it matter? She surveyed Caesar's burial mound. Cried. Pointed one of the guns at her head and needled her temple, then swung the barrel to face the woods, swirling it. Out? In? She couldn't decide. With her other hand she sifted fingers through the moist dirt of Caesar's grave. There was truly nothing left for her. Not anymore. Down on the road, a car whizzed by—people going places, going on as if there was a point. Lyn knew better. This place was the safest place, with the barrel pointed at her temple. Who would miss her? Silas? Her students? Leif? Oh, to close the book for good.

Into her awareness came the soft squish of leaves, of sticks pulled and snapped back. Steps. Someone approaching through the woods. The pace was cautious and muffled, but after the enormous silence of Caesar's death, Lyn's ears were tuned. Caesar would've heard it first had he been alive, but what mattered was Lyn *did* hear. No one friendly would come at her from this direction.

The steps halted. She listened. Lyn had the advantage, not that she needed it. Her dead nerves were steady. Leif had taught her well. She trained her sight on the sound, certain she'd hit first. She'd strike the moment he showed an inch of target. With one eye closed, she focused her other eye on the perfect rectangular bucket of the gunsight. Whoever moved into the site's bucket, it would be the last thing he did.

She adjusted her grip, moving the sight to march in lockstep with the footfalls of her prey. When he halted, so did she. A branch cracked. In that instant, he made his mistake. He was close enough; he was inside the sight. She caught the flash of movement. Khakis or some earthy camouflage. She breathed out and waited to the end of the exhale, then pulled the trigger.

And again.

The shots blasted birds from hiding and launched Lyn into a scramble for cover behind the tree. Apparently, she *did* care whether she lived or died, else why not stay where she was? What she wanted was to hear the sound of him falling. Or see him dead. Dead like the morning days ago—no, weeks ago. Forever ago, when he feigned death in almost that very spot. Right here. He wore a hornets' nest. She should've shot him then. This time, Lyn would. She would empty both guns into whoever lay in the wood.

But the steps still came for her, faltering, the gait uneven. She'd hit him; no doubt about it. She peeked around the trunk, keeping her gun trained on the unsteady and now-careless footfalls. He no longer tried to mask them, but was drawn to her. This standoff had to happen. Of course it would happen here, where it had begun.

Sweat dripped into Lyn's eye and stung. Her attempt to wipe it made it worse, for her hand was bloodied from the slide bite. She never remembered to keep her hand out of the action. The steps marched on, and in her momentary blindness, she wondered if he'd still take her by surprise. She wiped savagely at her eyes and blinked to clear them. He was right there, coming out of the copse, the brush swishing back like a curtain on some grand stage.

Chapter 41

A BUCK. A TEN pointer.

Lyn had hit him twice in the chest. Twin blood trails wended down the brown pelt. Blood spots stamped each step of his trail. He wobbled to the forest boundary and gave up. His legs buckled; his cage hit the ground. Only his head was in the grass on her property. Faint puffs of breath burst from his nose, last efforts. Then, one overlong exhalation. Silence.

From her memory, a man's voice rang in her ears and cut into the deepest parts of her. *It's never right to shoot when you don't know what you're shooting at. Your fear is dangerous, Lyn.*

Leif. Leif's voice was in her head.

Shafts of muted sunlight dropped through the holes where no leaves reached. Lyn went to the buck and knelt beside him and laid her hand upon his pelt. With each stroke she murmured "sorry." She traced every bit of muscle and contour, awed and saddened by her proximity to something so splendid and wild. Something she had no right to touch. Tears welled at the thought of what she'd done to the creature. And also at what had been done to her. Everything had been taken from her.

But had it?

There, the shaft of golden sunlight. She had that. She had the trees and the birds and squirrels clacking the branches and chittering. She had the magnificent animal at her knees. She'd made a mistake in killing it. She had that, too.

A car pulled into the drive. The gravel spat and popped. Lyn instinctively aimed her gun at the sound, but thought better of it and pulled her weapon into her chest. Had she not learned the lesson?

The car was parked and running, and the knocks reverberated through the woods. Lusty knocks. Leif's? Her heart quickened. Could it, after all this time, be Leif returning? Lyn pulled her legs under her and tried to stand. The whiskey yanked her back down. Not to be thwarted, she tried again, took one step, acknowledged the sparklers of a sleeping foot, and crumpled like a paper doll.

More knocking.

Should she call out? What if it was him, her enemy? What if it was Nolan? Or Finn? She didn't want to talk to anyone except Leif. But what if it was…Leif? And though her heart hoped it was him, she doubted. She shook out her sleeping foot and took careful, limping steps. She rounded the far corner of her house and peeked through the hedge that rimmed the porch.

Gone.

The sound of tires on gravel and stones said she was too late.

As Lyn listened to the car drive off, her cell phone rang. She could hear it through the walls. She dashed inside but missed the call.

Finn O'Malley.

Over the course of the night she had twelve missed calls from Finn, no voicemails. This morning she had three texts from Silas.

> Are you okay?

> Where are you?

> I'm calling the police.

Oh please, not the police. The last text had come two minutes ago. Lyn's call to Silas went straight to voicemail. She texted.

> No police! Get me a sub. Caesar died.

Rather than wait for a return text, she dialed Silas and got his voicemail again.

What was up with Finn and all those calls? Why not leave a voicemail?

The night Leif took Finn's call, Lyn had told him not to answer. What if Finn's call would have gone to voicemail? Leif wouldn't have left. What Lyn wouldn't give for five minutes with Leif Andrews. Five minutes.

Lyn didn't know everything about Leif Andrews, but she believed he had been a friend, a friend not made of words. The moments they spent together were better than any book. Lyn finally heard what loss had been trying to tell her in Jude, in Caesar, in Leif. Take them all away and still, they were with her because Lyn lived and breathed and could carry them around in her memory. Jude had given her love. Leif showed her strength. Caesar, loyalty. She held the phone and gazed in wonder and confusion at her walls, at the books she had ransacked that had been all replaced. She wondered why someone would clean up her mess, put everything in order, and she realized: her enemy didn't care which reality Lyn lived in: order or chaos. Lyn's enemy wanted to make sure her reality was the exact opposite of whatever she wanted it to be. This light bulb moment made her smile at figuring out the puzzle, and she was still smiling when fifty-thousand volts entered her neck from behind.

The voltage pulled Lyn into a rod of agony, wrenching her wistful smile into a slack jaw. From behind came a hand and a cloth or a paper towel. She couldn't tell. It was wet and smelled sweet. She could only watch as it was clamped over her nose and mouth. *Chloroform* was the last thing she thought before she slept.

Chapter 42

Finn

Finn ditched his police cruiser and "slept" in the Kia he had stolen, still wearing his uniform. The girl at the twenty-four hour drive thru gave him his coffee and a glazed donut for free and thanked him for his service. It brought tears to Finn's eyes, thinking it would likely be the last time someone honored him as a cop.

Going to Lyn's place was dangerous, but Finn didn't have delusions of escaping his fate. He did, however, want to stay free a while longer. He needed answers, and some things about the last few days didn't make sense no matter how much he puzzled over them. He had intended to get answers from Leif but lost his mind and shot him. And Lyn didn't answer her phone, which really burned his balls.

Lyn's Land Rover was in the driveway. So she was home. Why hadn't she picked up the phone? Why hadn't she gone into work? Because of that other car parked by the road, maybe. Finn was willing to bet it was the librarian's. Hmpf. Looked like she was in danger all right, of getting shagged. The idea of Lyn with someone not-Leif made Finn smile. He wished he could bring Leif back to life, show him Lyn in bed with the librarian, and shoot Leif again.

He parked down the road, preferring the camouflage of a walking approach.

A text came through from Shayla asking where he was and apologizing, again. Finn had made a point of scaring the shit out of his unfaithful wife before he left for work yesterday morning. It felt—not good, but powerful—to tell Shayla the chief was of the mind that Leif Andrews could be dead. Shayla's tears were what hatched the unthinkable in Finn: to kill his partner if he wasn't dead already. How dare she cry for Leif? Did she think her apology would make it all go away?

Finn made it go away.

Finn would have given his life for his partner. What if he'd taken a bullet for that son of a bitch, laid his life down for his so-called "friend," not knowing what Leif had done? How he had been betrayed? That was the thought that pulled the trigger. Leif allowed Finn to be wrong about his wife, about his life, about everything that mattered. The two people who should have cared about Finn had conspired to keep him stupid. It was too much, how Shayla had worried about Leif when he went missing. Finn knew how relieved his wife—*his* wife—would be when Leif Andrews was found. And he couldn't bear to see her relief.

Now he had hours, at best, before the mess he'd left at the Seven Baths caught up to him. A thought of Tawny made Finn wince. Of all the paramedics, it had to be her?

Father in heaven, don't let Tawny be dead. She doesn't deserve that. She was in my way.

Finn shut off his thoughts. He had to focus, and the ability to limit the scope of thought had been trained into Finn, would serve him well today, of all days. Finn was a fine fucking patrolman, and he would spend his last few hours getting answers from Lyn Darrow, the only person he knew of who had them.

He decided to case her place. It might be the last time he got to be a cop, and Leif thought she was in danger. A ridge across the road would give a perfect view into Lyn's living room and bedroom windows. He went back to the Kia for his duty belt, mostly for the binoculars.

The first thing he noted was the ridge was full of tracks, that Finn was not the first peeping Tom to use this spot. He trained the binocs on the bedroom window and was disappointed to see a made bed. Of course, they could do it anywhere. What did a made bed mean?

Next, he peered into the front window. The sheer curtains were closed, but he could make out hazy shapes beyond, if he zoomed enough. The couch was empty. The room looked like a library, what with all those books lining the walls. He remembered thinking what a bookworm she was. How pretentious, all those books.

He swung his circle of vision into the dining room where he caught movement on the table. An enormous silver mound was on top of the dining room table, the shape of it taking up the whole thing. Looked like a silver mummy, honestly, with some pink things that moved on its side, undulating like sea anemone. *What the hell?* Finn rubbed his eyes and tried again. And again, and still, all he could make out was a large lump on the dining room table. The silver and the table and the fact that it was wiggling made no sense. He rubbed his eyes.

"What...is that?"

It was only when he clambered down the ridge and got a view through the side window that he could make it out. The silver mound was actually people, duct taped to the dining room table like mummies. Two sets of shoes stuck out from one end. They kicked. The pink things at their sides were fingers.

Chapter 43

THERE WAS AN ALARM. No, a scream. It dug into Lyn's skull. Something jostled her.

"Lyn!...Lyn, wake up! Lyn...can you hear me?" The panicked whisper was close. The tone troubled her, the urgency, but crowding out everything was the blade of pain that slid into her head as she regained consciousness. Each second the pain expanded, until she was sure her head would crack apart like flawed clay in a kiln. She tried to open her eyes, but it was impossible. The more she tried, the more it hurt. She moaned and gave up.

"Lyn. I *need* you to wake up."

That voice. She knew that voice. Turning her head was impossible. She didn't know why. Only, when she tried to move, something kept her head straight. Something inflexible. It made an almost inaudible squelch when she pushed against it. Same with her arms and legs. And it tugged her skin in a burny way. Gritting her teeth against the pain, she tried again to open her eyes.

That was when she realized, they were stuck shut. Like when she was a kid in the psych unit, and the drugs weighted her eyelids. Only this time there wasn't even a slit, no sliver of light to give her hope. Now it was Lyn who screamed.

Chapter 44

Finn

ON HEARING THE SCREAM, Finn hesitated. Shit was getting real in there. A cop who wanted to see tomorrow waited for backup. As luck would have it, Finn didn't give a rip whether or not he saw tomorrow. Tomorrow sounded pretty bad, actually, what with him killing Leif and shooting Tawny and all.

Another scream.

Finn looked around, adrenaline kicking his heart into gear. Was he willing to risk his skin for this woman who was stupid enough to fall for Leif? He could call this in and run. He'd buy himself time but not answers.

He could do his job. Didn't that make him good, ultimately? Every day Finn protected the deserving and undeserving alike. (Until his friend's betrayal had swept away his morals and inhibitions like so many chess pieces.) Any guy who'd sleep with his partner's wife—could he be redeemed?

No.

But Finn could be redeemed. He would go in after Lyn Darrow because it was the job. That simple. Finn squared his shoulders and lifted his chin. He chose this last act as a patrolman. Finn was, first, a rescuer. He enjoyed killing law-breaking amoebas, cleaning up the world.

He decided to go around back and find a window, get a clear view of the assailant. The element of surprise was on Finn's side if he could get eyes on him.

The next window showed the librarian wasn't holding up well. His head was all over the place, like he was going crazy being tied up like that. Finn knew the look. People in extreme situations either rose to the challenge or fell to pieces. The librarian was a pieces type.

After checking several angles and windows, Finn was pretty sure he wasn't dealing with somebody's idea of an edgy sex game. What troubled him was that he hadn't gotten a look at the assailant. Whoever tied them up was either smart enough to keep clear of windows or—more likely—was lucky. The chief said *they didn't catch the smart ones.* Chief meant that the law was on the side of crime, that a criminal with a wee bit of brains could find ways to thwart cops. Finn was insulted. In his decade on the force, he caught the dumb and the smart—had caught them *all* and was home in time for dinner with Shayla, the bloody whore.

Finn tramped deep into the backyard.

More screaming from inside the house.

Finn rolled his eyes and double-timed it.

His foot dropped into a spot of soft, shifty earth. He barely managed to right himself before face planting into the freshly-dug grave.

Chapter 45

Lyn cried until the tears pooled in her eyes and escaped through a crease in the tape. Someone nearby was laughing a mad, unhinged howl.

Her.

The anger and agony of Caesar, the disappointment of Leif, the still-knifing grief of Jude—all her pain thrust out of her until she was too exhausted to cry or cackle anymore. And although she heard the frantic male voice begging her to stop, calling her by name, she didn't have space for it yet.

Who did the voice belong to? She licked her lips, and the bitter tang of iron filled her mouth. She had bitten her tongue. The sound of buzzing was unmistakable. She had a feeling she knew who it was beside her.

"Nolan?" Lyn ventured.

"Oh-thank-God-you're-alive," he said.

"I can't move anything."

"We're tied up, with duct tape."

"How?"

"I don't know. He came from behind and put a choke hold on me, tased me,"

"My eyes are taped. I can't see." Lyn used all her arm strength to push against the tape. It didn't give at all. She was out of breath and the pressure on her head was excruciating.

Nolan squirmed beside her. "Why would there be a bees' nest in here?"

Lyn felt Nolan strain against the tape, his movements shaking the table but not budging it an inch.

"They're for me," she answered. *They're revenge.* Something buzzed close to her ear, as if on cue.

"For you? Why?"

Lyn needed far too many words to explain, so she said nothing.

Nolan's response was to try again to break through the tape, to continue to struggle. He yelled and cursed. It was a disturbing sound coming from the usually placid librarian, a cocktail of rage and fear and frustration.

"I came...to check on you," he said.

No good deed goes unpunished. Nolan was in danger because of her, plain and simple. Like Simon's mom all those years ago, an innocent person was going to pay the price for Lyn's transgressions. By allowing people into her life, she put them in harm's way. Leif, Nolan, even her beautiful Caesar. And Jude? Was he run down intentionally? As payment for her sins? In the years after Jude's "accident," Lyn had elected not to participate in life, to bury herself in her books. Her mistake was to think she could escape her own self.

"I'm sorry, Nolan."

It was his turn to be silent.

"Do you know where he is?" Lyn whispered.

"No. I think he left before you came to. I can't be sure, but I heard the door slam, and a car. I heard a car. Who would do this?"

"I think it's someone from my past."

"Who?"

"A long time ago, I hurt someone."

A patch of silence, then: "Go on."

"This kid I knew when I was young. I'm sorry you got mixed up in it. I was a stupid kid and did a stupid thing. This is revenge for my revenge."

"I don't get it."

"Simon's getting me back."

"Simon?"

"I hurt his mom. It was an accident. I...put hornets in his car."

"Why do you think it's him, this *Simon*?"

"Because of the hornets." Lyn braced herself each time one flew by her ear.

Nolan took a deep breath. He didn't say he was shocked or horrified about the hornets. He didn't condemn her. Nolan would have made a good friend. All those times he invited her to the book group and she declined. All the book suggestions. His bold and outright pursuit of her in the last few days. She couldn't imagine herself ever loving him, but she regretted not allowing him in. She regretted not living life fully, because she understood her life was about to end. Nolan did, too. It was all over him; even without eyes Lyn could feel his escalating struggle against their bonds. She understood why he yelled, though it was foolish. The only person around to hear would be Simon.

Chapter 46

Finn

Through the binoculars, Finn watched the librarian scream. The sound wasn't much muted by the walls, and he could tell the librarian was losing his mind by the way his mouth opened crazy-wide and his face contorted. Weren't librarians supposed to be quiet? Lyn had thick silver tape over her eyes, but he recognized her hair. Besides, who else would be taped to Lyn's dining room table? The librarian—his eyes weren't taped. Now that was interesting. Why bind the both of them and not tape the guy's eyes? Did the perpetrator want the librarian to witness something? Sickos often got their rocks off at the second victim's look of horror while they tortured the first. Terrorized eyes were a deep orgasm for sociopaths.

The librarian swept his gaze around the room, as if he were searching for something. Or more likely, someone. The same someone Finn craned to see. Whoever assaulted the couple knew enough to keep clear of the windows. Lyn's lips moved, which meant she was alive, at least. Her fingers worked to rip the tape. Wasn't the woman usually the one doing the screaming?

Shayla. He winced. Since she confessed her and Leif's "mistake," Finn's hold on his emotions had unraveled. Wasn't life grand for the charming Leif Andrews? Badge bunnies falling all over him. He could have anyone, and he stole Shayla. *Finn's* Shayla. The image of Leif dead in the forest did not sadden Finn because he had grieved the death of his partner and friend before he pulled the trigger. Alone and unseen, Finn cried at the death of trust, camaraderie, innocence—fucking everything good in the world died when Finn learned the truth. *The truth will set you free.* Words he had learned at church when he was a boy. Wrong. *The truth will set you on fire.* His revenge had not filled him with a rush of satisfaction, peace, or victory, as he had hoped it would. Instead, as the blood pumped out of the hole he put in Leif's chest, Finn looked down on his friend-turned-enemy and said, "I *know.*" Not spoken with victory, but with utter despair.

And Leif tried to say something in return, but blood bubbled up and crested his lips. Leif was gone. And Finn swore he could feel the jaws of hell snapping at them both.

Finn glanced at Tawny, face-down in the dirt. He felt bad about shooting her, but he trusted she'd be all right. Probably need physical therapy and be working a desk for a while. They'd find something for her to do while she healed. He couldn't let Tawny stand in the way of his revenge.

Finn willed his focus back to the now. What he couldn't figure out was, why tie up the librarian, too? Why not just off him? Lyn was clearly the target. Had a jealous ex caught them in the act? If Finn had caught Leif and Shayla, well, he could almost, *almost* imagine toying with them like this. But more likely, Finn would have put a bullet between Leif's eyes before he could blink.

Duct taping the two of them to the dining room table meant that somebody had spent serious time planning and scheming.

Finn hustled to the last window and got a crisp view inside with the binoculars.

And there Finn O'Malley—who would have said a week ago that he was never surprised—was surprised yet again. He saw the hand. He saw the knife. And he could hardly believe it.

Chapter 47

THE MORE LYN PULLED at the tape, the more it chafed her wrists and knuckles. Deep breaths kept full-blown panic at bay, but being immobilized and blind poured fresh adrenaline into her every time she allowed her mind to be pulled back into their hopeless situation. *How many lives will you destroy because of me, Simon?*

Nolan had taken a break from pushing and squirming. He'd fallen into an almost-silent monologue or was praying, coping in his own way, she supposed. His mumblings were difficult to understand. Lyn listened for any clue as to where Simon was. All was silent except for the tick...tick...tick of the cuckoo clock—

—until the front door crashed open, shuddering the house. The thunderous fire of gunshots and the simultaneous, violent shift of the table flipped on its side, the tape preventing Lyn from being dumped. How any of this happened, Lyn had no idea, blind as she was, but the shock of it tore a scream from her. The tape held her in a sling and must have stopped her head from slamming on the floor. More gunshots. Each one made Lyn shrivel, and wonder why she didn't feel a hit. Wood snapped near her ear, peppering the side of her face with splinters. A thud and a moan followed.

"Nolan?" She bit her lip. There was no answer, and she wasn't surprised. "Simon?"

Keys jingled. Something dragged across the floor.

Simon would come for her next. Her heart slammed so hard it vibrated the table, and her stomach threatened to wretch. Soon it would be over. That was what she told herself. Soon she wouldn't feel anything. That was probably a lie. All this trouble. Simon would want to torture her for sure.

The tread of steps approached. Someone spit. There was the unmistakable snort of spit and the little splat as it hit something. Then the soft drop of knees against the floor. He was next to her. Looking at her. The cuckoo clock took over again. Simon was close enough she could hear him breathe. A strand of her hair was plucked off her cheek, and she trembled at the touch of fingers.

"Who are you? Simon?"

A finger touched her lips to shush her.

Next came a tugging at her top side and the unmistakable sound of cutting. Her body dropped incrementally until the tape tore and dumped her on the floor. She was no longer stuck to the table, but her arms were bound, her legs taped together. Someone dragged her out the front door and down the steps, banging her head on each one.

She screamed in hopes that someone was around to hear. Someone grunted as she was hefted then dropped onto a scratchy rug that smelled of...Caesar. A trunk slammed. Her Land Rover. Next to her was another person; she wriggled closer and tweezed clothing in her fingers. And something sticky, too.

"Oh, Nolan..."

There was no answer.

An iron tang bloomed in the air around her. She pinched the bit of flesh she could reach on the person beside her in the trunk, hoping for a reaction, a sign of life.

Chapter 48

LYN SUFFERED IN THE trunk for what felt like hours, jarred by bumps and turns. She'd become accustomed to the smell of blood in her nostrils, but the scratchy trunk carpet felt like sandpaper on her face. The duct tape pinning her hands to her sides was impossible to stretch or break, which meant the tape on her eyes wasn't going anywhere, either. Eventually, the car stopped. The radio that had been blasting Bon Jovi's "It's My Life" cut off. A door opened and closed. Footsteps retreated, returned. She braced at the sound of the trunk lock opening.

Hands lifted her out, delicately placing her on a soft surface like a bed or couch. A finger traced her neck, her ear. It was leisurely and feather-light. Gooseflesh broke out all over her, and she shivered with disgust. The sensual touch was more foreboding than a blow. The finger teased her lips, and she resisted the urge to purse them. Someone lifted her lip and traced the blade of her teeth. She could chomp down on that finger, draw the wrath of her abductor. Why not? Part of her wanted to get the torture over with and get dying already.

The fingers waited for her to bite, and when she didn't, left her. The slight tug against the tape was her only warning. It was ripped from her face, taking hair and eyebrows and lashes with it. Her eyelids were pulled nearly out of her head and snapped back as the glue released her flesh. In spite of her determination to remain silent, she screamed and blinked against the agony and the blinding fluorescent lights. Tears ran down her face, making it hard to discern where she was lying, but whatever she was lying on had side rails like a hospital gurney. The residual glue on her eyelids kept sticking them together, making blinking a brutal act. She forced herself to open them to see Simon's face, to regard the man who for so long struck at her from anonymity.

But she was not to get any satisfaction. A plastic mask leaned over her. White skin, pink cheeks, black jagged eyebrows, and a leering goatee. Guy Fawkes. Of course, the British conspirator who would have revenge for wrongs. Is that who Simon saw himself as—Guy Fawkes?

"Where am I? What'd you do to Nolan?"

He shook his head and gave the gurney a shove, taking her along an unlit hallway. Fluorescent tube lights garlanded with shaggy cobwebs lined the ceiling, and a sweeping flashlight beam caught frayed and hanging cords and cratered drywall. The screech of wheels and footfalls echoed in the tomb-like hall, and the occasional bump caused the gurney to lurch and blew the air from her lungs. Wherever they were, it had been long abandoned. At a doorway draped with thick plastic, Guy Fawkes held it back and guided the gurney through.

A gas lamp sat on a bedside table between two single beds, both made. Next to the lamp and bathed in its glow was a stack of books. A mural of Van Gogh's *Starry Night* had been painted over the blacked-out windows. When Lyn took in the wall opposite the beds, she nearly choked on her tongue. It was her. Like the whiteboard. Like at Leif's house.

"Simon?"

Guy Fawkes tilted his head.

"Why the mask?"

He slapped her. His breath came fast. It rattled inside the mask. He wheeled Lyn to one of the beds and lifted her from the gurney into the bed. She wiggled, trying to fall to the floor, anything to thwart him. But he caught her and pinned his body over hers. For a while he lay there, saying nothing. His weight on her lungs made it difficult to breathe. She tried to recognize the eyes through the mask holes, but they were just irises. Blue. The eyes alone held no clues.

Finally, he slid off her. After rummaging in a duffel bag, he pulled out a roll of duct tape.

"No..." Lyn begged.

He nodded and pulled a long piece.

First, he wound some around the bed bar, then he threw it over her and crawled under the bed to pull it around the other side, again and again until she was a mummy. He tore off a small piece. She knew what that was for. He held it up, like he wanted her to ask him not to do it, but she wouldn't give him that. Instead, she squeezed her eyes shut.

He grunted his dissatisfaction and pressed it deep into her eyes.

Not seeing, knowing he stood over her...she steeled herself for what was coming next.

She heard the mask drop to the floor. Breath, close to her ear. Lips brushed against her cheek, kissed it, kissed down her raw neck around the tape. Lyn's breath hitched and she gulped air. She clenched her teeth.

The lips became a tongue, swiping along her skin, making her flesh crawl. It traced her collarbones, her chin, burrowed into her ear. First one, then the other. The sting of cinnamon hit her when the tongue flicked her nostrils.

Lyn screamed, but the tongue didn't stop. It found her lips and sucked on them, nibbling on her open mouth and her screams. The mouth sealed against hers and the tongue penetrated until it choked. She snapped her jaw shut and tasted blood.

That did it.

He was off her and attending to himself. A zipper sounded. A hand roved around, knocking against supplies. Fingers gripped her eye tape and tore it off. The second time hurt worse than the first. Seeing was nearly impossible. She could make out that he had the mask on.

Like a disappointed mother, he shook his head and tick-tocked his index finger in the no-no gesture. The whir of the bed's machinery brought Lyn upright to face her own horrifying likeness on the opposite wall. Blood ran down her chin. His blood.

"I have dreams, too." The mask distorted his voice.

"Why?" Lyn managed.

"That hurts. All these years I've dreamed about you...and you forgot me."

Lyn shook her head.

"I came to you. Twice. You looked right through me. Didn't even recognize me."

"Simon, if I could take back—"

"NO, LYN. FORGET HIM. HE'S NOBODY." The man paced. He shook her bed in a fit of rage. He bowed onto her, laid his masked head on her stomach and sobbed. Like a gavel, one fist came down on her thigh, charlie horsing her, as he struggled with his emotions. For many minutes he lay there, the mask between them.

"The hornets. Only Simon would do that."

"What about your precious Leif?"

Leif. There was jealousy in Guy Fawkes' voice. "Leif didn't know about the hornets until *after* that morning they were put in my yard."

He stood and walked a few paces away, his back to her. "Was I that much of a nothing to you—that you don't remember?"

"I'm sorry."

"SORRY? You're sorry!? THERE IS NO SORRY BIG ENOUGH FOR THIS." He ripped off the mask, and spit. Lyn stared at the back of his head, dreading and curious. He shook with sobs, ran his hands through his hair and gripped fistfuls of it. He seemed afraid, too. Maybe he didn't want to turn around. She'd looked through him twice before, he said, but she didn't know what he meant. He seemed to fear she'd look through him again, and *she* was afraid she'd look through him again, that she wouldn't be able to fake whatever he wanted to see. What would he do to her, then?

The man gazed at the mural of Lyn, his halting body language told her he was undecided about his next move.

She blinked and studied him.

She did know his form. The way he stooped a bit. The wavy hair. The way he ran a nervous hand through it. Even before he turned, she knew, but could not believe.

"Nolan."

He sighed, a big heavy thing. His eyes were full of unshed tears. "How many stories did I send you? I went right through you. Do you know what I've done, how long I've waited for you to remember me?"

"Nolan, who's in my car?"

"See...you care more about who's in your car than you do about me. It's happening again. You always always always ALWAYS pick the *other* one, not me. You care more about a stupid pig than me."

Lyn closed her eyes. *A stupid pig?* Her eyes shot wide open. "Leif?"

Nolan picked up the scissors. "Leafs are inconsequential, little green things." He dug the point into the tape. The blade dipped too deep, and Lyn gasped at the slice in her thigh.

"Ouch," he said. "Sorry. Sorry. Some things don't have a big enough sorry, do they? Mom told me, 'Say it all you want, Nolan, but some things don't have a big enough sorry.' Your dog was the first pet for our pet cemetery. Remember our pet cemetery?"

Lyn turned her face away.

"Tell me you remember."

Lyn shook her head. Oh, she remembered. Now she remembered. But he'd changed so much. How could she have known?

"Say my name."

"You killed my dog?"

"Everybody around you dies. But not you."

"Stripes," Lyn whispered.

"What?"

"STRIPES. From the hospital."

He screamed, an unintelligible sound that tore from his throat and flew at her. "DING! DING! DING! She gets it. Give her a prize. Your prize is a dead dog. He was a good dog. Don't worry, he'll go to heaven. All dogs do. Have you seen the movie?"

Lyn shook her head. Stripes. The boy who would be Stephen King. Nolan was Stripes. Stripes was Nolan. He had played at being tied up beside her. But if it was Nolan who drove the car, who had been beside her in the trunk?

"You left me," he pouted, as if that explained everything. "And when I turned everything inside out for you, did you come to me, your friend who gave you all the best books? No, you chose a dim-witted traffic conductor."

"Leif...did you—"

"I'm not a monster, Lyn."

Chapter 49

From what was obviously an old but serviceable hospital bed, Lyn surveyed her surroundings while trying to maintain the illusion she was listening to Nolan—to Stripes. The room had been renovated. The broken and water-damaged ceiling panels of the hallway were not found here. They had been replaced and painted black. The light fixtures hung on long wires, dosing the room in smothered light. Plywood bookshelves stood side-by-side and were choked with books arranged according to the colors of the spines. A fluffy white blanket was thrown over a plush orange couch. Garish tapestries covered nearly every inch of wall, hiding the pock marks and chipping paint, no doubt. Lyn's hospital bed was in what was once a kitchen area. She could see a utilitarian sink and evidence of cabinets peeking through between the curtains. A bloody piece of gauze was on the counter, probably used on Nolan's tongue.

Was Lyn at Sacred Heart Hospital? It had closed down years ago.

"Where are we?"

"I love when you say *we*."

Lyn tried to find Stripes in the man standing over her, made fuzzy by the muted lighting. She could not see Stripes. "You lost weight," she said.

"Lost weight. Got lasered." He rubbed his cheeks. "That's no excuse. You promised. We'd always be friends, you said, always have each other's backs. You left me to rot in that place, and when I tried to talk to you, you looked right through me."

"I was thirteen. I got released."

"You were in high school."

"What are you talking about?"

"You ripped my movie ticket in half and put it in my palm. I can still feel it." He rubbed his palm. Sometimes I have to spit to get it like it was that day, all clammy. I was so nervous. You were talking to some guy on the other side of the entrance, going on about a party, and he was flirting and you were blushing, and I almost turned back. But I'd turned back before. Bought a ticket and not gone through with it, I don't know, twenty times. Each time I'd get close to the entrance, I'd chicken out. But one day you saw me, and you smiled. I thought you recognized me. I could barely breathe when I held out my ticket. Here..." He reached in his pocket. "I still have it." He held an oval-shaped scrap of gray paper. "You squinted at my ticket and said you couldn't read it. The sweat from my hands had worn the ink away. I couldn't talk. You looked right at me. I thought I might die, but at least you were looking at me. *She's going to see me now,* I thought, but you asked me which movie I was there to see. You couldn't give me directions because you couldn't read the ticket, you said. You laughed. You laughed *at me.* You held it up like it was gross because it had my sweat on it. I swiped the ticket from your hand and vowed I'd kill you someday. I wished you dead like the others, but you wouldn't die. Lyn, she doesn't die."

Lyn shut her eyes.

"Now, do you remember?"

Lyn didn't open them. "I wondered what was wrong with that kid, why he was so nervous about a movie. I figured he was about to see a scary movie or a girl had broken his heart."

"A girl had."

Another memory came back to her, the day she'd met Nolan in the far back aisles of the library. The day of Jude's presentation. Nolan seemed nervous, but she chalked it up to librarian introversion. Then, the book. The one with the horrible scene of Jude's death. The scene *was* there. Nolan must've switched out the books that day at the library. He'd dropped it. She remembered now. He dropped it and then the scene was gone.

"The books, they were changed," Lyn said.

"Don't you want to know how I did it? With *Bookworm?*"

She couldn't help but nod.

"Atticus, glue, and a knitting needle," he said.

"I don't understand. Somebody named Snow wrote that book."

"It takes a long time to type 90,000 words, but Lyn is worth it. Atticus is a book writing software. I ripped out the original pages and glued mine inside. I kept much of the book intact and wove your life into the stories...do you think that was easy? The last thing your husband did was slog up a hill, reeking of sweat, gulping breath. Almost there. Almost to that pretty wife of his, to a shower, to dinner waiting in the oven, a glass of wine—and bam! Killed your darling."

"Did you kill Jude?"

"I wrote about Jude."

"But did you kill him? Was it you who hit him, Nolan—I mean, Stripes?"

"Stephen King."

"Stephen King," Lyn repeated.

"I AM STEPHEN KING."

"I'm sorry I didn't recognize you."

"Sorry. Sorry. Sorry. Everyone says *sorry*. But sorry's only a word and it doesn't make anything better, does it? It didn't make it better for the Brother, and it doesn't bring anyone back."

Lyn squeezed her eyes shut. She didn't want to see, wished she didn't have to hear.

"Here's a confession: the Jude genre, I made it up."

Lyn gave him a withering look but said nothing.

"At first, I gave you some of his checked out books, but then I thought, *What good does that do anybody?* So I gave you books I liked, the ones I wanted you to have."

Something broke inside Lyn. It was as if a terrible pair of glasses had been placed before her eyes, revealing the world in all its razor sharp clarity. She wished for blindness again, for an innocent book in which to bury herself.

"Bet you'd like to get your hands on this." He slid her gun's action back with expert precision and sighted down the barrel at Lyn's head. "You and me—we're up close now, aren't we?"

"Give me my gun and we'll get close. Did. You. Kill. Jude?"

He shoved the barrel into Lyn's navel, hard. "I am *not* a monster."

Chapter 50

IN THE ACCENT CHAIR across from Lyn sat Nolan—Stripes—reading from his opus, *Bookworm*, the one that terrified Lyn the morning she found his "body" in her backyard.

Nolan's face was bleached by flashlight, warping his features, making him ugly.

"You were in my yard that morning."

He stopped reading. "Duh. I wanted to watch you read, but your stupid dog gave me away. The hornets were for your doorstep, but I used it to cover my face. I'd had it forever, so I knew the hornets were dead. Still. The King wrote a blistering short story about a man who put a hornets' nest on his face, and it fused to his skin..."

Nolan went on and on, spinning the story he, Stephen King, wrote. She didn't want to interrupt him, but she knew he'd done the blood in her classroom, too.

"You bought the blood online," Lyn said.

"Exactly. Told you, I'm not a monster."

"You shot at us, that day at the park."

"What? No."

"You killed Caesar."

Nolan shrugged. "Yeah, the pooch had to go. He'd given me away one too many times. I gave him three strikes. Not a monster."

"Not a monster..." Lyn mused, remembering the little boy Stripes, who she considered a friend. She and Stripes had shared their griefs and regrets, had passed them back and forth like trading cards under the tented sheets in the psych ward at Sacred Heart. And yes, she had left, but she hadn't abandoned him. Did it matter? He felt abandoned. The little boy who couldn't interrupt an adult, who was so full of manners and fear. The traits his mom diligently cultivated were the ones that killed her son and made her other son into a monster. Sorry, Nolan. Your actions make you a big, fat, hideous monster.

All those years ago, she had asked Stripes why he was there, at Sacred Heart, and he told her. Being full of her own pain, she didn't listen closely when he told the story. She was young. Selfish. She had only lost her moths, not everything. Now, his words came back to her again.

Nine-year-old Nolan waited for the adults to see him. He shifted his feet, leaned in, fear collecting in his eyes. Little Nolan was too far below the line of adult vision. He displayed all the signs of impatience without crossing the line into rudeness. Two directives had warred inside his younger self, he had told Lyn. One, get help for his brother. And two, don't interrupt an adult. Ever. But when he got their attention, when they heard "brother," "pool," and "can't swim," their eyes bulged. They scrambled like he'd pulled the fire alarm, and they ushered him faster, faster, faster down the hallway to the hotel swimming pool, where in their haste they shoved him down, and he broke his glasses on the pool deck. Women strangers jumped in the water, fully clothed. He'd never seen anything like it—fishing his limp brother out and using words it was not okay to use, ever...that's when he knew his little brother was dead. And there would be no sorry big enough for it. He'd learn later. No sorry big enough to bring him back.

Lyn remembered now. Stripes had told her under the tented sheets with a flashlight casting eerie light. She thought he made it up, like his other stories.

Lyn shook her head at the one who, like her, hid his sorry self in books. He poisoned Caesar. Painted her classroom in blood. He even straightened her books. Whatever she'd tried to hold, he swiped it away, wanting to be what she reached for next. Perhaps he wanted Lyn to feel the grief he had felt every day since the day his little brother drowned. She hated him and she understood him, and she hated that she understood.

Because I've done a terrible thing, I can empathize with people who do terrible things.

We've all done terrible things, Lyn.

Leif's words.

As soon as her memory of Stripes finished playing, she glanced at him, at Nolan, at the two people who were really one but not yet, not in Lyn's mind. She needed more time to assimilate them. But that was not to be. Lyn shook her head and squeezed her eyes shut against the pity she felt. Tears tracked down her cheeks as he read and read and read. When he got to the part about Jude getting hit by a car, she hardly felt a thing. Last time she read those words they zapped her like a thousand volts. She had hurled the book across the living room. But now, after all she'd been through and lost, they were just words. They held no power over her. Lyn pitied Nolan, but if she was going to survive, she could not let it show. Instead, she'd have to rock him with uncertainty, surprise him. She'd be the opposite of what she felt, the inverse of what he expected.

Lyn asked, "What happened to Athena?"

Consternation and internal reckoning settled on his face. "She committed suicide."

"Stole your thunder, did she?"

"Shut up."

"You can't hold a candle to King. Are you trying to kill an English teacher with shitty writing and bad gram—"

He was up and out of his chair, backhanding Lyn with enough force to send blood splattering.

She'd struck a nerve. "Stripes, get on with it and kill me. You're killing me slowly with your reading. I walked out of that hospital and never looked back at the fat little pajama-clad boy with his delusions of fame. You were nothing to me."

His face went through a metamorphosis. It twitched. Splotches of red bloomed. His lips became a bloodless line. He fisted both hands. Lightning quick, he sliced the tape under the bed and shoved Lyn off. The gritty tile floor met her forehead without mercy.

It worked.

"Lies! ...Liar, liar pants on fire! We made stories together. You cried on my shoulder. You—" Stripes said other things, but Lyn only heard the thud of her head against the tile, the clank of her rattled teeth.

Exhausted, Stripes slumped down, one arm slung across Lyn's mummified chest. He turned his head away and cried. "I know what you're doing. I've had therapy. You're trying to make me mad. But oh *no*. I'm not going to be tricked. No one's getting discharged today."

Chapter 51

Nolan

NOLAN KNELT OVER LYN. Starting with her legs, he cut the tape. Where the tape was fused to her jeans, both tape and denim peeled away like onion skins. Her shirt, too. When he pulled the tape, everything came.

Nolan sucked in his breath. "This is not what I imagined."

Lyn's eyes were shut tight.

"I thought you'd be screaming, that you'd tell me how sorry you are."

"Sorry." Lyn grunted.

He gave her a vicious slap. "Liar." He took the scissors and sliced deep into Lyn's cheek, intently studying the way her flesh flayed open. A fun little sound exploded from her, one he'd never heard before. He hoped he could make that happen again.

He searched the landscape of her body, deciding to play with the side of her ribs by cutting a deep gash, noting how the blade dipped in the spaces between rib bones. The bone wouldn't permit a deeper cut. It was true: the rib cage protected vital organs.

"Now if I twisted it and slipped the blade between the ribs..." He looked to see what sort of reaction he got out of her. Her teeth were clenched and sweat had broken out over her face. She pressed her lips together, obviously trying hard not to give him *that noise*, the one he wanted. The most erotic, the one women made in only three, delicious circumstances. One, while bearing down and pushing life out from between their legs. Two, while getting life thrust into the swallowing, warm space between their legs. And three, they cried it out to HIM when he brought out his sharp toys and sticky tape. She knew what he wanted and was denying him.

He brought up his hand, covered in Lyn's blood, and swiveled it, awed. "Your blood smells nice, better than the cold stuff I got online." He licked his hand.

From behind them came a noise, wheezing breath, shuffling feet. Annoyance flamed in Nolan as he turned.

In the doorway, hanging onto the plastic curtain for support, was the Irish pig. Where Nolan had shot him in the shoulder was a sash of blood. His gun was trained on them, albeit tremulously. "Put down the knife and put your hands in the air."

Nolan casually turned. The knife was poised, tip away from Lyn. He'd been gesturing with it and froze at the Irishman's words. Two shots of chloroform should have gotten him good. Those Irish. They didn't stay down. First Lief Andrews. Now this guy. If Nolan never saw another pig again...

Lyn glanced from his face to the Irish cop's. Nolan relished that they were both waiting on him. He could turn the tip down and stick it into her neck and die of a gunshot right over her beautiful body. It would be like Romeo and Juliet. It would be perfect. He, Stephen King, controlled the ending.

The Irishman swore at him and demanded he put the knife down, as if saying *fuck* was going to be the tipping factor. *Oh, now that you've raised your voice and called me a motherfucker, now I'll cooperate.* Nolan couldn't help but sneer and shake his head. Pigs were so predictable.

Lyn had a gloss of sweat on her face and neck, and her skin looked like wet china. Maybe he'd been a little zealous with the knife.

"Meh meh meh. Put the knife down." Nolan would put the knife down when he was good and ready. He surveyed Lyn, how he'd wrapped her like one of her stupid moths. He could just fall. Fall on her, point down. It would be all over. The Irish pig's mission to save her would be a failure. He shot a challenging stare and swiveled the blade to point at Lyn's neck, at the little depression he so wanted to spit in and dig at with his thumb. His grip tightened as he considered his move.

Not surprisingly, the Irishman responded according to his training.

Three loud pops in succession exploded from the doorway. The joke was on the pig though, because blood loss buckled his legs at the firearm's report. Cop didn't have enough strength to aim true. He lay on his side with his hand extended toward Nolan as if he were about to accept a gift.

"That was underwhelming," Nolan said, turning back to Lyn. A few tears tracked down her cheeks.

Nolan licked them.

A strange expression materialized on Lyn's face. It was...almost...composure.

Nolan felt suddenly and from out of nowhere that he'd been punched several times. The blows didn't hurt much, but he instantly weakened and dropped the blade. Warm liquid spread down his arm.

Blood.

On Lyn's face appeared a spattering of more blood. The Irishman snake-crawled toward them and viciously shoved him off Lyn. Nolan had no strength to resist, and the floor met his cheek. He felt only the coldness of the tile, the smoothness. A strange, icy sensation gripped him and spread outward. He watched with growing detachment as the Irishman swiped the scissors and cut Lyn free, looking over his shoulder every few seconds. "Move an inch, you scrote, and I'll plug your fucking eyeballs." To Lyn he said, "Nice job."

Nolan had not been punched. Lyn shot him. The pig's gun was in her grip. How'd that happen? The pig must have slid it across the floor as he fell. Sneaky, Irish pig. Lyn held the gun to her chest and took deep, gulping breaths like a fish. Nolan touched his own chest and felt warm, thick wetness. He waved bloodied fingers before his face. No pain, what a relief. He thought there would be pain.

The Irish cop patted Lyn's head.

"Everything's going to be okay," he told her.

That gesture, what the cop did to Lyn, was all Nolan had wanted from her.

No. He wanted more, much, much more, but a velvet touch on his cheek would have been a beginning. Wasn't that why he'd planted the stories? To get her to see him? Nolan managed to pick up the knife. He patted his cheek with the flat side, as she had patted the pig's cheek.

"Oh no you don't." The Irishman swiped the knife and chucked it across the room. He got in Nolan's face. "You're bleeding out."

Nolan's choked laugh brought blood spilling from his lips. Acceptance and ice were taking hold. He tried to make sense of things but could not. Lyn and all his cares began to fade.

The last words he heard were the Irishman's, and he did not understand them at all. "Been a cop all my life and I've seen my share of dead bodies, but I never watched anybody die. Today I watched two men die."

Chapter 52

For a few minutes, all Lyn could hear was the clamor of her heartbeat where it didn't belong—in her ears. As her pulse slowed, she became aware of the burn of her cuts and Nolan's lifeless, open eyes.

Lyn was not dead. How surprising. Nolan said it: Lyn doesn't die. Everyone else dies, not Lyn.

"Why you?" Finn asked.

"We have history—childhood history."

"Go on..."

"I'd rather not."

Finn shook with the effort of sitting up. "I knew there was chemistry between you and the lib—"

"Oh for fuck's sake, Finn. I didn't recognize him. He pretended to be someone else."

"Oh, to be somebody else," Finn mumbled and shifted his body and groaned. "Nice job, catching my gun when I slid it to you. Most cops wouldn't have reacted as fast as you did."

Cops. Leif. Where was he?

Finn continued, almost to himself, "So it had to be this piece of shit who called Leif and pretended to be me. Mystery solved."

"Finn, do you have your radio on you? Nolan's house should be searched. Maybe Leif's there..."

Against her, Finn stiffened and cleared his throat. "Can't we sit a while longer. I'm not in a hurry to call this in."

Lyn eyed him. The hair on the back of her neck stood up.

Finn's face was a troubling mixture of hate and defiance that she initially mistook for shock. His uniform was stained with blood over his shoulder, torso, even down his leg.

"Leif's not the good guy you think he is," Finn said.

"What are you saying? Do you know where he is?"

"I would have taken a bullet for him. You know that?"

Lyn nodded.

"But that was before." Finn snorted at a thought. "If it weren't for you, I'd still be in the dark about Leif."

Like the day Jude died, Lyn had a dark premonition. It was with a choked throat that she asked, "Finn, you said you watched two men die today. Who else died today?"

"Let me get something out, okay? Remember that day in the woods—someone shot at you and Leif? I shot at you from the woods. I wanted to see him scared. I painted his house in ketchup, too, to make you hate him. I did those things, and I'm not sorry."

"You could have killed us."

"If I wanted to kill you, you'd be dead."

Leif had made that very point, that day. "And you put fake evidence in Leif's house to throw shade on him—why?"

"Not the pictures. The ketchup. To look like your classroom. You can't throw shade on a black hole, Lyn."

A black hole. He meant Leif.

"You're tougher than I thought. You're going to be okay."

"I don't understand."

"You're better off. Trust me. Leif would've been bad news for you. A man who can lie to his best friend can lie to anybody."

Lyn didn't care if Finn was hurt or that the blood from his uniform got all over her hands. She clutched his shirt in each fist and shook him. "WHERE'S LEIF, FINN?"

He tried to pet her hand, but she released her hold and crab crawled away from him. He sighed, "I tried to find in my partner, my *friend*, a sliver of remorse or guilt, but Leif acted like everything was right-O. We could talk without speaking, we knew everything about each other—or so I thought. You know how I found out? Shayla hears about you and Leif and she loses her mind. I'm thinking: Why is my wife losing her mind over this? 'Why aren't you happy for Leif?' I ask her. And there it is on my wife's face." Finn punched the floor. "Fucking bloody whore."

"Finn...where's Leif?"

Finn didn't meet her eyes.

"Finn?"

Finn shook his head and pursed his lips. The shadow of some thought darkened his face.

Lyn put her hand over her mouth. The world crashed into her yet again.

Chapter 53
One Week Later

LYN TRIED TO KEEP her eyes off Maura Martin's aluminum foil covered head and the drips of hair dye running down her neck, but it was distracting. She told herself to focus, FOCUS on the older woman's eyes. Maura insisted Lyn drink some tea, decaffeinated Earl Grey, and Lyn was grateful for a teacup to look into. The citrus aroma mingled with the earthy smell of henna hair dye and decades-old furniture.

"Just baked yesterday." Maura offered a plate of orange cranberry scones.

Lyn declined, though they looked delicious. The lump of nervousness in her throat would not let anything pass.

From its place on the far wall, a picture stared accusingly. Simon, senior year. Looking cocky and fine as Lyn remembered him. She could imagine Simon telling her off, asking what the hell she thought she was doing, drinking tea with his mother?

"Simon's doing well," Mrs. Martin said, as if she read Lyn's thoughts. "He was trouble for a good while after my accident, as you probably know, but he got religion and he's been clean ever since. He even leads the alcohol meetings, sometimes, when the regular guy can't make it." Her pride was contagious, and Lyn found herself smiling, too, a tentative smile.

"He got a job as a toolmaker. Good money. *Good* money. He comes for dinner every Sunday. Pork roast. That's all he ever wants. Pork roast, corn, mashed potatoes, and of course my rolls. I don't mind, though. Just glad to see my boy." She sighed. "He told me about you."

Oh no.

"What he did to you when you were kids. Long time ago, he told me about it. You know how you're supposed to air your dirty laundry as part of them alcohol meetings? I remember because I was shocked my boy would be a jerk—excuse my French."

"They were just moths." Lyn didn't mean it, but she wasn't sure how to respond.

"Nonsense. They were your first babies. You were a little girl, figuring out how to nurture things. I know how it goes. For me, it was a glass jar full of ants. You'd a thought I birthed them for how I worried over whether they had enough leaves and sand...and when my pa made me dump them into the garden...ooh no. I threw one of my best fits that day, so I know what I'm talking about with little girls and their littler critters." Mrs. Martin went back in time, back to her ant farm.

Lyn helped herself to a scone, but only to have something to hold. Suddenly the floor became interesting. The accent rug had once been white and had silhouettes of poodles in varying shapes of play, all blue. She had to say what she came to say, but beginning was hard, so hard.

"What happened to you?" Maura pointed to Lyn's cheek.

"That's why I'm here, actually. I did something I'm not proud of, and I think this was my punishment." She touched her stitches and stopped to see if Maura's face would reveal whether she knew about the can of hornets, if Simon had suspected and told her.

But no. Blank and open curiosity stared back.

"I thought it was Simon, who did this." Lyn tapped her stitches again.

"Well what would make you think that? You got to forgive him. He was a dumb kid."

"*I* was a dumb kid."

"Kids are mostly dumb."

"I have a confession, Mrs. Martin, about your car accident."

"Oh."

Lyn wanted to disappear into the poodle rug or be sucked into her plush chair, to become one of the gazillion dust mites. But she had made a promise to herself. She sucked in a breath. "I know you lost control because you were stung by hornets."

"Everybody knows that. I hate them. I hate all things with stingers."

"I put them there."

Maura's mouth dropped open.

"I put the hornets in Simon's car because I was trying to get back at him for what he did to my moths. I'm sorry." A phrase came to Lyn just then, and it was so true she had to say it. "There's no sorry big enough for what I did. I know that, but I'm here to offer it because that's all I can do." Lyn could barely finish, her throat kept catching.

Maura nervously reached up and touched her head, realizing her aluminum for the second time. "Oh...my. That is a...now I don't know...you purposely put those hornets in my car?"

"*Simon's* car. I didn't know you would drive it."

"But you could've killed him. How could you do such a thing?" She gripped the sides of her chair.

The sound of the interstate filtered through the thin walls. A semi belched and smaller engines buzzed. Lyn very badly wanted to be in any one of the vehicles, anywhere but in Maura Martin's living room.

She stood to go. Maura didn't acknowledge her, but seemed to be in a memory, re-watching her accident and its after-effects through a new, darker, more malevolent lens.

Lyn cleared her throat. "I'm glad to hear Simon is well. Thank you for the tea. I'm sorry. The words are not enough, but I had to say them and wanted you to know the truth."

Maura shook off her memories. "Well, you didn't have to come here and confess. I would never have known. Here's what I'd like. Tell a lonely old lady what happened to you? Your face, I mean. Who did that?"

Lyn sat down and told her. Everything. About Jude and Leif and Caesar and how she thought it was Simon getting her back for the hornets. Maura's eyes filled when Lyn told her about Jude, Caesar, Leif and Finn, Nolan and his brother and how his mom couldn't love him after the drowning she blamed him for. How nobody could.

"How'd this Nolan know about the hornets?" Maura asked.

"I was on so many meds at the hospital, I must've told him."

"That's some story. You should write a book."

Lyn gave her a rueful smile.

Chapter 54

Two Weeks Later

WHITE COTTONY FUZZIES STUCK in the fresh paint as they lazily fell. Lyn picked at them and resumed painting the porch. Every day since confessing to Maura two weeks ago, Lyn wondered if Simon would come and get his revenge for her revenge. Maura had assured her it was no one's business but theirs and would remain buried. Each day that passed untroubled, Lyn's trust in the older woman grew. On parting Maura had said, "The past is a grave. You can either dig it up, or plant flowers and visit it once in a while. I know which I'd rather do."

Fresh spring leaves rustled at the wind's bidding and made Lyn sigh as she swirled cottonwood seeds into her paint bucket.

"Maybe you were right." Tawny sneezed and swatted at the fluffy, snow-like seeds. "We should've waited to paint."

Lyn and Tawny had met a second time as roommates in the hospital. News 5 did a story on them with the headline: **Renegade Cop Kills Partner, Shoots One Woman and Saves Another Hours Later**. The subheading was **Together in Recovery at Park Hill Hospital**. At first, their shared experience bound them together, but as the days passed, a friendship developed. When they were released from the hospital, Tawny suggested painting the exterior of Lyn's home. A dramatic change was in order, Tawny had said. Painting would signify a fresh start (and, Lyn suspected, would keep her from succumbing to depression). The still-healing paramedic had leaned into the wet paint enough times to whiten her hair before taking a break, reclining in an Adirondack chair beside the fire pit. She nursed a beer.

"Hey, lazy bones. This was your idea, remember?" Lyn said.

"These bones are not a hundred percent. Damn, but I can't wait till they heal. Doctor says they'll be stronger than they were before they were broken. How about that?"

Lyn dipped her brush and painted a swab across Tawny's arm. "I know what you're doing with your imagery. You a paramedic or a therapist?"

"I have no idea what you're talking about."

"I'm the broken bone," Lyn said.

"Aha...speaking of broken, you hear about Finn?"

Lyn stopped painting, the brush bent against the shingle. "No."

"He got his ass handed to him, even in the county jail. Broken jaw, ribs. Cops never do well behind bars. I'll be surprised if he makes it to his trial."

There was ice in Lyn's eyes. "Maybe he should have thought that through before killing his partner."

"The man was out of his mind, Lyn, I mean, he'd have to be to shoot *me*." Tawny pointed her brush for emphasis and inadvertently swabbed Lyn's neck. "Sorry."

Lyn made a small, sad laugh.

"What?" Tawny asked.

"I hate that word, *sorry*."

"Leif and Caesar, they never coming back. Sorry don't bring them back—that's the problem." Tawny purposely drew a line of paint on Lyn's arm. "Now if I say sorry for that, it don't mean shit because you can see it in my eyes I'm not sorry. Nolan, he meant to hurt you. Finn O'Malley, he didn't. Sometimes we fools go off the rails. I know I have."

"Ever kill anyone?" Lyn dabbed some paint on the back of Tawny's hand. She was half-joking.

But Tawny drew a deep, serious breath through her nose. "I saved a whole lot more."

"Oh."

"Never going to balance the scales," Tawny whispered. "But the only other option is to curl up and die, see? You got only two options when you fail spectacularly. Start making the world better or take yourself out, permanently."

"I'm angry Leif wasn't the good man I thought he was."

"The good man you thought he was? Hell, the man saved lives. He was a better man than you knew him to be. And worse. Don't judge him by his worst moment."

Something Leif had said came to mind, now it made more sense. *We all make mistakes. I hope I'm not judged by the worst decision I ever made.*

Lyn brushed a stroke of white paint down Tawny's cheek. Tawny gave back, careful not to go near Lyn's stitches. Soon the pair were ghosts.

The postman arrived but didn't come close. He wore the wary look of mail carriers who put up with more than their share of dogs and weather. Psycho women covered in paint was probably a first.

Tawny waved him over. "Just drop them on the ground." She nodded toward Lyn. "She needs something to do."

With a grin, the postman placed the mail on the empty Adirondack chair and continued his route.

Tawny frowned at the ads and envelopes. "When I get out of this thing, we're going to have a proper fight, not paint wars. Just 'cause you younger doesn't mean I can't beat you up."

Lyn spritzed her with paint from her brush, making little white spots in her hair.

"Do you know what it takes to get this hair? No. You obviously don't, else you would have respected the hair."

"You already leaned into the paint. You should see the back. Besides, the white makes you look wise," Lyn offered.

Tawny scoffed, "*Look* wise. I *am* wise." She sorted through the ads. "Junk, junk, junk, bill, junk, junk—hmm...this one's interesting." She waved a white envelope that bulged with something inside. "No return address. Postmarked Bryson City, North Carolina."

Lyn set her brush down, saw the handwriting, and gasped. "It's her!" Lyn ripped it open, and a bead lizard with green eyes fell out.

"Oh...how?" Lyn held up the bead lizard.

"What's that?"

"It was Leif's." Lyn pored over the contents, not caring she got paint on the paper.

"Hey." Tawny gently scolded. "Share."

"Oh. Sorry. *...since I had to stop to take care of some blisters—*"

"Wait." Tawny interrupted. "*Who*'s it from?"

"Delaney, of course."

"*Delaney-of-course.*" Tawny mimicked Lyn with a sing-song voice.

"She's walking the Appalachian Trail. She got some blisters and had to stop. I guess that's a common thing." Lyn continued reading. "*...blisters from the rainy weather. I saw you on the news. And your paramedic friend...*" Lyn stopped reading out loud. Her lips moved over the words.

"Oh no you don't." Tawny went to swipe the letter but Lyn was too fast. Banged up as she was, she still had the advantage of standing, while Tawny was folded into her chair.

Lyn's eyes shone with mischief. "She thinks we're a couple."

Tawny rolled her eyes. "Girls caaaaan't be just-friends no more. Got to be a couple. Even if I was gay, you are not my type. Too skinny."

Lyn continued, "Delaney says, *I knew you'd be with a nerd, like you, but I thought you were straight...*" Lyn dropped the letter and pursed her lips.

"Kid's right. You do give off a nerd vibe." Tawny slapped her thighs. "But please, continue."

"...but I'm glad you're doing you, and I thought you might like to know I'm okay. No. I'm better than okay. I meet lots of interesting people on the trail. Nobody thinks I'm weird here. We help each other with advice and we trade snacks and stuff. I almost never hike alone. I don't know how far I'll get because I don't have money, but I don't care. The trail towns need workers during the hike season. I'm not gonna lie. My favorite job was working the beer tent. Free beer. I hope you're not disappointed.

I don't even know if Mom's alive. And, I know this sounds bad, but I don't care. You were the only person who gave a fuck about me, Mrs. D. Maybe I'll come visit you someday, if that's okay. We can talk about our favorite books. I get most of mine from swap shelves at the trail towns. It was hard to leave it, but Watership Down is a heavy ass book.

I carried it through Georgia and I took a lot of shit about why I'd carry a book I'd already read because that's not trail-smart, but I wanted to keep it because it was from you. I know. I stole it, but I feel like you'd understand. Am I right? I want to be like the rabbit Hazel. I cried when he died, Mrs. D. And I never cry, not even when I saw what happened to your cop friend. (I'm so sorry, btw. The lizard was in his truck. I thought you'd like to have it.) Anyway, the book made me cry, which is why I love it. And I'm glad you're alright because I think I might have cried about that, too. Don't worry. I'll go back to school. Someday. For now I want to actually learn stuff. And do stuff. And read things that aren't stupid, like <u>Watership Down.</u> That's one great book. You were right about that. Reading is my second favorite thing to do. Hiking is first."

Lyn pressed the letter against her heart and whispered, "She's a broken bone, too."

The finished, painted house had a texturized look—cottonwood fuzz painted right into the wood—but every time Lyn looked at the blemished siding, she thought of the day she and Tawny worked together and of Delaney's letter. Joyful moments like that day were few, so Lyn cultivated them, brought them into her focus and beheld them in her mind's eye. Sweet moments with Jude, laughing with Leif, playing with Caesar—she brought out memories the way one brings out jewels and lays them out, just to see them sparkle. When the horrible memories threatened to invade her mind like smoke oozing from beneath a closed door, Lyn wrote letters to Jude, to Leif, to Caesar, even to Delaney. Anything to lasso her thoughts. Once her mind was put right, she used the letters as tinder in the fire pit.

She wrote more than she read.

Chapter 55

A Year and a Half Later

THE FOREST PLAYED A joyful song Lyn had never heard before. Or maybe she'd not had the ears to hear it. The same instruments were present: the birds, the rhythmic thud of her steps, the constant refrain of locusts heralding the end of summer. Shafts of gold slashed through where the trees allowed. Leaves danced and touched, filing against one another in a faint, unbroken chord.

Saturdays when the weather was fine, Tawny brought croissants from Bear's Bakery, and Lyn made cappuccinos. Some days Lyn spiked them with Tito's or peppermint schnapps. The two women often ate breakfast together and hiked the trail.

Like today. Around one hand Lyn held a small garter snake she'd found sunning on a rock in the stream. She'd held it long enough that it had relaxed and twined in her fingers, flicking its delicate tongue every so often.

"Well...what do you think?" Lyn tried to get a read on her friend's face.

"Snakes are gross."

"I'm not talking about the snake," Lyn said.

"About what, then?"

With a playful shoulder shove, Lyn said, "Delaney."

"Oh right, our favorite runaway." Tawny winked. "You wanna fight? That ass-whooping I gave you last week wasn't enough for you?"

Tawny had been teaching Lyn mixed martial arts, and Lyn found she liked it. It made her sweat. It made her strong. And it made her strategic.

Delaney ran out of money and was unable to finish the Appalachian trail. She had not returned to school. Instead, she moved to Wyoming and took up rock climbing, so said her most recent letter. Letters came every month or so with no return address, which meant no way for Lyn to write back and try to convince her of the importance of going back to school. Lyn wanted to track her down, hire a private detective.

"I think she doesn't give you her return address for a reason. She knows the teacher in you is eager to drive the bohemian from your bohemian student."

"She probably doesn't even know what a bohemian is. If she went back to school she might learn—"

"Hey, I got an idea. How about *you* take a page out of Delaney's playbook."

"Hmph," Lyn said. She crouched and let the snake go free. Both women watched it slither into the wood.

Tawny squeezed Lyn's hand. "Delaney's living her best life. She's learning what she wants, meeting all kinds of interesting people who don't see an orphan or a freak...Let the girl go."

Letting things go was not exactly Lyn's strong suit. Exhibit A: Jude's wood. Lyn continued to circumvent it with the mower and used an edger to cut around where logs lay scattered, tossed by Jude all those years ago, logs clothed with mushrooms and sinking into the earth.

"Want to make s'mores tonight?" she asked. "We can invite Silas and Tom. I have some very old wood I need to burn."

"Only if you convince Silas to invite the police chief. The man's fine." She patted her butt. "Like me. And he mountain bikes, at his age. You know I dig older men with a crazy streak."

"What? The s'mores aren't enough—"

A rustling drew both their eyes. Several yards into the woods, a dog wound its way between the trees, bounding in a merry canter. It noticed them, stopped, and wagged.

"What a long nose," Tawny remarked.

Lyn drew in a breath. "And those markings. Must be part Shepherd."

They stopped. The dog's pink tongue lolled. When it panted, a smile seemed to play at its chops.

"Hey, boy," Tawny said.

The dog wagged harder in response.

"How do you know it's a boy?"

"All dogs are *boy* 'til you know," Tawny replied.

Lyn searched for an owner, assuming a hiker was coming along behind and had allowed the dog to roam. Something ahead on the path caught the dog's attention, and it dashed into the trail, gaining speed and grace on the relatively smooth surface. Soon it was only a bounding black shape shrinking in the distance. It turned a corner and was gone.

Tawny's question was evident in her eyes.

Lyn knew the question. For months Tawny had been trying to convince her to adopt a dog. She had texted picture upon picture of adoptable dogs.

"I told you, getting another dog feels like I'm betraying Caesar. He's irreplaceable." They walked a while in amicable silence, Lyn craning for the sound of the dog. None came.

When they arrived back at the trailhead, Lyn threw up her hands. "I wanted that dog to be a stray."

"So you *are* ready to move on," Tawny said.

"I'm ready to love a dog that falls into my lap, but I'm not going looking for one."

Tawny grabbed a fistful of Lyn's t-shirt and got in her face. Lyn had never seen her friend so fierce.

"I wasn't going to break it to you, but old, rotten wood don't burn so well. You waited too long. We can have s'mores, sure, and a fire, but we'll have to use mostly the other wood. Hear me? You waited too long, and now the wood's useless." Tawny shook Lyn by the shirt to make her point. "You done good, Lyn. I'm not saying you haven't. But I'm afraid I'm going to need to knock some sense into you if you don't hear me now. You made a mistake, hiding in books, thinking it got you closer to a dead man. Jude wouldn't want that for you. From what you tell me, he lived his life to the fullest, to the last moment. Did Nolan kill him? Or a stranger who accidentally hit him and ran off? You're never going to know the whole truth, and that's okay. You know why? Cause it has to be. Because you ain't turning into God any time soon, and Nolan's dead."

Lyn blinked back tears.

Realizing she'd been stretching Lyn's t-shirt, Tawny uncurled her fist and smoothed the cotton. "You go find the ugliest, most unadoptable dog possible and take him home. Give him a good life. You can read your books, but don't you live in them no more."

"You done?" Lyn asked.

"Maybe. Why?"

Lyn wrapped Tawny in an embrace that picked the larger woman up off the ground. "You're ten times better than a friend made of words."

As they hugged, the dog appeared, jumped up, and put its paws on them. Up close, Lyn could see he had no collar and was skinny. It didn't surprise her a bit when he, yes, *he* jumped into the back seat of her Land Rover.

THE END

Acknowledgements

This story has been through scores of iterations and passed under the eyes of many readers. My husband read early and late versions and is my true north in matters of plot. He unknowingly inspired the opening scene when he was late returning one evening from a bicycle ride. I'm pretty sure I read him the riot act before crying in his arms.

While I was writing this book, my dog, Abbott, died. Writing the burial scene for Caesar helped me work through my own grief. Abbott's been gone five years, and his picture is still on my lock screen. I wanted to write a character who thought she lost everything, lost even more, and then made peace with her life.

I appreciate my friend circle who were willing to invest in the story while it was under construction: the Beach family, Cindy Carlo, Shaun and Ashley McKinley, and Denise Friend. Your thoughtful suggestions were instrumental in making a clean and clear story.

I credit my Alpha readers, the Reds, with making my writing life the joy it is and helping me flesh out the ideas for *Bookworm*. Mary Turzillo, Rebecca Moon Ruark, Diane DeCaprio, Cynthia Hilston, and Laura Kennelly—your fingerprints are all over my work. This story would not exist without you.

Meetings with my horror buddies are the halftime locker room speeches for my writer's heart. Talking to you: authors Neil Sater, Sean

Seebach, and Ann Heyward. You scare me, challenge me, and keep me full of great and bloody ideas. Thank you for shining up my book with your expertise.

Heartfelt thanks to my therapists, Mike and Amy, who helped me understand the concept of agency and why it matters. My characters will be bolder thanks to you. *Bookworm* began as a horror fairy tale. I'm glad to say my helpless damsel story matured into *not an easy happily-ever-after but a thriving in spite of the world*. (Thanks, Shaun McKinley!)

Adoration to my Lord and Savior, Jesus. May this story serve a greater good. Imagine how different Lyn's life would be, had she not taken revenge on her childhood bully.

About the Author

KL Griffiths lives in her imagination and also in Northeast Ohio with her husband. They are proud parents to four amazing children and grandparents to doggies, kitties, and chickens. In addition to writing, Kelly works at the local library and is daily grateful to have been granted a life so full of stories, ideas, and the interesting people who share them.

Want to join her conversation on everything deep, dark, and droll? Or check out her suspense thriller, *Spiked: Here's to Revenge?* Head on over to klgriffiths.com or use the QR code below.